Vanishing ACT

Charm & Deceit

JENNIFER ALLEE *and*
LISA KARON RICHARDSON

WHITAKER
HOUSE

Publisher's Note:
This novel is a work of fiction. References to real events, organizations, or places are used in a fictional context. Any resemblances to actual persons, living or dead, are entirely coincidental.

Vanishing Act
Charm & Deceit ~ Book Two

Jennifer AlLee
Web Site: www.jenniferallee.com
E-mail: jallee725@hotmail.com

Lisa Karon Richardson
Web Site: lisakaronrichardson.com
E-mail: lisa@lisakaronrichardson.com

Authors are represented by MacGregor Literary, Inc., and The Steve Laube Agency.

ISBN: 978-1-60374-906-0
eBook ISBN: 978-1-60374-907-7
Printed in the United States of America

Whitaker House
1030 Hunt Valley Circle
New Kensington, PA 15068
www.whitakerhouse.com

Library of Congress Cataloging-in-Publication Data

AlLee, Jennifer.
Vanishing act / Jennifer AlLee and Lisa Karon Richardson.
pages cm.—(Charm & deceit ; bk. 2)
ISBN 978-1-60374-906-0 (alk. paper)
1. Single women—Fiction. 2. Kidnapping—Fiction. I. Richardson, Lisa Karon, 1978– II. Title.
PS3601.I39V36 2013
813'.6—dc23 2013019311

1 2 3 4 5 6 7 8 9 10 11 W 19 18 17 16 15 14 13

Dedication

From Lisa
To Helen Shoemaker. Gone, but not forgotten.
She lives on in every word I write.

From Jen
To the Saturday Night Game Group: Nate and Cora, James and Kayce, Kyle and Emily, Billy, and junior members Isaac and Perrin. Our times of food, fun, fellowship, and nearly nonstop laughter recharge my creative batteries more than you know. You are all dear to my heart, and I thank God for each one of you!

Acknowledgments

Thanks so much to the creative team at Whitaker House for their encouragement. Your excitement for our story makes it so much more fun to write. You are fantastic! And we would be remiss if we didn't acknowledge our agents extraordinaire, Tamela Hancock Murray (Lisa's agent) and Sandra Bishop (Jen's agent). Their invaluable help frees us up to actually create, and we couldn't keep up without them.

—Lisa and Jen

Chapter 1

May 6, 1862
Washington, D.C.

Juliet palmed the thin stack of note cards on the table and slid them up her sleeve. Her fingers trembled as they always did before a "show." No matter. They'd be steady when it counted.

Grandmotherly Miss Clara smoothed Juliet's pale skirts. "You've got a new sitter. A young fellow."

"Do we know anything about him?"

"Artie's checking now."

Juliet pressed the heel of her hand against her stomach. The queasiness would pass, too.

"This is all I found. It was in the lining of his hat." Miss Clara passed her a folded ticket stub for Ford's Athenaeum and a battered-looking letter with countless creases.

Juliet accepted the offerings and opened the letter. No, not a letter. She raised an eyebrow and looked at Miss Clara. "This is a pass that allows the bearer to move through Union lines."

Miss Clara glanced up from her examination of a tiny stain on Juliet's hem and met her eyes.

"So, he's doing war work?"

"Apparently important work. It's signed by President Lincoln."

Miss Clara took the paper from Juliet's trembling fingers.

Why would anyone carry such a document in a place as obvious as a hatband? Though ostensibly he was in the heart of Union territory and it wouldn't be required, the pass granted access anywhere. That meant he'd come from beyond Union lines, in rebel territory. But, in rebel territory, who would want such a pass on him? Juliet sat down at the kitchen table. Something about this man felt dangerous. The pass identified him as Carter Forbes. The name meant nothing to her, and yet something niggled at the back of her mind. She *should* know about him.

Artie clattered down the stairs, his brown hair disheveled as usual, and leaped over the last few steps, landing with a thump. "Nothing."

"Did you try to cross-reference him?"

Artie tilted his head and scowled in response.

Juliet held up a hand. "I had to ask. It seems that I should know the name." She rubbed the furrows from between her eyebrows. She hated blind readings; they were so tricky. "Did he say how he learned of my sittings?"

Artie shook his head. "I don't think so. The Professor never said anything."

The Professor entered at that moment. "They're all ready for you."

"Do you know anything about this Carter Forbes fellow?"

The question seemed to pain the old gentleman, and Juliet winced at her own callousness. The Professor used to draw enormous crowds through the power of his observations about people; but now, his eyesight was shrouded by milky white cataracts, which meant he noticed very little.

"He came to the front door and asked if he could attend today's sitting. He spoke well, and when I took his hat, I noted it was of fine felt. I asked if he had been referred by one of your clients, and he said no. He didn't seem to want to offer any further information."

It wasn't an unusual reaction. Many new clients were hesitant and wanted her to prove her skills by astonishing them with information about themselves.

Juliet inhaled and held the breath for a long moment before letting it out in a rush. She could do this. She had to do this. If she turned away clients, it wouldn't be long before she and her makeshift family were turned out of their home. She just couldn't go back to the vaudeville circuit. Not if she was to have any hope of keeping them all together. One day, she would find a better way to support them. But for now, well, she had no choice.

Carter covertly examined his companions around the smooth oak table: a half dozen well-dressed ladies, most of them older than he, all but one of whom were in mourning; and a tall, rickety man with a snowy beard that reached his waist. The individuals in the group appeared to have at least a nodding acquaintance with one another, and they sat in companionable silence as they waited for Miss Avila.

The peaceful hush proved to be too much for a twittery sort of elderly lady to Carter's right. She wore a full dress of black bombazine that looked far too warm for the summer heat. Her hair was frizzled into the semblance of ringlets that wilted on either side of her cheeks. She leaned closer to him and smiled kindly. "I don't think I've met you before. Is this your first visit to Miss Avila?"

One of the ladies sniffed at this breach of social etiquette, but the others looked interested and friendly, as if the mere fact of their gathering in this room conferred a special kind of privilege.

Squelching the desire to educate them on the certainty they were being duped, Carter pasted on a smile for the lady and nodded. "Yes, ma'am. Is she as impressive as they say?"

"More so, I think." She beamed at him. "Miss Avila has such a way about her. She's so mystical and otherworldly. I completely see why the spirits choose to seek her out."

The bearded gentleman cleared his throat. "She's not like some as you'll find—them show-offs with their painted-up faces and tricks. She's a good little gal, the kind my Emmeline would have taken under her wing. The kind I would have wanted for my boy." His words choked off, and he blew his nose into a large handkerchief.

Carter wanted to pat him on the shoulder or offer some reassurance, but he couldn't allow himself the liberty. The fellow was austere and proud in his grief. Any expression of pity would likely inflict further hurt. How could someone take advantage of these poor people?

The door opened, and a slip of a young woman entered. Her dark hair was pinned up in a neat chignon. She wore a simple cotton day dress with stripes of soft white and pale purple, unadorned except for a strip of lace edging the collar and running from the bodice to the belt line. The sleeves were certainly long, and roomy enough to hide all sorts of goodies. But he didn't see any telltale bulges. He and the other gentleman stood at her entrance.

"I'm sorry to have kept you all waiting." Her voice was well-modulated and cultured. There was a whiff of foreign climes beneath the excellent English, but Carter couldn't quite place the accent.

She circled around the table to the only available seat. Carter had engineered matters so that she would be seated right beside him. Miss Avila lightly touched the elderly gentleman's arm as she passed. "Mr. Greenfield, how are you today?"

If Carter didn't know better, he would think she was genuinely concerned.

"Thank you for asking, my dear. I am much as usual."

"You haven't had bad news from the War Office about Ben, have you?"

Aha. She was fishing for information.

"No, I've had no word. Been at least four months since his last letter." His voice cracked.

Miss Avila reached out and squeezed his hand. "We will pray for his safekeeping. But, in this case, no news is good news. Keep up your faith."

She approached her seat but stopped in front of Carter. "You must be Mr. Forbes," she said pleasantly.

"I am."

"I am Miss Avila." She smoothed her skirts as she lowered herself delicately into the chair. "Is there someone in particular you are hoping to reach today?"

"I thought you'd be able to tell me that, and all the mysteries of the world besides," he shot back.

A sharp gasp came from the lady on Carter's other side. The disapproval in the room radiated toward him in waves.

Miss Avila, however, maintained her calm. "I'm afraid I cannot read your mind. I suppose there are some who may be able to do so, but my gifts do not lie in that direction. If you wish to get the attention of those on the other side, it would be best for me to know whom to ask for."

"My father, Jonathan Forbes," Carter blurted out. Immediately, he regretted it. He didn't want to sully Father's memory with anything this woman might say about him. But another idea sprang to mind. "And my sister, Emily." He smiled then, trying not to bare his teeth in the process. *Just let her try to get out of this one.*

Miss Avila had a knack for giving a person her full attention. When she turned her lovely dark eyes to her manservant and motioned for him to close the curtains, it was as though a lighthouse beacon had moved away from his soul.

As the room darkened, she leaned forward to light the single taper in the middle of the table. The manservant departed through a noticeably squeaky door. The candlelight flickered, casting grotesque shadows on the walls around them.

"We must now join hands."

It took all of Carter's self-control to keep from rolling his eyes. Of course, if they held hands, no one would be free to catch whoever might cavort about in the darkness beyond the edge of the candlelight to help the woman create her weird effects.

He took the hand she offered in his and held it tightly, to be certain she could not pull away. She made no attempt to do so. Her small, soft hand rested warmly in his, neither grasping nor trying to break free of his grip. Her eyes drifted closed.

Carter sat rigid, straining every sense to discover her means of trickery. Except for the occasional tiny pop from the candle, there was no sound in the room. The silence allowed the sounds outside to press inward—a city symphony of rumbling carriage wheels, clip-clopping hooves, and shouting street hawkers. Somewhere across the street, a piano played a popular ditty. The world was going on all around them, but, shut away in this dark and silent room, they were set apart.

At last, Miss Avila began to speak. She brought a message from the dead to each of the ladies in turn—words of enduring love, whether from a parent, husband, or child, that made them dab at their eyes with lace hankies. Finally, she asked for Catherine Greenfield.

The old fellow shifted, sitting taller. "Catherine? Catherine, are you there?"

"I'm here, Harlan." Miss Avila now spoke with a slight Southern accent.

"My Catherine. I've longed to hear your voice again."

"We talked before I left. You promised you wouldn't grieve like this."

"I know. But I'm just not sure how to get on without you. And now, Ben's gone off, and...and I'm scared he won't come back."

"You must live on, Harlan. Ben's children need a man about to help keep them in hand. Look to the living, my dear. Look to the living."

Carter raised an eyebrow. That was not the message he'd expected.

Mr. Greenfield leaned toward the candle, his features taut with anxiety. "Are you telling me Ben is there with you?"

"No, dear."

"You're sure?"

"Harlan Greenfield, I think I'd know my own son."

Tears glistened on the old fellow's face. "Oh, thank God. Thank God."

Miss Avila spoke again. "Catherine is gone. Is there an Emily Forbes there who will speak with me?"

Carter searched the woman's face, but it gave away nothing. She waited patiently as the silence in the room again allowed the outside world to intrude.

At last, she shook her head. "I'm sorry, Mr. Forbes; the woman you seek is not on the other side."

Carter clamped his lips together. She was cunning, he had to hand her that. He had counted on her revealing herself as a fraud by claiming to talk to Emily, who was very much alive and well.

He forced himself to continue the charade. "And my father?"

Once again, Miss Avila appeared to consult with an invisible host.

"He is there but unable to speak to me directly."

Carter hid a sneer. "He suffered so much during his final illness. I want to make sure he is no longer in pain."

"There is no illness or suffering in the other world. He says you should not worry about him." Though she didn't open her eyes, Miss Avila's delicate brow furrowed emphatically. "Nor should you be concerned about your disagreement prior to his passing. It was a small matter, and you must not allow it to prey on your mind."

Carter nearly let go of her hand. How could she possibly know about that?

Miss Avila's frown deepened, and she shook her head a couple of times. Then her eyes popped open. "They are gone." She began to tremble from head to foot and slumped slightly, as if the contact with ghosts had sapped her strength.

She clapped her hands lightly, and the door opened again with another squeal. Carter was nearly convinced that was by design, for all the other appointments in the establishment were in perfect taste. Why would she abide a squeaky door, unless it was a deliberate flaw designed to reinforce the idea that the sitters were entirely alone—that no one else could have entered or exited?

Miss Avila bid her guests farewell, shaking their hands and giving each one a few personal words. She asked about family members and various ills. Took notice of a new bonnet and complimented a handsome necklace. The sitters seemed to brighten under her attention, as if she'd lit a lamp within them.

At last, Carter alone remained with her. He realized afresh how small she was; how her eyes, though dark, were bright and... kind. Once again, she surprised him, and he fumbled for words.

With practiced ease, she stepped in to save him from embarrassment. "Thank you for coming today, Mr. Forbes. I hope you found it enlightening."

"To be honest, I had hoped for more."

"Perhaps you are unaware that a sitter's attitude can affect the ability of the spirits to communicate clearly. Tell me, did one of my clients refer you?"

"In a manner of speaking."

She cocked her head prettily, waiting for an answer.

Carter decided it wouldn't hurt to let her stew. He smiled back wolfishly but didn't elaborate further.

Miss Avila stilled like a rabbit scenting a nearby predator.

Juliet didn't dare move for fear she would give away her agitation. Mr. Forbes was even more than she'd bargained for. A tall man with neatly combed light brown hair and a well-groomed mustache of the same color, he was the sort who might be dismissed if one were fool enough not to notice the intelligence in his gray eyes and the muscular build beneath that stylish coat.

Juliet was no fool. She would not underestimate this man. He wasn't the type to approach a medium. That meant he'd had a very definite purpose in seeking her out. If that purpose had anything to do with the work that had earned him a pass signed by President Lincoln, she could find her goose cooked.

On the other hand, it could very well have to do with his not-so-dearly-departed sister. As soon as he'd mentioned Emily, Juliet had made the connection. No wonder the name Carter Forbes was so familiar. But did he know of her acquaintance with his sister? At that moment, Juliet remembered something else Emily Forbes had mentioned about her older brother: He was a Pinkerton agent working for the government.

That certainly explained the pass. What it didn't explain was what he wanted with her.

"I always like to get to know my new clients," she finally said. "Would you care to join me for tea in the sitting room?"

His smile was thin-lipped. "I'd be delighted."

Juliet led the way. "Please have a seat. I just need to speak to my housekeeper a moment."

Once out of sight, she all but ran for the kitchen. Miss Clara and Professor Marvolo were seated at the table.

"All done, dear?" Miss Clara slid a tray of cookies toward her.

"Forbes is a Pinkerton and he wants something. I know it."

Professor Marvolo turned his clouded gaze toward her. "Describe him."

Juliet had spent years under the professor's tutelage. As quickly as she could, she described everything the Pinkerton had said and done, in addition to his appearance. "I had a bad feeling about him from the beginning, so I kept the sitting very simple. No spirit writing. I didn't want to do anything that he could seize upon."

"Very wise." The professor nodded over his fingertips, which he had pressed together as if in prayer. "He's here on a personal matter."

"Are you sure? How can you tell?"

"If this were an official investigation, he wouldn't still be fooling around with tea and verbal sparring. Besides, the Pinkertons are all working for the war effort, in one way or another, and we don't have a thing to do with that."

"What should I do?"

"You have to go back in there and talk to him. Find out what he wants. This could be a good thing. Having a Pinkerton on our side might be beneficial."

Miss Clara patted her arm. "I'll bring in tea directly."

Juliet clenched her hands into fists. She could do this. She had to do this. They were counting on her. And while she was not certain they would benefit from having a Pinkerton on their side, it would be a total disaster to have a Pinkerton as an enemy.

She returned to the sitting room. Once again, Mr. Forbes stood as she entered.

"I apologize for the delay. Tea will be brought directly."

"That sounds good." He sat as she did. "I'm curious, how long have you had this gift of being able to talk to spirits?"

She smiled. "Anyone can talk to spirits. They are the 'great cloud of witnesses' that surround us. The real trick is being able to hear them talk back." She decided to press her luck. "Mr. Forbes, now I must ask you a question."

"Certainly."

"Why did you try to make me believe your sister was dead?"

He slid back in his chair. "I think you know the answer."

"It was a test, then?"

He nodded. "You passed that one with ease."

Juliet watched him warily. "That one? Was there another test?"

"Oh, yes," he said smugly. "My father didn't die of a lingering illness. He was murdered."

Now Juliet settled back in her seat. "Perhaps you should think over the conversation again. I merely said that there was no illness on the other side, and that he said not to worry about him."

Artie entered, carrying a tray of tea things.

Alarmed, Juliet sat forward again. She didn't want him anywhere near this man. "Artie?"

"Miss Clara asked me to bring this to you." With his back to the agent, he gave her a broad wink.

Juliet refrained from making a face at him.

"And who is this strapping young lad?" Mr. Forbes asked in a too jovial voice.

"This is my son," Juliet said evenly. "Artie, make your bows."

Forbes looked from her to Artie and back again.

Juliet answered the unasked question. "He is adopted."

"I see. It must be difficult, supporting such a large house, as well as a family."

Juliet felt as if a hand had tightened around her windpipe. "Artie, go on back to the kitchen and help Miss Clara." Her eyes warned him not to argue.

When he was gone, Mr. Forbes stood. "Miss Avila, I grow tired of sparring with you. We both know you are a fraud. If I have to, I will send agents by the dozens until someone exposes you. Then I will smear your name in every salon and parlor in the capital. You will never have another client."

Mouth dry as parchment, Juliet tilted her chin up a notch. "May I know what I have done to earn your enmity?"

"I have a young person I am responsible for, as well. My sister, Emily, whom you introduced to spiritualism."

Juliet frowned. "Emily sat for me only once, and she was brought by a neighbor."

"Once was far more than enough. She now believes that she can, in a way, resurrect our parents and keep them close at hand. She's been taken in by a spurious English nobleman who claims to have powers remarkably similar to your own."

Juliet knew immediately of whom he spoke. "Lord" Shelston was gaining quite a following in the area, but he could be cruel and exceptionally greedy, as well, draining his clients of their resources and then discarding them.

"If your worry is with Shelston, why come after me?"

Carter shook his head. "I am not a complete idiot. If I attack her pet directly, Emily will simply consider me too protective. I must tackle this problem at the root."

"And you believe I am the root of the problem?" She laughed roughly. "Mr. Forbes, my influence is nowhere near as great as you take it to be."

"Not at all, Miss Avila. I realize your clientele is small, by most standards. But, by shutting down your operation, and those like yours, it lights a fire under Shelston's feet. He'll soon find Washington a very inhospitable place."

Mind awhirl, Juliet sought a way out of this dilemma. "I know Shelston, and I agree with you as to his basic character. I don't want to see your sister involved with him any more than you do. So, I have a proposal."

Carter raised a questioning eyebrow, so Juliet rushed on.

"I'll go with you and tell Emily all I know about him and how he achieves his illusions."

"And what do you want in return?"

"Your word that you will leave my family and me in peace."

She could imagine Forbes's thought process: weighing the pros and cons; deliberating what his sister's well-being was worth to him; contemplating whether he could live with himself if he let a small fish swim free in order to catch the larger fish he was after.

Finally he held out his hand. "You have a bargain, Miss Avila."

She grabbed it before he could change his mind and pumped it forcefully. The deal had been struck.

Chapter 2

He'd made a pact with the devil, and now he was escorting her into his home.

"After you." Carter held the door open and motioned for Miss Avila to enter the modest brownstone. As she removed her gloves, one slow finger at a time, she looked around the foyer. No doubt collecting whatever information she could about him and his family for future use.

"You have a lovely home." She turned to him, the stone set of her jaw belying the pleasantness of her voice.

In no mood for banal chitchat, he angled his head toward the closed parlor doors. "Are you ready to speak to Emily?"

Miss Avila frowned. "How do you even know she's in there?"

He glanced at the stately grandfather clock on the far wall. "It's half past two. She will be sitting on the settee, doing needlework." It didn't take a spiritualist to know that. Ever since the accident, his sister had been as predictable as the rising sun.

Lips pursed, Miss Avila nodded. Carter walked past her and pushed open the double doors.

Sure enough, Emily was perched on the edge of the red brocade settee, her head bent over a canvas stretched taut in a wooden hoop. She looked up, brow wrinkled in confusion. "Carter. You're home early."

"I ran into a friend of yours." Motioning behind his back, he summoned Miss Avila into the room.

She moved with ethereal grace, as though her feet didn't touch the floor. The moment she walked in, she slipped right into her façade. "Hello, Emily."

Recognition sparked in Emily's eyes. "Miss Avila. How nice to see you again." Emily put aside her needlework and struggled to rise, grimacing as her wooden leg hit the floor with a loud thump.

Carter wanted to rush forward and help her, but she hated it when he did; she accused him of coddling her. So, instead, he held back and watched as she jerked and pushed herself into a standing position.

Miss Avila didn't seem fazed in the least. She waited patiently, hands clasped in front of her. When Emily finally made it across the room, the medium opened her arms and embraced the young woman. "How are you, my dear?"

There it was again—that note of genuine concern in her voice. If Carter didn't know better, he'd think she actually cared about Emily. But, of course, she didn't. A woman like this preyed on the weak and unsuspecting. She wouldn't let emotions stand in her way.

"I'm quite well, thank you." Emily stepped backward and looked over at Carter. "I see you've met my big brother."

"Indeed." Miss Avila threw him a smirk. "He's very protective of you."

Emily tilted her head in an exaggerated fashion. "Oh, no. Carter, what did you do?"

Every muscle in Carter's body tightened. They were not even five minutes into this exchange, and somehow the spiritualist had manipulated the situation to put him on the defensive. "I did nothing."

A most unladylike snort came from Emily. "I find that hard to believe."

"It's a brother's job to look out for his sister. You should count yourself lucky to have someone who cares for you so." Miss Avila took Emily's hand and gave it a consoling pat. "Come. Let's sit so we can talk."

Miss Avila walked slowly, adjusting her pace to allow for Emily's halting gait. When finally they sat, Emily looked up at Carter with eyes so round and innocent, they broke his heart.

"Miss Forbes." Miss Avila laid her other hand atop Emily's, drawing back the young woman's attention. "There is something of great importance we must discuss." She took a deep breath, then continued. "Your brother tells me you've made the acquaintance of Lord Shelston."

Emily's eyes brightened, and she sat a bit straighter. "I have, indeed. Do you know him?"

Miss Avila nodded slowly. "I do. Quite well, in fact."

"Isn't he amazing? So cultured, and he has such strong ties to the mysteries beyond this world. He's helped me a great deal."

Carter scowled and crossed his arms over his chest. When Miss Avila looked his way, he saw the anger in her creased brow, the fire crackling in her onyx eyes. She knew exactly how serious the situation was.

She turned back to Emily. "I'm sure it appears that way. But he's not what he seems. He is dangerous."

"Dangerous? In what way? How in the world could he hurt me? Why would he?"

Carter could keep silent no longer. "By getting your hopes up." He moved to the settee and went down on one knee, his hand on Emily's forearm. "By telling you he has a mystic connection to our parents."

"But he knows things—things he couldn't possibly have found out unless Mother or Father had told him."

"Blast it, Emily! People cannot communicate with the dead."

Emily yanked her arm away from him, wrenching free of Miss Avila's grasp at the same time. "Yes, they can. Miss Avila does it all the time." She turned to her. "Tell him."

Carter pinned Miss Avila with his eyes, entreating her to make good on her promise. "Yes, Miss Avila, tell me how you talk to the dead."

Miss Avila's cheeks bloomed red. She closed her eyes, and soot-black lashes fanned out across her pale skin. For a moment, her appearance called to mind a princess in one of the Grimm Brothers' fantastical tales. Yet when she opened her eyes, he saw not a princess but a woman determined to do the thing she least wanted: tell the truth.

When Juliet was young, about Artie's age, she'd worked as an assistant to her uncle, a magician. He had taught her the one ironclad rule of the trade: Never reveal professional secrets. Her breakfast tumbled round and round in her stomach. She was about to share all the tricks of the trade. If not for the weight of Forbes's eyes on her, she might have made a dash for the door. But she'd given her word, and she would keep it.

"Miss Forbes, your brother is correct. I hate to speak ill of someone who should be a colleague, but Lord Shelston does not communicate with the dead."

Emily blinked slowly, her head listing to the side. "Why would you say such a thing?"

"Your brother has good reason for his concern. Lord Shelston has ravaged the fortunes of several of his clients."

"No. When he spoke…he sounded just like Mother and Father."

"No doubt he listened carefully to your accent and mannerisms, and built upon what knowledge he might have had about your background." Emily had a northerner's clipped cadence and brisk formality. Shelston would have extrapolated from there. Her parents' accents would likely have been the same. Add a dash of feminine lightness—or masculine authority, as the case may be—and a big scoop of hopeful expectation from the sitter, and the client believed what she wanted to believe. Juliet knew that from experience.

Emily pushed herself back on the cushion, moving as far from Juliet as possible. "How could you? Are you jealous of him?"

With a sigh, Juliet looked down at her hands, clasped tightly in her lap. "This has nothing to do with how I feel. I'm trying to share facts with you. He may seem like he is giving you solace, but the truth is, he's preying upon your desperation by telling you what you want to hear."

"For a price," Forbes muttered.

"Yes, for a price." She glared at the Pinkerton.

Emily again struggled to her feet; but this time, it was a bit easier, thanks to the availability of her brother's shoulder. One hand pressed down on him, fingers digging in, while the other grasped the side of the settee. She stood upright, teetered for a moment, then moved across the room. It seemed she used her entire body to compel her artificial leg into forward momentum.

"Emily, I can tell you how he achieves his effects, if you will listen."

The nurturer in Juliet wanted to rush to her and erase the worry and pain that creased her face. But that same nurturer knew there was something more important at stake. With any luck, she'd accomplish what she'd come here to do—save her family—and also help Emily in the process.

Emily stood across the room, her fingers trailing lightly over the keys of an upright piano. "He's taken clients from you, probably." Her voice, as thin and tight as one of the instrument's strings, barely carried to her.

Before Juliet could stop him, Mr. Forbes rose to his feet and moved to his sister. She was fairly certain anything he might add would only make matters worse. But the man was determined to drive home his point.

"I asked her to come talk to you," he said, "so you'd see that his spiritualism patter is nonsense."

Emily looked at him, eyes narrowing. "How did you manage to find her?"

Even from her place on the settee, Juliet could see the man blanch. She held back a smile. Of course he didn't want his sister to know he'd attended a sitting, regardless of the reason. But he had asked Juliet for honesty. She saw no reason why she should hold back on this point.

"Mr. Forbes came to my salon for a sitting." She rose and sashayed across the room. "Not to contact a loved one, mind you, but to set a trap for me. He even asked that I try to contact you on the other side." She tapped Emily on the shoulder with the gloves she still clutched in one hand.

Emily frowned at her brother, then looked back at Juliet. "Why would you agree to help him after that?"

"Your brother can be very...persuasive." Her shoulders rose and then fell in a defeated shrug. "And, as I said, I have a family to support."

Just as Juliet had hoped, Emily became visibly upset. Her jaw clenched, spine stiffened, and fingers curled into tight fists. Creating tension between brother and sister would help ensure that no harm would come to Juliet's family after she left this place. Emily's kind heart would require her brother to keep his word, and he surely wouldn't risk her displeasure by doing otherwise. It was perfect.

"He threatened you, didn't he?" Emily jammed her fists on her hips and swung her ice-like stare from Juliet to her brother. "You threatened to hurt her family if she didn't help you. Carter, how could you?"

He held up his hands in surrender. "I never threatened her family."

Strictly speaking, that was true. But when he'd threatened her livelihood, he'd threatened them all. Still, there was no reason for his reputation to be sullied.

"Miss Forbes, your brother is only acting out of loving concern for you. I hope you understand now why you cannot trust Lord Shelston."

Emily eyed Juliet askance, as though she'd just sprouted a second head. "What I understand is that my brother brought you here under duress and made you say these horrible things about Lord Shelston. And I forgive you, though I'm not sure I'll ever forgive him." Tears flooded her eyes.

Juliet stammered for an answer. "But…but after what I've told you, surely you see…I can tell you how he performs his tricks."

"I will not listen to this…this base calumny any longer. Please don't say anything you'll regret. Certainly not now, since Carter's scheme has already been shown up."

Pressing a hand to her plummeting stomach, Juliet swallowed. This was no longer going according to plan. Not at all.

Forbes reached toward his sister, but she moved away before he could touch her. His hand fell to his side. "If you would just listen with an open mind, then you'd understand."

"If *I* would have an open mind! What about you?" She poked him hard in the chest with one finger. "You refuse to believe there might be something beyond what you can see."

"That's not true. I have no doubt that God exists and watches over us, every moment of our lives."

A bitter laugh escaped Emily's lips. "Yes, God. You'll forgive me if I don't find much comfort in the knowledge that He was watching over me when I was shot, and then when I lost my leg and my parents."

Juliet kept her outward expression calm but cringed inwardly. To be injured in such a manner was tragic. It was no surprise Emily questioned God and had gone looking elsewhere for comfort and guidance.

For his part, Mr. Forbes couldn't have looked more crestfallen had his sister slapped him across the face. "You don't mean that."

"Yes, I do." Emily's shoulders fell, and she looked suddenly exhausted. "Please, both of you, just leave me in peace." She turned her back to them, one hand still braced on the edge of the piano.

Mr. Forbes opened his mouth, but Juliet motioned sharply for him to stay silent. Nothing more they might say would help the matter. Not now.

Eyebrows drawn together, he snapped his mouth shut, turned, and walked out of the room. Juliet followed him, her mind reeling. She'd done exactly what Forbes had asked but hadn't achieved the outcome he desired. As a Pinkerton, it was possible he would keep his word and leave her family alone. As a concerned and upset brother, he might very well decide to sully her name simply out of a need to do something.

He stood with arms folded across his chest and glared at her. "Well played. I cannot believe I actually thought you would do the right thing."

Juliet pulled the door firmly closed behind her. "I did exactly as I promised. I didn't know she would leap to such a conclusion. How could I possibly have guessed that?"

He stepped forward. "It's what your sort does, isn't it? You help people believe what they want to believe."

Juliet's eyesight went jittery for a second with the surge of anger pulsing through her. "How dare you! I did what you wanted. Now you have to hold up your side of the bargain." She stepped forward, too, until they were toe-to-toe, even though she had to crane her head to look him in the eye.

"Oh no, you don't." He sneered. "I'm not letting you get away with this. You're going to help me expose Shelston."

"I am not. I wouldn't be able to continue working in this town if I betrayed a fellow medium."

He scowled down at her. "I can guarantee you won't continue working in this town if you don't."

Juliet fought the impulse to kick the big brute in the shin. How, how, how was she to get out of this mess? She closed her eyes and counted to ten. Drew in a deep breath. Thought of her family and of Emily. Finally her eyelids popped open. "If I help you expose Shelston, will you swear to leave me in peace?"

The Pinkerton's posture relaxed ever so slightly. "I promise." He raised a hand and pointed right at her nose. "But if you pull another fast one, you will live to regret it."

Chapter 3

Standing in front of Miss Avila's two-story brick home, Carter wiped his damp palms on the front of his trousers, steeling himself for what might ensue. He was not a man given to fits of nerves, but he'd wrestled with his conscience most of the night, which had made sleep hard to come by. Contrary to what Miss Avila seemed to think, he did not enjoy bullying young women. He just had to find a way to deal with Shelston, especially now that Emily was angry. She was in high dudgeon to the point she was liable to do something they'd both regret.

On reflection, he didn't really think Miss Avila had manipulated the conversation with Emily as artfully as he'd first suspected. As she herself had said, no one was that good. At least, no one in his experience.

Taking a deep breath, Carter pulled back his shoulders and rapped on the door. Moments later, it opened.

The aged butler tilted his head slightly to the side. "May I help you?"

"Carter Forbes, here to see Miss Avila."

"Yes, Mr. Forbes. So good to see you again. This way, sir."

From the milky haze clouding the man's eyes, Carter doubted he saw much of anything. Still, the butler moved with the steady gait of someone who knew exactly where he was going and was in no hurry to get there.

Once in the parlor, the butler extended his hand to a sitting area. "Make yourself comfortable, sir. I will announce your arrival to Miss Avila."

The man walked away, and Carter seated himself gingerly on the settee. His right leg bounced in a ceaseless rhythm. He ought to apologize to her, but he wasn't sure he could bring himself to do it. To apologize might imply that he condoned her line of work, and he couldn't—

A gray-haired lady doddered in, bent so far over her cane that she stared at the ground. Carter stood, hat in hand. "I'm sorry, ma'am. It seems there's been some mistake. I'm here for *Miss* Avila."

"So much for the all-seeing eye of the Pinkertons." The figure straightened and transformed before his eyes.

"Miss Avila?" He peered more closely at her.

She smiled. "I told you I'd be blackballed if anyone realized I'm the one who helped expose Shelston. So, I took some precautions."

He couldn't help being impressed. "I never would have recognized you."

"That's the idea."

"Where did you learn to change your appearance like that?"

"My misspent youth. We'll need to hurry if we're going to make his noon sitting."

Carter nodded, deciding not to comment on her abrupt change of subject, though he tucked the reaction away for further consideration later. He offered her his elbow. "Well, come along then, Mother. I've a carriage waiting."

"After you, Sonny."

He wasn't sure, but he thought he caught a flash of a smile before she hunched over again. This was going to be one interesting afternoon.

Juliet stared out the window at the evidence of war as they drove through Washington. Men in uniforms were everywhere. Rows of Wiard guns awaiting deployment occupied the nearby park, where couples had formerly strolled. Red, white, and blue bunting hung in limp bunches, looking as dispirited as much of the populace. All too many of the pedestrians trudging down the sidewalks wore black.

Their carriage passed beneath the incomplete monument to George Washington, poking awkwardly at the sky like a jagged, broken tooth. Mr. Forbes remained ominously quiet. Not that she wanted to talk to him. She was just as happy to sit in silence. Still, she couldn't help but wonder what was going through his mind.

At last, he turned from his private perusal of the landscape. "Did you ever work in the theater?"

Juliet decided she liked him better when he was quiet. "I can't see how my background could be of any possible relevance." That wasn't strictly true, but he didn't really need to know how she had come to learn illusionists' tricks.

His jaw stiffened, but he did not argue. "Do you at least have a plan?"

"Of course I have a plan."

"Would you care to enlighten me?"

"No, I wouldn't. The less you know, the better off we are."

"How could that possibly be?"

"If I tell you my plan, you might give it away—and then blame me when it doesn't work."

His chest jutted out as he pulled his shoulders back. "Why would you even think—"

"I think it's a possibility because you had to keep sticking your oar in with Emily. You ruined the whole conversation, then blamed me for manipulating things."

"I did no such thing. I was just trying to help her understand."

"She doesn't seem to want your help."

"That much is clear." He grunted and rubbed his fingers over his mustache a few times. "Do you think she'll listen, even if I—*we*—prove this fellow a fraud before witnesses?"

The genuine concern in his tone made Juliet bite back the flippant response that sprang to mind. She patted his arm. "I don't know if she will listen or not. People have a way of discounting information they don't like. But once Shelston's exposed, if there are enough witnesses, I don't think he'll stay around. He'll want to move on to an easier harvest."

Mr. Forbes nodded, his eyes still troubled, but he did seem to have found some solace in her words. "Can I trust you?" The question seemed directed at himself as well as her.

Juliet met his gaze. "If you have to ask, then nothing I say will offer much reassurance."

"Just don't betray me."

His earnest plea gripped her heart, but she was spared the need to reply when the carriage came to a stuttering stop in front of Shelston's residence.

Mr. Forbes blew out a heavy breath, then hopped down and helped her from the carriage as solicitously as if she really was his mother. A manservant met them at the door, and Forbes handed over the one-dollar sitting fee for both of them.

Juliet pushed a pair of faux spectacles up her nose and peered around the hall. Shelston obviously had some well-fixed clients. The house was full of useless yet expensive-looking *objets d'art*; every door was adorned with plush curtains of bottle-green velvet; and ornate rugs thick enough to swallow a shoe covered the floors. It all had a heavy, muffling effect that made Juliet feel she ought to whisper, which, in turn, made her want to shout.

They were ushered into a sitting room so swathed in fabric, it appeared padded. The couches and chairs had been pushed back against the walls to make room for a round table of glossy mahogany. Juliet cast a critical eye on a large cabinet standing in one corner of the room, with doors painted so as to give the illusion of being elaborately carved. It also featured round crystal knobs set close together near the center of the cabinet. *Excellent.*

The manservant pulled out a chair for Juliet, and she settled into it slowly.

"What name may I give his lordship?"

"Eh?" Juliet scrunched up her nose and squinted at him through her spectacles.

He raised his voice, shattering the too-hushed hush. "I said—"

"Mortimer." Forbes cast Juliet a sidewise glance, and she winked at him. "You may tell Lord Shelston that Mr. Mortimer and his grandmother, Mrs. Noying, are here to see him."

Juliet sniffed at having been aged another generation. She poked Forbes in the ribs with the end of her cane. "Speak up, Eustis. Granny can't hear you."

The detective smiled wanly at the manservant, and the fellow scuttled off, apparently delighted to get away from an imperious old biddy.

No sooner did the doors close behind the fellow than Forbes rounded on her. "What are you doing?"

She shook her head in warning. He was a fool if he thought they were alone. He raised one eyebrow in question, and she used her chin to indicate the cabinet. A deep frown scored his features, and she could almost see him debate whether or not to go fling open the doors. Once again she gave a small shake of her head. He may not trust her, but he had to acknowledge that she knew more of this arena than he did. If they were to have any hope of catching Shelston, he needed to listen to her.

Forbes grimaced, his fists tightening, but he stayed put. "Grandmother!" He'd raised his voice. "I said, what are you doing? I've asked you not to chew tobacco when we go out."

Juliet turned her snort of laughter into a gurgling cough. "Sonny, I'm eighty-four. I figure I'm old enough to do what I please at this stage of life. Speaking of which, I'll be going to see my kinfolk what passed on soon enough. Why'd you insist on this foolishness?"

Despite his apparently low opinion of her, light danced in Forbes's eyes. "Don't you want to see Granddad?"

"I saw 'im every day for sixty-five years. A break isn't such a terrible thing 'fore we face eternity together."

The detective bit his lip to keep from laughing and hid his grin behind his hand, his fingers massaging his temples in a show of exasperation. A thrill sparked through Juliet at the effect her teasing had on him. He seemed much more approachable when he smiled.

The manservant entered again with several more sitters, and they all waited quietly for "Lord" Shelston to make his appearance. After an interminable delay, the fraud swept into the room, wearing a floor-length black velvet cape over a full evening kit.

He must have been roasting alive; indeed, his face was redder and shinier than ever. Though it looked ridiculous, the costume was highly practical. There was no telling how many little pockets were sewn into the cape, and the black would mask his shape from the sharpest eyes in the darkened séance room.

Shelston offered the group a low bow. "Good day to you, my friends, my adventurers together into the dark and mysterious realm beyond this humdrum life. There are many things about the great beyond that remain unexplained, but I assure you that with me as your guide, there is no danger. You have nothing to fear from most spirits, and I would give my very life to protect my charges from any wicked entity we might encounter."

With a flourish of his cape, he took his place at the table. The manservant reappeared, bearing a trumpet and a drum, which he placed in the center of the table.

Shelston continued his monologue. "Unfortunately, not all spirits are able to speak clearly with those of us on this side of the veil that divides us from death. The instruments before you are provided to allow the departed other methods of communication."

Juliet barely kept from rolling her eyes. She wasn't any better than Shelston, morally speaking, but at least she didn't set out to insult the intelligence of her sitters.

The curtains were drawn, the candle lit. The manservant made his way noisily out of the room. Shelston instructed everyone to hold hands. Around the table, the sitters obeyed.

"O great spirit guides, hear me now. Attend to us and listen to my call." He continued on in that vein, growing louder and more insistent, until his head lolled to one side. Then he straightened in his seat as a high-pitched voice lisped from him: "Lord Shelston, you honor us with your presence again. What do you wish to know?"

Shelston went around the table, allowing each sitter a turn to ask questions of the spirits. As he spoke, white wisps began to float around the room. During a pause, the trumpet levitated from the table and began to play as if of its own accord.

Juliet squeezed Forbes's hand, signaling him that she was stepping away. Leaving behind the sand-filled glove grasped firmly by the person seated next to her, she silently moved back from the table.

This was the trickiest part of the whole proposition. She had to navigate the room in the dark without bumping into anyone or anything. She had studied the layout carefully, though, and now she made for the cabinet as quickly as possible.

As expected, the doors gaped open. Also as anticipated, the hinges were well-oiled; they made not a sound as she closed them. She slid a half-inch-thick band of India rubber down her arm and looped it twice over the two crystal knobs.

"I felt a breath on my cheek!" one sitter cried out.

"A hand on my shoulder," said another.

Juliet hurriedly retraced her steps. Pulling her expression into one of appropriate awe, she resumed her seat and again took Forbes's hand. He gave her fingers a squeeze, obviously wanting to question her, but she ignored him. There was no way to communicate now.

Next, she yawned once, then again, more loudly. As Shelston continued to drone on and on, she made a show of falling asleep. At her first snore, the fraud faltered for a fraction of a second. He made a valiant effort of trying to talk over her, and he even sped up his speech, until, at last, he conceded defeat. With a moan, he pressed a hand to his head and began to rouse from his trance. From the corner where the cabinet stood came a thump and a bump, followed by what sounded distinctly like an "ouch." The otherworldly tendrils of white that had been streaming away from the table as if the ghosts were departing dropped in a heap on the floor and lay there, unmoving.

Juliet nudged the detective.

Mr. Forbes needed no other cues. He jumped to his feet. "Lights!" An instant later, he flung open the nearest set of curtains.

Everyone winced at the sudden illumination, but it quickly dawned on the sitters that sometime during the séance, they had been joined by two men dressed all in black, including black gloves on their hands and knit masks covering their faces. One of them had dropped a pile of cheesecloth as he'd tried to crawl under a couch.

As outraged gazes turned from the black-clad figures to Lord Shelston, he began to bluster. "How did you young fellows get into my house? Just what do you think you're doing here? Have you been playing pranks on my guests?"

Forbes moved in. "Lord Shelston, I'm Pinkerton agent Carter Forbes. I would suggest you take your leave of Washington before word of this fraud gets out."

Shelston opened his mouth as if to spout some defense.

Forbes forestalled him. "And I believe we all deserve a refund."

Head high, Shelston pulled his cape around him and swept from the room. His henchmen followed on his heels.

A society lady in lavender silk shifted, as if about to stand, but she couldn't quite find her feet. "Well." The word seemed to sum up the feelings of the entire group.

The manservant reentered. "His lordship has been affronted and will not return this evening. He has asked that you all leave."

"And our fees?" Forbes wasn't going to let go of that point.

A little tic started in the corner of the servant's right eye. He stepped to the side and produced the bag into which he had dropped the monies he had accepted at the door. The sitters lined up to get their fees back as they departed.

As the carriage pulled away, Forbes whooped and tossed his hat up. It bounced off the ceiling and dropped to the floor, but he didn't seem to care in the least. "How did you do it? What did you do?"

Juliet grinned at his exuberance. "Charlatans often have accomplices who either hide in large pieces of furniture or enter the room through secret panels. Since the cabinet was the only likely hiding place, and the only object behind which to conceal such a panel, I closed the doors and put a band of India rubber around the handles, which effectively locked the cabinet. In the dark, it would have been difficult for the fellows to figure out what was wrong or to find another means of escape without alerting the sitters. So, we caught them flat-footed."

"The plan was brilliant, but what if there had been another door?"

Juliet offered her most enigmatic smile. "I had other options."

The Pinkerton shook his head. "I'm not even sure I want to know."

"Do you think Shelston will skedaddle?" Juliet adjusted her false nose. The combination of gravity and the heat was taking its toll on her disguise. "Did we do enough?"

Forbes leaned his head back against the seat and closed his eyes. He still hadn't bothered to pick up his hat. "I'll give him every reason to take off and never look back."

"And you will honor our bargain?"

One eye opened a crack. "I'm a man of my word."

Juliet didn't bother to point out his change of heart the day before. "I'd like something else."

"What?" He straightened, looking suddenly wary.

"I've been endeavoring to expand my clientele among the better circles. I want your promise that you won't try to undermine my efforts."

"I promised to leave you alone. How is this different?"

"It isn't, as long as you are willing to abide by that promise."

He looked her over from head to foot. "If I agree to this, I need to know how you became so skilled at disguises."

Juliet suddenly realized that authors who described a character's mouth as "falling open" were not necessarily exaggerating. "What about being a man of your word?"

"I still am. But I also have a duty during wartime. I can't allow someone who could be a potential spy to continue operations."

"Do you seriously suspect that I might be a spy?"

"Not if you have a reasonable explanation for your skills."

Juliet glared out the window. If she wasn't extremely careful, this Pinkerton would soon know all her secrets. But this was a small matter. A little digging, and he could get the information for himself. "Growing up, I traveled and worked with my uncle. He was a magician on the vaudeville circuit."

The Pinkerton finally bent to retrieve his hat and slapped it on his knee. "A magician's assistant. That explains it."

"Yes, well, I've answered your questions. I expect you to uphold your end of the bargain." Even as she said the words, Juliet suspected the Pinkerton hadn't finished meddling in her life. He was quick, and his faraway smile indicated he was probably already figuring out how to turn the information to his advantage.

Chapter 4

A warm breeze rustled through the trees as Carter reined his horse to a stop in front of the Executive Mansion. He dismounted, his foot barely out of the stirrup when a stable boy appeared and reached for the reins.

"Afternoon, sir."

"Good afternoon, Daniel. How's your mother?"

The young man's smile lit up his face. Daniel was a free Negro who earned a wage for his labors, yet he obviously wasn't used to receiving common courtesy from white men. It was a sad state of affairs when people stopped treating each other as human beings, equal in the sight of God.

"Ma's feelin' better today, thank you, sir." He patted the horse's neck then reached inside his pocket and pulled out a piece of carrot, which he offered to Red on the flat of his palm. The horse all but inhaled the treat.

"You certainly know the way to his heart," Carter said with a chuckle.

Daniel grinned and kicked a rock with the toe of his worn shoe. "Cook lets me have the stubs." He laughed as Red rubbed his velvety muzzle against his cheek. "I save 'em for the special ones."

Carter nodded and touched a finger to the brim of his hat. "I leave him in your capable hands."

With the steady clop of Red's hooves behind him, Carter turned and took in a quick breath. No matter how many times he climbed the front stairs and walked between the grand white pillars, he always experienced a moment of awe. But a moment was all he would allow himself. He had important work to tend to. It wouldn't do to wander around the Executive Mansion like a starry-eyed schoolboy.

His knock on the door was immediately answered by a short, thin doorkeeper in formal dress. He bowed slightly. "Good day to you, Mr. Forbes."

Edward had been in charge of the door since Zachary Taylor sat in the president's office, but his voice still held a tinge of an Irish lilt.

"Good day, Edward." Carter glanced up the stairs. "Is he in?"

They'd done this dance for more than a year, so Edward knew the man Carter inquired about was not President Lincoln.

"Yes, sir. He's waiting for you in the Green Room."

Carter frowned and strode past the doorkeeper with a brisk "Thank you." Mr. Pinkerton had never waited for him before. And certainly not in the Green Room.

Allan Pinkerton turned around the second Carter's foot crossed the threshold. With eyebrows so thick and low over his eyelids, the man seemed to wear a perpetual scowl. But today, Carter feared the scowl was real.

With no preamble, Pinkerton pointed past him. "Close the door behind you."

Carter pulled it shut. "Is there a problem, sir?"

"I'll say there is. With Mrs. Lincoln."

Now their location made sense. As mistress of the manor, Mrs. Lincoln took her role seriously, and she wasn't one to let a closed door keep her out of a room—with one exception. Her young son Willie had died of typhoid fever earlier in the year, and his body had been laid out and prepared in the Green Room. She hadn't entered it since.

"Is there a threat to Mrs. Lincoln?"

"Only the one she poses to herself." Pinkerton frowned. "She insists on consulting with that charlatan spiritualist Lord Shelston."

Carter made no outward reaction to hearing Shelston's name. Inwardly, however, he had a flash of Miss Avila playing the part of his doddering old grandmother, and had to hold back a laugh. "That's a problem, sir."

"Oh yes. At best, the man's a fraud. At worst, he's working for the other side. We've already foiled one assassination attempt on the president. How are we supposed to keep him safe if Mrs. Lincoln insists on opening the door to anyone who claims he can contact her dead son?" Pinkerton took a breath, bowed his head, and made a quick sign of the cross on his chest. "God rest his soul."

Carter followed suit. "Amen."

Pinkerton picked up as though the moment of deference had never happened. "If she were in her right mind, I might be able to make her understand. But she's having none of it. She insists we bring Shelston to her. Now."

Mrs. Lincoln's emotional state had always been fragile. But, since her son's death, it had been shattered. If she believed Shelston could contact Willie and bring her a message from beyond the grave, then nothing Mr. Pinkerton or anyone else said would dissuade her. What would she do when she learned Lord Shelston had made a hasty departure from the capital? And what if Carter's part in it became public knowledge? This was turning into a bigger tangle of trouble than he'd anticipated.

"Sir, I have it on good authority that Shelston is leaving the city."

Pinkerton's eyes narrowed to the point of closure, and he muttered something under his breath. "She won't accept that. She'll just go looking for another medium. Heaven knows who she'll run to."

A plan took form in Carter's mind. "If I may, sir. In my dealings about town, I've run into a woman who could be of great help to us."

"Another spiritualist?"

Carter wasn't prepared to disclose the true nature of his acquaintance with Miss Avila, but he wasn't about to lie, either. "An actress, of sorts. And a skilled illusionist. I believe she could pose as a medium and perform a mock séance."

Pinkerton scratched the wiry hair covering his jaw. "Can you trust this woman?"

"I've not known her long, sir, but I believe she can be trusted. To a point."

"And beyond that point?"

"Let's just say I have certain leverage. It's in her best interests to follow my orders."

"So, we provide Mrs. Lincoln the comfort she desires and, at the same time, protect her from opportunists. Not a bad idea, Forbes. Not bad at all."

Carter allowed himself the ghost of a smile. To quote an old friend, "Everyone should have an ace in the hole." And Miss Avila could be his.

"The first lady? Have you gone mad?"

Leaning against the wall in Juliet's private sitting room, arms crossed over his chest, Carter Forbes frowned. "I thought you would be excited to secure such a prestigious client. I don't see the problem."

Juliet paced the length of the worn carpet, arms pumping, fingers curled into tight fists. Of course he didn't see the problem. He was an upright, honest man. Walking into the Executive Mansion was no different to him from walking into the average home. He couldn't imagine how many things could go wrong. But Juliet could.

"My reputation is at stake."

"Let's talk about your reputation, then, shall we? You continue to tell me your main focus is providing for your family. Think of what will happen when word gets out that Mrs. Lincoln, the first lady herself, has come to you for a sitting."

Juliet bit her lip and stared at the empty fireplace. An endorsement from the president's wife would give her credibility that could take her years to achieve on her own. The most fashionable parlors in Washington would welcome her. Even though many people in the capital didn't care for Mary Lincoln, they still liked to emulate her. Juliet's worries over keeping her little family together would be eliminated.

But it could work to her disadvantage just as easily. If anything went wrong—if Mrs. Lincoln labeled her a fraud—Juliet would never work in Washington again. It would be the end of her career, such as it was, and the dissolution of her family.

And there was another thing that niggled at her. "Why would you want to do anything that might help increase my business?"

He hesitated for a moment, as if weighing just how honest he should be. "Truthfully, I don't. I consider you the lesser of two evils."

Complete honesty, then. Impressive, if a bit insulting.

"Mrs. Lincoln demands to see Shelston," he continued. "Thanks to your assistance, that's impossible. Frankly, I find it distasteful that I'm required to produce a mystic of any kind. But I'd rather it be someone I trust than a stranger."

Juliet stopped her pacing and turned to face Forbes. "You trust me?"

One corner of his mouth lifted in a lazy grin. "More than any other spiritualist I know."

A backhanded compliment, indeed, but she'd take it. From what he'd said, it was just as important to him that Mrs. Lincoln believe the ruse as it was to Juliet. She could use that, and the fact that he seemed to like her, in spite of himself, to her advantage.

Slipping into the character of Madam Avila, she glided to an upholstered French chair and sat gracefully. "Since this won't be a genuine sitting, I'll need as much background information as you can provide."

Forbes snorted and pushed away from the wall. "You're telling me your other sittings *are* genuine? That you talk to the dead?"

She smiled sweetly. "Of course they're genuine. I provide a conduit between those who grieve and their loved ones. Nothing more, nothing less."

"Like you did for Mr. Greenfield?" Forbes sat in the chair across from her.

The fine hairs at the nape of her neck stood at attention. What was he implying?

"I noticed what you did with him. When he asked about his son."

Juliet shook her head. "I never said Ben was dead."

"No. And you never said he wasn't." The detective leaned forward, hands clasped. "You gave the man hope without making a promise you couldn't fulfill. It was a kind act."

She released a breath and hoped that a rosy flush didn't give away the heat blooming in her cheeks. "He is a sweet man." A sweet man who'd already experienced enough pain. If Juliet could ease the sufferings of people like him with a cleverly worded phrase, an exaggeration, or even a "conversation" with a deceased spouse, then that was exactly what she would do. She wished she could explain it to Mr. Forbes—make him see she wasn't entirely the kind of deceitful person he thought she was.

"I don't agree with your choice of profession, but at least you appear to care about the feelings of the people you dupe."

The warmth of her cheeks grew from a bloom of gratitude to a blaze of anger. "Now look here...."

She half rose from her chair, but Forbes motioned for her to sit. "Calm yourself, Miss Avila. This isn't the time to discuss the ethics of what you do. Regardless of what happens in your other sittings, this one will be carefully planned, down to the last jot and tittle. Now," he rubbed his palms together, "shall we begin?"

"You're being ridiculous. This isn't some sort of theatrical performance to be played out in front of an audience. The sitters are participants. They will take things off script faster than you can blink."

His jaw tightened, and she sighed, bracing herself for some cutting observation on the nature of mediums. "I've been tasked with making sure Mrs. Lincoln doesn't fall into the hands of charlatans who could take advantage of her and her position. If I can find someone who will also offer her a bit of comfort...well, I guess that's why she wants a spiritualist in the first place. But I will not give you free rein. I must know what you will say."

Juliet concentrated on presenting a calm façade. "The best script in the world is useless if the other person doesn't know her lines. However, I know what people usually ask when they come to me."

He watched her intently, and she tamped down the desire to fidget with her dress. "Well—"

Juliet held up a hand. "I know you haven't a high opinion of my morals, but I promise not to pry into any sensitive government details—including information about the war, lest you still think me a spy. I'm afraid that's the best assurance you'll get from me." She bit the inside of her lip, then decided to throw in all her cards. "If you don't like it, you can find another spiritualist."

Juliet pressed her dry lips together, trying in vain to moisten them. She couldn't stop moving, so she bustled around the sitting room, plumping already plump cushions and correcting every tiny imperfection that caught her eye.

What if this was a trap? What if Forbes had set it up, determined to prove her a fraud? Could he be that devious?

Miss Clara came in with a vase of fresh flowers from the back garden, where she tended the blossoms as if they were children. "You will be fine, Juliet. Stop fussing."

Juliet ceased her frantic rubbing of a nearly invisible spot on the table. "I'm not fussing."

Miss Clara raised both eyebrows, then turned and set the flowers on the side table in front of the wide window.

"I'm a little nervous, that's all." Juliet smoothed down the front of her skirt.

"And a hurricane causes a breeze." Miss Clara tweaked an iris into a prettier attitude. Then, apparently satisfied that the arrangement couldn't be made to look any nicer, she left the flowers and gave Juliet a hug. "Of course you're nervous. The president's wife is coming for a sitting."

Outside the window, the clop of hooves and jangle of metal announced the arrival of a coach bearing the first of the afternoon's sitters. Juliet swung out of the room. "Professor, they're here."

He was already in the hallway, standing tall and smoothing the front of his frock coat. "I know how to answer the door, Juliet. Why don't you go on into the kitchen?"

"I'm sorr—"

"Go on, child. Don't want to spoil your big entrance."

Juliet did as bidden. Still, she couldn't keep still. She paced and paced the kitchen, her stomach clamped in a tight knot. "Why are they taking so long?"

Sitting at the battered wooden table, Artie cast her a sideways look but didn't respond. He bolted the remains of a piece of strawberry pie, then slid out of the room without a word.

A fresh pang struck Juliet. She knew she was making them all crazy, but she couldn't seem to help herself. She needed to do something. She would be calm once she could do something. In the meantime, her family suffered.

She pressed her ear to the kitchen door. Well-bred voices murmured in the hall. Crinolines rustled. Feet shuffled. The sounds faded as the guests were ushered into the sitting room.

Another knock. Juliet nudged the kitchen door open a crack and peered out. Professor Marvolo opened the front door with a flourish. A short woman entered, clad in deepest mourning, her face covered with a black net veil. On her heels came Forbes. It could only be Mrs. Lincoln; though, as planned, the woman believed herself to be incognito.

The gap Juliet peered through was no more than half an inch wide, yet Carter seemed to sense her presence. He looked directly at her and offered a little smirk, as if amused at her reticence. But she noticed that he had polished his boots, and his shirt appeared freshly laundered and starched. He was proud of his association with the president's family. He wouldn't have brought Mrs. Lincoln here unless he thought she would be safe.

The realization provided some relief.

Juliet stepped away from the door. She forced herself to sit and take slow breaths, in and out, in and out. She would do this. It could be the beginning of a whole new era for her family. Mary Lincoln may not be extremely popular in Washington, but that didn't mean people weren't avid to know what she was up to. If Mary Lincoln became a regular at Juliet's, they would flock to her.

But first, she had to get through the private sitting, which included a handful of Mrs. Lincoln's friends and her sister Elizabeth Edwards, who had crossed the battle lines and come north to comfort Mary in her grief over her son. None of these other sitters had been to a séance before. There were undoubtedly a few who were willing to be impressed, as well as a few who would love to debunk Juliet as a fraud.

The professor swung open the door. "They're ready for you."

Juliet stood and drew a breath deep into her lungs. "Thank you." Affixing a smile as enigmatic as Mona Lisa's she moved down the hall, followed by the professor. He opened the door for her, and she glided in, trying to look ethereal, mysterious, and wholesome in equal measures. The sitters ceased their quiet chatter.

She caught the Pinkerton's eye as she entered. At least she knew that one person present truly wanted her to succeed. "Good evening. Thank you all for coming." She claimed the last seat at the table and stood before it, hands clasped at her waist. "I could give a speech about the afterlife and the world beyond this one, but most of my guests prefer to talk to spirits from that realm rather than listen to me."

As she spoke, Professor Marvolo drew the curtains across the window. The brilliance of the sunset was cut from the room. Juliet lit the taper in the center of the table and seated herself. "I sense there are several new, unhealed griefs among you. Some of terrible weight."

Mrs. Lincoln lifted her veil and dabbed at her eyes with a black-edged handkerchief.

Juliet's heart went out to her. Losing a child must be agonizing. A mother-son relationship was such an intimate one, and the fact that untold numbers of mothers across the country were experiencing the same pain surely didn't ease Mrs. Lincoln's own sense of grief. "I hope that, by the time we are finished this evening, you are able to find a measure of peace. Perhaps we could all join hands."

She took the hands of the individuals on either side of her and waited, letting the silence grow. Then, in a soft voice, she began her instructions. "Gaze into the candle and focus your thoughts on the space between life and death. Think of the person to whom you most wish to speak. Conjure that person's image in your mind."

Gently she wound the spell of her voice around them, lulling and soothing, as she had been taught by Gaston, the great mesmerist. After several moments, their eyes began to go glassy in the candle glow. Even Forbes appeared less alert.

Juliet continued her spoken lullaby. "Imagine your essence floating free of your body. We are approaching the veil that separates life from death. Rising with the candle smoke. You are looking down at yourself, and with new, inner eyes, you wake to other presences."

Small wisps of ethereal whiteness materialized, first here and then there. They seemed to swirl and dance around the perimeter of the table. Juliet watched carefully as the expressions on the visages illumined by the glow of candlelight turned wondering.

She closed her eyes and frowned. "I sense the presence of a young boy. He longs to speak. He wants to reach out to his mother." With exquisite timing, Artie dropped the dark cloak that had covered him head to toe. Even though she knew it was a boy draped in cheesecloth, a chill ran through Juliet at the sight of the ghost child standing there. He reached toward Mary with one hand, and, in a voice just above a whisper, he said, "Don't cry, Mother. I am well here. I found Eddie."

Mary Lincoln leaped up with an inarticulate cry. Then she slumped backward. Luckily, Forbes was there and caught her before she could fall.

Juliet glanced back and watched the apparition melt into thin air as Artie crouched down and crawled beneath the cloak again. He made his exit quickly, darting with a single flutter of trailing cheesecloth for the cabinet at the end of the room.

Jumping to her feet, Juliet gave every semblance of haste as she moved to turn up the gaslights. But she allowed Artie plenty of time to make his escape. Her stomach, which had calmed down at the beginning of the performance, now flopped like a landed fish, while her heart beat against her ribs in desperate rhythm. Forbes was not going to be pleased.

As the lights came up, Juliet could see a tableau of concerned faces surrounding Mary. Forbes crouched on the ground, still cradling her shoulders in one arm, while he gently patted her face with the other hand.

One of the ladies pulled smelling salts from her bag and passed them down the line until they reached someone close enough to wave them under Mary's nose.

She tossed her head from side to side at the stench, then her eyes popped open.

"Are you all right, Mrs. President?" Forbes asked.

The others clustered around her echoed his concern.

Mary let out a small moan and raised a hand to her head. "Did you see him? That was my Willie. My Willie. He spoke to me."

Forbes nodded. "We all saw him."

A chorus of amazed confirmations followed his pronouncement.

"Where is she?" With the Pinkerton's help, Mrs. Lincoln struggled to her feet.

Juliet drew back against the wall, but there was nowhere to run as everyone turned to stare at her.

Mary pushed through them, hands extended. Tears shone in her eyes. "You brought my Willie back to me. I told Lizzy he had visited me, and she thought me quite strange. But now I am not alone in seeing him." She clasped both of Juliet's hands in hers. "How can I thank you?"

Juliet struggled to assimilate the fact that Mary wasn't angry. She leaned forward, allowing herself to be embraced by the shorter woman. Behind Mary, Forbes stood, assessing her anew.

It had been a success, but now she owed the Pinkerton, and there was no telling what he'd demand in return.

Chapter 5

July 4, 1862
Washington, D.C.

Carter scrubbed a hand over his unshaven cheeks and cricked his neck to the side. He'd be almighty glad to get home and take a bath. He dismounted, pulled his saddlebag free, then handed Red's reins over to the livery stable groom. A quick rummage in his pocket turned up a nickel, which he flicked to the lad as a tip.

Three more blocks, and he'd be home. His body ached almost as much as his mind. He'd ridden hard but hadn't managed to outpace the images of the dead and dying on the banks of the Chickahominy. Seven days of hard fighting had left a band of carnage just south of Washington. Carter had tried to correct McClellan's misapprehension of the size of Lee's army, but to no avail. The cautious Union general had stalwartly insisted that he was outnumbered. An image of Miss Avila flashed in Carter's mind, as had happened a surprising number of times over the past two months. Maybe she'd been right when she'd said that people believed only what they wanted to believe. McClellan obviously wanted to be able to blame his reluctance to engage in decisive action on something other than his own unwillingness to commit.

Carter pushed through the front door and dropped his saddlebags to the ground. He slid his hat off and ruffled his hand through hair sticky with sweat. "Em?"

A thump and then a scrape sounded from the sitting room. When he thrust open the door, she met him with a look of delighted surprise salted with relief, but the curve of her lips quickly reversed, evidently because she'd remembered she was still angry. His sister suspected he'd had something to do with Shelston's precipitous departure from Washington, and she'd been making her displeasure known ever since.

She stooped awkwardly to retrieve a large book from the floor. "Oh, you're back."

Even pretended, her indifference stung. He tried not to let it show. "Safe and sound, but in desperate need of a bath. Could you ask Hayes to start water boiling?"

She sniffed but set her book aside and stumped from the room.

He sighed. Eventually she would forgive him.

Probably.

He made his way next door to thank the neighbors for keeping an eye on Emily in his absence. And then, at last, he retreated to his room. The bed called to him, as alluring as a siren. He took a step forward but stopped short as he glanced at his filthy clothes. Lying down now would just be a waste of a good bedspread. Hayes had already brought in the standing tub, at least. That meant the promise of sleep wasn't too far off.

Carter sat on a cane-back chair and pulled off his boots, letting them thunk to the floor. Then he stood, groaning at the biting pain of sore muscles, and shed his shirt and pants in a heap.

Hayes arrived with the first buckets of steaming water. "It's good to see you home, Mr. Carter. Miss Emily's been missing you something fierce."

Carter grinned. "Don't let her find out you told me so. She's still mad."

A half dozen trips later, and the manservant had filled the tub half full. Carter climbed in, wincing and sighing at the same time, as the heat stung his many cuts and scrapes while simultaneously easing some of the knots from his muscles.

He held his breath as Hayes poured the next bucket directly over his head. The manservant handed him a bar of soap and a linen square, and Carter set to getting rid of the worst of the grime. Hayes moved to lay out a clean nightshirt, then nudged Carter's dirty clothes with the tip of his foot. "I'm thinking these should be burned."

"Whatever you say."

"Mm-hmm."

"What's Emily been up to while I've been gone?"

"Not much of anything, far as I could tell. She hardly leaves the house. Hardly speaks to anyone. Hardly eats. I know Shelston wasn't no good, but that child has been miserable since he up and left." He handed Carter his razor and a mug of shaving lather.

"Now that this assignment is finished, maybe I can spend more time with her. Distract her some."

Within fifteen minutes, Carter had finished his bath and donned his nightshirt. After Hayes tactfully retreated, Carter pulled back the covers and slid between the sheets. A groan escaped his lips as his head hit the pillow. Nothing had ever, ever felt this good. Ever.

A furor of voices floated to him from downstairs. A clatter of quick footsteps sounded in the hall, and he cracked open one eye. *Please, God, no.*

A knock rattled his door. He yanked the pillow from beneath his head and covered his face.

The knocking persisted.

"What?" he demanded.

"There's an emergency." The voice didn't belong to Emily or Hayes or either of the other two servants. "Mr. Pinkerton is on assignment out West, and President Lincoln asked specifically for you."

Carter bolted from the bed. "Coming." In less than three minutes, he was dressed. He flung open his door. "What's wrong?"

A lanky ensign snapped to attention. "Tad's disappeared." He offered a belated salute.

Carter sucked in a quick, whistling breath. After the death of Willie, he knew the loss of another son could kill Lincoln. "Where?" he demanded.

"This way." The coltish young man dashed down the stairs, Carter just behind him.

Carter followed hard on the heels of the ensign to Lafayette Square Park, where a tight knot of officers and officials had gathered in a gesticulating mass. President Lincoln stood off to one side, having somehow extracted himself from the cluster of men, and stared at a newly constructed review stand facing H Street. Whitewashed and draped in festive bunting, the structure was raised off the ground and sported two rows of built-in seats. It was covered like a gazebo, with an American flag perched at the peak of the roof.

Carter and the ensign went around the men, whose voices were rising. He had no desire to be caught in a brawl. Instead he came up beside the president. "What happened, sir?"

Lincoln glanced over, looking even more gaunt and drawn than usual. "I don't know."

"Why were you here? I thought you were going to address Congress."

"I sent a message to Congress. I was doing a troop review. For the holiday. There was a band." He waved absently. His brow was furrowed, as usual, but he seemed far away. Carter knew he was turning over some conundrum. He always got that pensive look when he wrestled with a thorny problem.

"Mrs. Lincoln and Tad were both with you?"

The president turned to look at Carter then. "He was right there. Right there between us." Again he gestured at the stand.

Carter put a hand on his arm. "Let's go up and look."

Lincoln followed, though he looked as if a stiff wind could blow him over. All the starch had been taken out of him.

"You were sitting here?" Carter drew the president's gaze toward the seats of honor in the middle of the platform.

Lincoln nodded.

"And you said he was between you and Mrs. Lincoln? He didn't get up and go past her?"

"No." Lincoln shook his head. "She said he didn't. Sometimes he likes to get down and march with the soldiers. But he didn't. He didn't go past me, and he didn't go past Mother." He sounded puzzled. "I forbade him to go marching today. He's had a chest cold. He wouldn't disobey. I wish Allan Pinkerton were here. There's no telling where Tad might have wandered."

Carter didn't respond, but he wished Allan were there, too. Something caught his eye, and he bent to examine the seats. A piece of black suiting poked from a crevice. He pulled on it, and it came free, allowing the light to shine through the gap.

"Mr. President, do you know what's behind this?"

"Behind?"

Carter made for the stairs, with Lincoln and the ensign tagging along. He swung around behind the grandstand and was confronted by a wall of sheeting. It had likely been hung in the interest of making the structure handsome from both front and back, without need of more lumber or paint. Carter slipped beneath the cloth.

He stayed bent to keep from knocking his head on the underside of the stand. Even so, he was immediately arrested by one of the strangest sights he'd ever seen. Suspended from the boards above, a chair hung upside down. Beside the chair was a lever. Carter pulled it.

Air whooshed as the chair flipped up out of sight, immediately replaced by another, which hung in identical fashion. The mechanism was as silent as oil and clever gears could make it. The tiny click as the second chair swung into place never would have been heard over the tramp of feet, the blast of martial music, and the cheers of the crowd.

Behind him, bent nearly in half in order to fit beneath the grandstand, the president stared at the contraption, transfixed. Still crouched low, Carter grasped his arm and drew him away from the sight.

"Sir, I—"

"This means he was deliberately taken." Lincoln's eyes were dilated with shock, and he'd lost his stovepipe hat somewhere.

"I'm afraid so."

"You've discovered more in ten minutes than those crows have in an hour." Lincoln waved at the gesticulating men. Grief had scored lines deep into his face. "I want *you* to find my boy."

Carter looked Lincoln in the eye. There was only one thing he could say. "I will."

Juliet sat with an arm around Mary Lincoln's shoulders, rocking her back and forth. Mary's keening had quieted to soft sobs, but she was liable to break out in wails again at any time. She was like a toddler in her grief—wild and savage and unprincipled.

Lizzy Keckley, Mrs. Lincoln's dressmaker and sometime confidante, tried to convince Mary to accept a little brandy to settle her nerves. This set her off again. She thrashed her head back and forth violently.

"No. No, I want Taddie. Where is Taddie? Oh God, why do You do this to me? Where's my Taddie?" Another round of inconsolable moaning and shrieking began.

Juliet stood and slipped from the room. Where could the doctor be? Mrs. Lincoln needed a sedative, something to help her sleep before she made herself ill with grief. Juliet descended the stairs to the foyer, but no one was there, save for the porter, Edward. "The doctor hasn't arrived?"

"No, ma'am. You know I'll send him straight up when he comes."

Juliet nodded. She knew. She just needed to do something of use.

Glass shattered overhead. Then something else. Mrs. Lincoln must be smashing the last few pieces of unbroken glassware in her room. Most of it had already been destroyed.

Carter Forbes emerged from the hallway, looking worn-out and haggard. She took a closer look. Was he wearing a nightshirt under his jacket?

"Miss Avila? What are you doing here?"

"Mrs. Lincoln sent for me. And you? You have a new assignment?"

"I'm going to find Tad."

Before she could respond, there was a pounding upstairs, and a door was flung open hard enough to crack the wall. They both looked up as Mrs. Lincoln appeared at the top of the staircase. "Miss Avila! Don't go. I need you to contact the spirits. They'll know where Taddie is. Stay with me, please. I'll be calm." She clattered down the steps in her dressing gown, heedless of the public nature of her home.

Juliet took her hands. "Mrs. President, I'm not going to leave you alone. You remember Mr. Forbes, don't you? He's the one who introduced us."

Mary focused tear-blurred eyes on him. Her breeding asserted itself as she made an effort to appear dignified. "Please excuse me, Mr. Forbes. I am distraught today."

Seeing that Forbes seemed unsure of how to respond, Juliet intervened. "Mr. Forbes is investigating Tad's disappearance. He will find him for you."

Mary's eyes grew round. "You will find him." It was more a demand than a question.

"I will do everything humanly possible."

Mary shook her head. "That's not enough. Not enough. You must work with Miss Avila. She can find him. She knows things. The spirits speak to her. You can ask Willie. I'm sure he knows where Taddie is. He always took good care of his little brother." Weeping took over again, and she crumpled in on herself.

Juliet got an arm around her. "Come along, dear. Let's get you back to bed."

"Let me." Dr. Robert Stone, the Lincoln family physician, appeared at Juliet's elbow, grasped Mary's shoulders, and helped her up the stairs.

Juliet watched after them. She felt she ought to go sit with Mary until she was asleep, but the woman's savage grief was exhausting. Juliet did not want to merely bear it with her; she wanted to alleviate it.

Forbes turned, as if to depart, but she shot a hand out to stop him. "You heard Mrs. Lincoln. She wants me to help."

He raised an eyebrow. "I am not going to go have a séance."

Juliet shook her head. "Surely, there's something more practical I can do? Please, I need to do something. Let me tag along."

He lifted his chin a notch but didn't immediately say no.

Juliet pressed the advantage. "It will make Mrs. Lincoln happy. Well, happier, at any rate, and will give her some peace of mind."

A strange look came into his eyes. "Didn't you tell me you were a magician's assistant at one time?"

"Yes." Juliet pulled back. "What—"

"Did you ever see a trick where a person was made to disappear by means of a chair that flips? Two chairs, actually."

Juliet felt as if she were facing some obscure entrance exam. "Both chairs are bolted to a section of flooring, and that's what flips, correct?"

"Exactly. Come with me." Without waiting for her acquiescence, he took her hand and all but ran from the building.

"Where are we going?" Her words came out in short bursts as she raced to keep up with him.

Forbes glanced quickly over his shoulder, his eyes hard as flint. "To the scene of the crime."

Chapter 6

The walk from the Executive Mansion to the park took no more than two minutes, during which time Juliet's mind never stopped asking questions. Who would want to kidnap Tad? For what purpose? And why in such a public manner? The device Forbes had described was more than a little familiar to her. Would her knowledge of how the perpetrator had carried out his heinous act reflect badly on her? Would she become a suspect? Did any of that matter when a little boy's life might be at stake?

Juliet had expected more lawmen to be about, the thought of which made her skin prickle as though breaking out in a rash. Perhaps they were already following up on important clues. Even so, she was glad for the light touch of the detective's hand on her elbow. She had good reason to be here. Oddly enough, she and the Pinkerton were on the same side.

Juliet listened to Mr. Forbes as they approached the grandstand, all the while taking in the structure and the surroundings. "This is it. There were two rows of chairs on the platform. We removed all but the one Tad was sitting in."

Even without anything to compare it to, Juliet could see that this particular chair was thinner, the back shorter, than average. To the casual observer, it would appear to be the perfect place for a child to sit. But not to Juliet.

"The smaller the chair, the easier it is to flip," she said under her breath.

Forbes turned his head sharply. "Excuse me?"

She hurried on ahead of him. "This illusion works best if the chair is small and the assistant is light." Before he could stop her, Juliet mounted the stairs and crossed to the center of the platform. Kneeling down, she examined the area closely. "This is very good work."

"So glad you approve."

Juliet held back a biting retort to his sarcasm, reminding herself that Tad was more important than hurt feelings or bruised egos. "The level of craftsmanship will help us identify who made the illusion. I meant nothing more."

Mr. Forbes squeezed his eyes shut, then nodded. "Forgive me, Miss Avila. The situation, combined with very little sleep, has put me in a bad temper."

Juliet rose with a smile. That explained his nightshirt, then. "Nothing to forgive, Mr. Forbes. I expect I'll snap a time or two before this is over."

"If you recognize the handiwork behind this contraption, can you identify the culprit?"

"Yes and no." Juliet bit her lip.

"What does that mean?"

"It means I believe I can identify who designed the device and built it. But that doesn't mean he's the one who kidnapped Tad."

Mr. Forbes blew out a long, low breath. "But he has to be involved in some way."

"Not necessarily. Just because he sold an illusion doesn't mean he knew what it would be used for. The men who create the hardware behind the magic very seldom use it themselves."

"You're telling me I'm looking for another man?"

Juliet nodded. "Most likely, more than one man. Carrying this out in such a public place with no witnesses whatsoever would require at least two people."

Forbes squeezed the back of his neck and muttered something under his breath. Then he looked at her, his eyes brimming with fatigue. "Walk me through it, please."

"All right. Let's say I'm Tad." She moved to sit in the chair, but Forbes grabbed her arm and stopped her.

"Are you sure that's wise?"

"As long as the lever is secure, this chair won't move." She sat down gingerly, then tested her theory by wiggling back and forth. Just as she expected, the chair stayed put. "Do you know exactly when Tad disappeared?"

"While the band played. He was sitting there, flanked by his parents. The next second, he was gone."

Juliet looked across the park, imagining the crowd of people, the noise of the band, the commotion all around. Nobody, not even those seated on the stage, would have heard the lever being pulled, the chair swinging down and being replaced by another. But why hadn't anyone seen anything?

She began to reason aloud. "We know that at least one man was positioned beneath the stage, to trigger the device and to subdue Tad. But he couldn't have done it without assistance. Someone had to be out in the crowd, watching for the right time to act." She stood up and pointed toward a rise of crape myrtle. "See there, where the ground is slightly higher? That would be the perfect spot."

Forbes frowned. "How can you be sure?"

Juliet held his steady gaze. "Because that's how I would have done it. It's classic misdirection, the most basic skill of any magician." She gulped down her fear, reminding herself that she had done nothing wrong, and soldiered forward. "Without the aid of an assistant, the lever man would have had no way of knowing if Tad's parents were looking at him, or even if Tad was sitting in the chair. Another set of eyes would be essential."

"Confounded trickery and deceit." The Pinkerton stalked across the pine boards, his boots falling hard. Then he turned and came back to Juliet. "Do you need to see the mechanism itself?"

"Yes, that would help."

Without a word, he crooked his finger. Juliet followed him down the stairs and around the back of the platform. He lifted up the skirting and motioned beneath it. "I've ordered my men to remove the works and bring them to the Executive Mansion. You can take a closer look at it there."

With the fabric held aside, sunlight found its way into the dark interior. "I'd prefer not to waste any time." Juliet gathered up her skirts and bent low.

"But your dress—"

"Can be laundered or replaced. The condition of my skirts is my least important consideration." She moved forward, taking care not to knock her head against the low-hanging support beams. She stopped by the upside-down chair. It was a fanciful, disconcerting sight. Her mind was invaded by the image of sweet, inquisitive little Tad Lincoln, disoriented and afraid, tumbling from the chair into a stranger's arms and feeling a hand clamp over his mouth. Her stomach twisted. She had to find him.

With great care, she examined the lever and the configuration of the gears. To most people, they would mean nothing, but to her, they were as clear as reading someone's signature. As she had hoped, they pointed quite specifically to one man.

Across from her, a spot of sunlight caught her attention. Close inspection revealed a hole in the wood no bigger around than her pinkie. Closing one eye, she pressed the other up against the hole. It gave her a clear, perfect view of the trees on the knoll.

"This is where the scoundrel watched for his accomplice." She turned, lost her balance, and fell forward, landing on her hands and knees.

"Are you all right, Miss Avila?" The note of genuine concern in the detective's voice was touching.

"Perfectly fine." She crawled out from under the bandstand and moved to push herself upright, but her fingertips brushed against something hard in the grass. "More than fine, actually. I found something."

She pulled a nub of pencil from the grass and handed it to Forbes. It seemed normal enough, except that it had been wrapped in a bit of India rubber. "What do you suppose that's for?"

Forbes stared at it. "Maybe it's a means of sparing the fingers of someone who writes a lot? It could have been here for weeks, or it could be a clue. Good work." He wrapped the pencil in a clean, white handkerchief and tucked it in his jacket pocket. "You're either the most perceptive woman I've met or just the luckiest. I'm not sure which."

Juliet was starting to get used to his backhanded compliments. "Maybe a little of both, Mr. Forbes."

He looked down at the ground, but his gaze stuck at the level of her knees. "You've been hurt, Miss Avila."

Juliet looked at the same spot on her skirt and was shocked to see a red smear on her dress. She poked at the fabric, looking for the tear. "Goodness, I must have cut my knee when I fell. But I didn't feel a thing. I—"

The sight of blood didn't normally turn her stomach, but this time it did. Her skin grew cold, and when she looked up at Forbes, she knew he read the horror on her face.

"What's wrong?"

"I'm not hurt. Not in the least. When I fell, I must have landed in it. It's not my blood." She shook her head wildly. "It's not my blood."

The Pinkerton's lips pressed together firmly, but he didn't speak. No words were necessary.

The blood was Tad Lincoln's.

He stripped off the woolen jacket, sighing with relief as the scratchy fabric left his body. The uniform had been a necessary disguise, one he hoped never to don again. But, uncomfortable as it was, it had been equally effective. The few people who'd looked his way had seen a brave member of the Union army. Men had saluted him; women had tipped their heads and smiled. Not one had considered that the large canvas bag he carried held their president's nine-year-old son.

So much respect at the sight of that uniform. If they knew what he knew, they wouldn't respect it. Neither would they respect the flag fluttering above the grandstand, nor the ineffectual man acting as president. If they knew what he knew, if they understood what was at stake, they would be filled with just as much hatred and resolve as he was.

A moan came from the corner of the dank cabin, where the small form of Tad Lincoln thrashed on a thin straw mattress. The effects of the ether had yet to wear off, but the boy's labored breathing spoke of a different problem.

"Has the bleeding stopped?"

"Yes, finally." A young woman crossed the room with a bowl of water and clean cloths. She shook her head, making her unruly, red curls bounce and swirl around her shoulders. "I only helped because you promised no one would get hurt."

"It was an accident, pure and simple. But a bloody nose is of little concern, in light of the blood that's been spilled in this war."

"Be that as it may, it's not helping with his breathing." She put her ear to the boy's chest. "There's a rattle in his lungs. I don't like it. You should send for a physician."

"No. No one else can know he's here." He frowned. Already there were too many people who knew pieces of the puzzle. Too many loose ends. They couldn't afford to bring in another. "Keep an eye on him. If you believe any medicines will aid him, I will get them."

She smiled, her eyes going soft and moist. "Thank you."

He shrugged. "It wouldn't do to let the president's son die, would it?"

Not until he was through with him, at least.

Chapter 7

Carter pressed the heels of his palms against his eyes, which burned with fatigue. He'd grown fuzzy around the edges, and his reflexes certainly weren't as sharp as they should be for him to enter a neighborhood like Swampoodle, where there were streets even the police refused to traverse. Yet not only did Carter go barreling in; he brought a young woman with him.

Beside him in the carriage driven by an ensign, sitting as primly as if she were the first lady, Miss Avila showed no concern. "Don't worry. Maguire's workshop is just a block or so from St. Aloysius. It's a decent area."

He grunted. Her knack for sensing a person's manner and moods sometimes made him think she really could read minds and do all of the other nonsense she claimed. The smell of stagnant water filled the air as they rattled over the H Street Bridge across Tiber Creek. It was the kind of hot, muggy evening that didn't allow for real rest. The kind of night that resulted in sharp tongues and short tempers. Through the fading light, the hulking mass of St. Aloysius Church came into view, overshadowing its humbler neighbors, literally and figuratively. Along the dirt road, a pig rooted in the rubbish. Chickens scratched in the fenced yard of the nearest home. Tinny music spilled from a bawdy house around the corner.

They passed the church and turned onto a narrower side street. The driver pulled his rifle into his lap, an impulse Carter appreciated. It was the same sense that had him touching his holstered revolver, just to feel its reassuring weight.

By contrast, Miss Avila looked almost placid. He couldn't tell if it was the result of naiveté or if there was more to it. She did seem quite familiar with the area. He'd never considered where she hailed from, though the name Avila didn't fit a neighborhood that was as Irish as County Cork.

As soon as the carriage came to a halt, Carter hopped down and held a hand up to Juliet. She ignored it, gesturing with her chin at the building behind him. "No lights."

He turned and stared at the shabby clapboard structure. Nothing about it indicated the workshop of a skilled craftsman. It certainly didn't look like it could belong to a fellow who fashioned the trappings of magic for a living. "Here?"

"Yes. He's had this place for years. It's bigger than it seems."

Carter raised an eyebrow but decided to take her word for it. "Looks like he's closed up for the night."

"I was afraid of that. It is quite late."

"Does he live near here?"

"He used to live at the back of the shop, but I heard he recently earned enough to move into his own house."

"Why didn't you say so? We'd have just gone there."

A single eyebrow quirked at his snappishness. "I don't know where it is."

"At last—something you don't know." He went to the front door and rattled the knob, then headed around to the rear of the shop to see if he could locate this Maguire fellow he'd heard so much about. He'd be hanged if he was going back to Lincoln empty-handed.

Miss Avila didn't deign to follow. *Well, who cares?* If ever there was a woman to try a fellow's patience, she was the one. *Always so calm and…and reasonable.*

The place really was larger than it appeared from the front, and it took him several moments to locate another entrance. When he did, he vented his frustration by banging the door with his fist.

By now, the sun had completed its own disappearing act, leaving the neighborhood engulfed in darkness. Music from at least three saloons, each melody different and out of tune, collided in the street. Carter swatted at a horsefly nosing around his face and unloosed another barrage of banging.

The back door of the neighboring house smacked open, and a shaft of feeble light stretched across the narrow lot toward Carter. "What's all that racket?"

Carter stopped his hammering, albeit reluctantly. He'd wanted to hit something most of the day. "I'm looking for Cormac Maguire."

"Ain't here."

"Do you know where he lives?"

"Aye."

"Where?"

"I'll not be telling the likes of hooligans who come trying to batter his door down, and that's the truth." The coot turned back to his house. "Now, stop that noise and get along with you."

"I'm a detective. It's very important I find Mr. Maguire."

The only reply was the slamming of the door.

Carter kicked the door in front of him. He'd have to ask some of the other neighbors. He marched back to the front of the house and passed the carriage.

"Where are you going?" Miss Avila asked.

He didn't stop. "To ask the neighbors where he lives."

The carriage springs murmured as she stood. "They won't tell you anything."

He didn't stop.

There was a creak, and he guessed she'd resumed her seat. At least she'd be out of his hair.

"Pigheaded." Though not spoken loudly, the word still managed to catch him between the shoulder blades.

He grinned perversely. At last, he'd managed to ruffle her calm. His satisfaction was short-lived. He wasn't normally so cantankerous. It was from lack of sleep, yes; but mostly it was Tad. He couldn't let him down. The world would be a poorer place by far without the little boy who kept the Executive Mansion in a constant state of uproar and schemed of ways to raise money for the Sanitary Commission. Nor could he let the president down. The man was overburdened with concern for the country and his cautious plans for emancipating the slaves. His boys were his sole delight. He loved them completely and indulgently. And he'd already lost one son this year. Carter considered again that the loss of another might kill him.

Doggedly, he worked his way along the street, though he knew Miss Avila was right. One householder after another denied any knowledge of Maguire or where he might reside. If he'd asked, they probably would have denied it was nighttime, for the mere principle of the thing.

It was closing in on ten o'clock when he finally conceded defeat.

He had avoided looking at the carriage while making a fool of himself. Now, like a contrite schoolboy, he climbed back in. "Let's go, ensign."

The fellow snapped the reins, and they were off, horse and driver surely all too glad to be headed out of Swampoodle.

A gentle hand rested on Carter's arm. He looked up into fathomless brown eyes. "I know you are worried about Tad. But we'll find him."

"Did the spirits tell you so?"

"No. We just have to find him. We don't have a choice."

Carter opened his mouth to say something but then snapped it closed again.

"Cormac will be at his workshop by dawn. We can talk to him early."

"There is no need for you to be involved in this any further, Miss Avila. I appreciate your help to this point, but I'm sure you have other things you need to do."

"He won't talk to a detective. Not without persuasion. I need to be there."

"What makes you think you can convince him to talk to me? You can't tell him what's at stake. President Lincoln was clear that he doesn't want people to know about the kidnapping. Information like that could start a panic, or, at the very least, cause people to doubt Lincoln."

She turned and looked at him more fully. "Why should it make people doubt the president?"

"Because Tad was kidnapped for a reason. He's a pawn. Someone wants to control the president. To force some decision upon him. People will inevitably wonder whether he'll choose his son over their own boys."

She dropped her head and rubbed at her temples.

He leaned toward her, trying to see if she was crying, and patted her awkwardly on the shoulder. "I'm sorry to be blunt."

She shook her head. To his relief, there were no tears. "I am glad you were honest. If they have use for him, they won't kill him. We have a chance of finding him."

Darkness had not yet entirely relinquished its grasp on the city when Carter arrived at Juliet's home the next morning. He had slept, but only because his body had demanded the rest. His mind, meanwhile, seemed not to have stopped churning for even a minute.

Miss Avila's elderly retainer answered the door and admitted him to the parlor. Carter was becoming as familiar with the room as if he were courting her. He snorted at the preposterous idea. They could never make a match.

For one thing, he had Emily to consider, and Miss Avila had her own family. Though, come to think of it, he had no idea of whom this family consisted, aside from the boy. Archie, or Artie, or whatever his name was.

Too keyed up to sit, Carter wandered to the window and peeked through the lace curtain. A man in rolled-up shirtsleeves with a hat pulled low stood with his hip propped against a hitching post, his gaze trained on the house. Smoke curled lazily from the cigarette between his lips. He looked like any of the thousand day laborers in the city, loitering until someone gave them some odd job to do. Except that he had a green handkerchief hanging haphazardly from the left pocket of his pants. And Carter had seen the fellow before, outside his own house, that very morning.

Carter straightened, and the fellow seemed to notice the movement. Their eyes met, and the fellow bolted.

Instead of running away from the house or down the street, he ran straight toward the alley alongside the house.

Carter dashed down the main hall and flew through the door at the end. It slammed open, striking the wall, and he found himself in the kitchen. Four sets of eyes, including Miss Avila's, turned to him. He paid them no mind. He darted through the kitchen, dashed out the open back door, and jumped down the stairs.

Just ahead, he could see a figure careening around a corner. Redoubling his speed, he tore after the fellow.

Juliet had nearly choked on her coffee when Forbes burst into the kitchen. The fierce gleam in his eye made her realize anew that he could be terrifying if he chose. He was gone before she could swallow.

"Good heavens!" Miss Clara gawked.

Juliet smacked her mug down and knocked over her chair in her haste to follow. By the time she reached the bottom of the stairs, he was already halfway down the alley. Holding her skirts high, she raced after him.

"What is it?" She wasn't sure if her cry even reached him. He swung around the corner without looking back.

She ran faster, heedless of what neighbors might say. The sound of a kicked rock reached her ears, and she glanced back. Artie was gaining on her. She rounded the corner and kept going. Then she glanced behind once more. "Go back, Artie."

He pretended not to hear.

When she looked ahead again, she barely had time to pull herself to a stop before barreling into Forbes. He moved slowly now, examining the side streets.

"What is it?" she gasped.

"A man followed me this morning. I hoped to catch him."

Artie pounded up to them. "Why'd you stop?" He wasn't even winded.

Forbes removed his hat and smacked his leg with it, then wiped sweat from his forehead with the back of his arm. His eyes continued searching the area. "I lost my chance."

"Why would someone be following you?" Juliet asked.

"There are a number of reasons."

She scowled at him. That was no answer at all, and he knew it. She turned and reached for Artie's hand. "Come along. Let's go finish our breakfast." She marched away, though Artie squirmed free of her grasp. Over her shoulder, she said, "You may join us if you wish, detective."

Artie, the little traitor, bounded around the Pinkerton like a puppy, begging for details of what he'd seen and wanting to know whether the man was some sort of criminal.

Miss Clara and Professor Marvolo awaited them on the back stairs.

"What in heaven's name is going on?" Miss Clara used the voice that had quailed a thousand chorus girls.

Juliet waved a hand. "Ask him." She stepped around them and went inside to the stove, to see if there were any more eggs in the pan.

There weren't, but there were a few biscuits left, and one sausage. She placed it all on a plate and made room at the table for their guest.

Forbes entered, her family swarming around him. His gaze took in the shabbiness of the room, and when he saw her at the table, she could tell he wondered what the mistress of the house was doing eating in the kitchen. Her cheeks burned as if he'd caught her in a lie. In a way, he had. The pretense of wealth she'd adopted to attract the best clients was as much a sham as her spirit voices.

But it was none of his business. She had never wanted to impress him, anyway.

She set the plate down at the place she had made. "Do you want coffee?"

He was as easy to read as a book. He really wanted to head back over to Cormac's. He probably hadn't eaten at home, either. "We need—"

"If you're going to be in any shape to run down villains, you need to eat."

"Just a cup of coffee, then," he said.

"I'll get it." Miss Clara bustled past Juliet. "Sit, child."

She did so, concentrating on her plate. With the Pinkerton's warning from the night before still ringing in her ears, she had not said anything about Tad Lincoln's kidnapping. Instead, she'd let them all believe Forbes was making her help him expose another medium. Now, trying to keep it all straight, she considered that it was possible to have too many secrets.

Despite his protestations, Forbes devoured the food Juliet had placed in front of him. Within a few moments, he was standing again, hat in hand.

Miss Clara cleared her throat and gave Juliet a significant look. Juliet made the appropriate introductions but offered no further explanation. Now she was as anxious to be gone as he was.

The ensign from the previous evening had evidently been detailed to assist Forbes. He waited patiently with the carriage, just as he had the evening before. The poor fellow must feel like he'd been demoted to driver, but he helped Juliet inside with a smile.

"Was that your family?" Forbes asked as he climbed in from the other side of the carriage.

"Yes," she said shortly.

His lips twitched with unasked questions, but he did not quiz her further. They rode to Swampoodle in silence.

Cormac's workshop looked just as it had the night before. After helping her from the carriage, Forbes tried the doorknob. It refused to budge. With an inarticulate growl, he turned and stalked around the side of the building.

He returned after a few minutes. "It's still locked back there, too. You said he'd be here."

Juliet had not waited idly. She gave the front door a delicate push, and it swung open.

He surged forward. "That was locked."

"Yes, it was."

"Did you have a key?" he demanded, looking ready to throttle her.

"I didn't need one."

Scowling, he wagged a finger in her face. "What do you th—"

"Oh, for heaven's sake, I picked the lock. I told you I was a magician's assistant. It's an essential skill of the trade. Do you want to go in or not?"

"I—yes. Thank you. Somehow you always catch me flat-footed."

"Don't mention it."

In the feeble morning light, Forbes made a survey of the workshop.

Juliet stepped in behind him. "Cormac? It's Juliet." She'd never known him not to be at his workshop by dawn. He always arrived before his assistants, to be sure they were there on time; if they weren't, he docked their pay.

"Hey, that looks like...." Forbes wove his way through piles of half-finished projects toward the back.

Juliet couldn't see what had caught his eye, so she followed.

"It's a trick chair, like the one in the grandstand." He crouched down and examined it. "I think you were right. This appears to be by the same workman. The joints are very fine." He circled the chair, then stopped short and sucked in a sharp breath. "Stay back."

Juliet halted where she was. "What's wrong?" She was within arm's length of the chair, and she cocked her head to see. Then she got a whiff of something metallic and primeval.

Forbes went down on one knee, reaching for something.

"It's Cormac, isn't it? He's dead."

"Someone's dead." He looked up at her with concern. "It's not a pretty sight, but if you think you can stand it, maybe you can tell me if it's Maguire or not."

She knew before looking. Her stomach lurched, wanting to go the opposite way her feet were carrying it.

Cormac lay on his side. At first, she didn't see a wound. Then she realized he'd been stabbed in the back several times. Her hand flew to her mouth to hold back the scream welling in her chest.

Forbes straightened and put a hand on her arm. "Maguire?"

She nodded.

"I'll have the ensign fetch the police."

"Wait. Do you think this is related to Tad?"

Forbes shrugged. "This is a rough neighborhood. I suppose it could be unrelated, but I think we'd be wise to assume there's a connection and to be extremely careful."

With great effort, she swallowed the lump in her throat and managed a nod. As the detective left, she stooped and took one of Cormac's hands in her own. She'd never wanted to talk to the dead as much as she did in that moment. "What did you get yourself into, Cormac? Did you even know?"

Her stomach roiled, and a prayer formed on her lips for the first time in ten years. "God, please help us find Tad before these evil men do the same to him."

Chapter 8

The harsh sunlight beating down on Swampoodle did nothing to make it more inviting. If anything, it emphasized the haggard faces of the locals standing in front of the shabby buildings, gawking, as two orderlies from the closest hospital removed the sheet-swathed body of Cormac Maguire from his workshop. Crime and death were nothing new in this part of town, but the interest of so many reporters certainly was. They were in the forefront of the throng, shouting questions at everyone who went in or out.

Mr. Forbes had banished Juliet from the workshop, stating that he must do his inspection first, before any evidence was disturbed. Thankfully, he'd allowed her to stay within the perimeter being enforced by the police. As news of the gruesome murder spread, the audience continued to grow, with people pressing against each other, all vying for a good view.

Juliet had ignored the reporters long enough that they'd stopped hollering at her. But she thought one had started sketching her picture. The fellow was taller than his compatriots, with light brown hair, a wide, mobile mouth, and pale blue eyes. She turned away, careful not to give him much of a view, even while she paced. After several moments, she tried to peek out of the corner of her eye at what he was doing. He waggled his eyebrows at her and gave her a broad wink. She decided not to look his way again.

As she perused the other side of the crowd, her eye was drawn to a figure in a faded black cloak. Odd that someone would wear such a heavy-looking garment during the heat of summer. Odder still that the hood was pulled so far over the head that it hid the face of the person beneath. A large man with the bloodshot eyes and red nose of someone who spent more time drunk than sober pushed his way forward, jostling the cloaked person, who turned on him with a cry of fright. The hood fell away, revealing a woman with brilliant red hair and wide, scared eyes.

"'Scuse me, lass. I did na' mean ta rumple ya." The man's booming voice, followed by an even louder burst of laughter, drew the attention of everyone around him. The woman shook her head as she hurried to replace the hood.

Juliet looked more closely. She knew that red hair. It was such a brilliant shade, it had to be the same woman. Why was she trying to keep her identity hidden? Could she have had something to do with the murder?

"Juliet!"

She turned briefly toward the sound of her name. Someone in the crush of people had called to her, but she needed to speak to the woman before she slipped away. When Juliet turned back, she had barely enough time to spot the back of the cloak as its wearer escaped through the crowd. Drat. Maybe if she followed—

"Juliet!" This time, a waving hand signaled the caller. Juliet let out a breath when she recognized the lad.

"Liam." She turned to a nearby officer. "Please let him through. He's the victim's nephew."

With a nod, he lowered his arm to let Liam pass, then held back the people who tried to surge through with him.

Juliet opened her arms to the young man. "I'm so sorry."

"I don't understand." He sagged against her, his voice ragged in her ear. "Why would anyone kill him?"

"I don't know. That's what we're trying to figure out."

"We?" Liam pulled back and looked around. "Are you working with the police now?"

"In a manner of speaking." Tad Lincoln's safety, and the welfare of the nation, depended on her watching her words. "I'm assisting a Pinkerton agent. It's quite a long, complicated story. But we came here to ask your uncle some questions about an illusion he manufactured. That's when we found him."

Liam frowned. "Was it the rotating chair?"

Juliet gasped. "How did you know?"

A growl escaped Liam's lips, and he spat out something unintelligible in Gaelic. "I told him that illusion would lead to no good. The man that ordered it was much too secretive, even for a magician."

"You saw him?" Juliet's heartbeat sped up. "You saw the man who ordered the illusion?"

"Yes, but—"

"Come with me."

She curled her fingers around his wrist and all but dragged him past the ensign keeping watch at the front door, ignoring his raised hand and Liam's protests. She had to find Forbes. There he was, hunkered down near the spot where they'd found the body, his brow furrowed in thought.

"Mr. Forbes."

He shot to his feet. "I asked you to wait outside."

"I learned something you need to know."

He looked from her to the fellow at her side, then down to the fellow's wrist, still grasped in her clutches. "Who is this?"

His voice was tight, and one eyebrow had quirked up—an odd reaction that resembled jealousy. Ridiculous, Juliet knew. "This is Liam." She dropped his hand and pushed him forward a step. "He's Cormac's nephew, and he saw the killer."

The young man blanched as he took a jerking step closer to Carter. Eyes dropping to the floor, he caught sight of the blood puddle and pressed his hand against his stomach. Carter felt sympathy for him but refrained from showing it. There was a chance, however slim, that Liam could be in league with the kidnappers. It was too early to dismiss any possibilities.

"When did you see the killer?"

"I never said I did."

Carter frowned at Miss Avila, then looked back at Liam. "Well, did you or didn't you?"

"No. I mean, yes. Maybe. I...." He raked his fingers through his hair. "I saw the man who ordered the illusion you're interested in. I don't know if he killed my uncle, but I never trusted him."

"He has to be involved." Miss Avila spoke with unwavering conviction. "If not with the murder, then—"

Carter held up his hand before she could say anything about the president or his family. "Please, let me handle this, Miss Avila."

"Avila?" Liam looked at Juliet in confusion. "When did you change—"

It was Juliet's turn to cut someone off. "That's for another time, Liam. What's important now is this customer you so mistrusted. What is his name?"

"I don't know."

Miss Avila's shoulders slumped at the same time that Carter blew out a frustrated breath. "This is a never-ending circle of unanswered questions. What do you know?"

Liam's jaw tightened. No doubt he was as frustrated as Carter. "The man insisted on meeting with Uncle Cormac in private. But my uncle wasn't one to take chances. He had me hide over there during the meeting." The tall cabinet he pointed to bore a striking resemblance to the one in Miss Avila's home.

"Did you see him?" Juliet asked.

Liam shook his head. "Not enough to recognize him. He was taller than Uncle Cormac. His voice was deep, rough."

He'd just described half the men in Washington. Carter reminded himself to move slowly, lest he spook an already skittish witness. "What color was his hair?"

"I don't know. He kept his hat pulled low and never really turned toward me."

Miss Avila stood close enough that her skirt brushed Carter's leg, and he could feel her impatience as she tapped one foot. "What kind of hat? What did his suit look like? Why did you find him suspicious?"

Carter held up a hand. "Give him time to answer."

"He can have all the time he wants. But it's his uncle who's been murdered. I know he wants to help."

Beside her, Liam had returned his gaze to the blood on the floor. Unless he was a remarkable actor, there was very little chance the lad had been involved with the crime.

"Son." Carter put his hand on Liam's shoulder and squeezed until the boy looked up and focused on his face.

"Yes."

"What was the fellow wearing?"

"An old black frock coat and gray trousers, kind of baggy around the knees. He had a black derby and a trimmed beard… brown, I think."

"Good. That's good, Liam." Miss Avila patted his shoulder.

The lad nodded, his Adam's apple bobbing.

Grant maintained eye contact with him. "I need you to think. Did the man say anything that might give us a clue as to who he is or what he planned to do with the illusion?"

Liam squeezed his eyes shut, as if imagining himself back in the dark wardrobe, eavesdropping on the conversation. "He wouldn't tell Uncle Cormac where he planned to use the chair, only that it was for a performance his audience would never forget."

Carter still hadn't quite made the connections he needed. "What made you distrust this man if the exchange was so innocuous?"

"I dunno." He scratched the back of his neck. "It was the way he acted. Like…like he was gloating. Not just like someone who's come up with a new trick, but mean-like. He…he seemed shady. Asked a bunch of questions about who Uncle Cormac talked to about his tricks."

"What did Cormac say?" asked Miss Avila.

"Told him we're close-lipped about our customers and what we make. Same thing he'd tell anyone who asked."

The workshop was becoming a broiler in the July heat. Carter wiped sweat from his forehead. "How did the fellow pay? Cash or a bank draft?"

"Cash. Half up front and half on delivery."

"And he was pleased with the work?" Miss Avila didn't even seem flushed by the heat.

Liam's mouth twisted in a grimace. "He was more than pleased. He was…triumphant. And he quizzed Uncle Cormac about secrecy again. Said he'd hear if Cormac blabbed about him, and then he lowered his voice and said something else I couldn't hear. Uncle Cormac repeated what he'd said before, and the fellow patted him on the shoulder and said he knew he could count on him. Then he said he was willing to pay for the consideration and peeled off a couple of extra sawbucks from a big wad and handed them over."

A chill ran through Carter. Without a doubt, they'd found the origin of the illusion used to kidnap Tad Lincoln. But the master builder was dead, and their only witness had precious little information of any use.

They had gleaned one valuable, albeit disturbing, fact: The man who had Tad was not merely a kidnapper; he was likely also a murderer. One look at Miss Avila, her hands clasped tightly together, her bottom lip clenched between her teeth, and he knew she'd made the same deduction.

With every second that passed, their chances of finding Tad alive grew smaller.

The carriage ride to the Executive Mansion was grimly silent. Juliet was thankful, for she knew that if she spoke, she would dissolve into tears. Right now, the most important thing for her to do was to gather her thoughts, pull her emotions together, and wrap them up neatly in her well-rehearsed character. As Miss Avila, she could put distance between herself and the pain of those she sought to help. That was because Miss Avila, the woman who could commune with the dead, was a sham, a part she played—a role that allowed her to conjure any emotion that suited the moment. It was a lesson she'd learned as a little girl: If you became a character, then no one could hurt the real you, because they never truly knew you.

She dared to glance at Forbes. The detective sat, stone-faced, elbows on his knees, staring at the tail of the horse pulling them through the city. Over the years, Juliet had encountered many an officer of the law, but she'd never known one quite like him. He was honest but fair. The fact that he hadn't run her out of town, when he thought so little of her vocation and those who practiced it, spoke of a man who measured his actions. He'd taken the time to get to know her, even though, at first, he had meant only to use her. He'd given her more consideration than some of her own flesh and blood.

"We'll find him." The words were out of Juliet's mouth before they had been formulated in her brain.

For a moment, she wondered if he'd heard her. When he turned his head, the anguish in his eyes broke her heart. But then he blinked, and his frowning lips leveled out into a straight line. "Yes, we will find him." He nodded once. "There is no other option."

The carriage came to a stop in front of the Executive Mansion, and a liveryman came to meet them. As they neared the front steps, Juliet heard a rustling at the side of the building. She reached out and grabbed Forbes's arm. He turned, and she put a finger to her lips before he could speak. She pointed to the bushes, even as another rustle sounded.

He motioned for her to stay behind him as he crept toward the noise, hand resting on the butt of his gun.

"Come out slowly," he ordered. "Keep your hands where I can see them."

There was more rustling, then some snuffling, and a Negro boy of about twelve or thirteen stood up and walked out of the bushes.

"Daniel." The detective's demeanor immediately changed. "What were you doing hiding in there?"

The boy's eyes were red, the skin below his eyes still damp from tears. "I was waiting for you, Mr. Carter. But I didn't want to bother you and the lady." His lip quivered.

"Daniel, what's wrong?" Forbes's voice was so soft and gentle, there was no doubt he cared for the boy.

"It's Ma. She took a turn, and…and…."

Unable to keep up his brave front any longer, Daniel dissolved into tears. In a move that totally disarmed Juliet, the Pinkerton put his arm around the boy and pulled him to his chest, offering comfort.

After a moment, Daniel backed away and wiped his nose on his shirtsleeve. "I'm sorry, sir. Ain't right for me to be so familiar."

"Nonsense." Forbes clasped the boy's shoulder. "We're friends. Friends comfort each other."

A wisp of a smile came and went. "Yes, sir. I'd best be getting home now."

Forbes frowned. "You can't live in that shanty by yourself."

"I'm a man now. Need to take care of myself." Daniel squared his shoulders. "Got nowhere else to go, anyhow."

"Yes, you do," she inserted.

Daniel and Forbes turned to Juliet, almost as if they'd forgotten she was there. Remembering his manners, Forbes motioned to her. "This is Miss Avila."

"Ma'am." Daniel nodded.

"My pleasure, Daniel."

Forbes cocked his head to the side. "Now, what were you saying? About Daniel having somewhere else to go?"

"Yes, of course. He'll come live with me." The boy looked at her as though he suspected her of playing a joke. "My family is very special. We had no one else until we had each other. It would be my honor if you'd join us."

Daniel looked up at Forbes, silently asking for his approval. He smiled and nodded his head. "You can trust her."

In the midst of his fear and pain, a little bit of calm came to the boy's face. The professor would shake his finger at her when he found out she'd done it again—taken in another stray, as he liked to call it. But Juliet knew that, deep down, he felt the same way she did. Life wasn't worth living if you didn't help those who had less than you. The thought warmed her heart, though not quite as much as the information Carter Forbes had just revealed.

He trusted her.

Chapter 9

Carter kept glancing at the bewitching woman. What was her angle? There was nothing she could personally gain from helping a lad like Daniel. At one time, he'd considered her mercenary, based on her vocation. But she'd made a home and a family for herself, seemingly out of nothing. And he knew she was fiercely loyal to them. Perhaps it was time to reassess his view of Miss Avila.

But it would have to wait. Now, it was time to face the president and report his lack of progress. No one in the neighborhood had seen a thing, at least nothing anyone would admit to. Cormac had plenty of friends, and any enemies had evaporated in the face of his untimely demise. The thought of seeing the disappointment in Lincoln's eyes stung like a raw wound. There was nothing to do but face it. Carter headed up the stairs to Lincoln's office, while Miss Avila turned toward the private quarters to check on Mrs. Lincoln.

He stopped on the third step. "Miss Avila."

She paused and looked over her shoulder.

"Do you have any idea where to go from here?"

She faced him fully. "I saw a woman I used to know outside Cormac's shop."

"Do you think she knows something? Did you talk to her?"

"No. But she was acting strangely—wearing a cloak despite the heat. I thought she didn't want to be recognized."

"Why didn't you mention this before?"

She drew herself up, her back straight as a poker, and didn't respond.

Carter tugged at his ear. "I'm sorry. I—"

"She left before I could speak to her. Then Liam arrived, and I brought him in to see you. I'm sorry I didn't mention it earlier."

"Who was she? Do you think we could find her?"

"Her name is Estelle Bines. She was a magician's assistant, like me."

"So, she would have known Cormac?"

"I don't know if she did or not."

"But she could have been coming to see him about something else entirely."

Miss Avila shrugged wordlessly.

"Do you think we can find her?"

Somehow she managed to find a game smile. "We can try."

He descended the three stairs and crossed to her, taking her hand. "Thank you. I'm sorry for snapping."

She met his gaze. "We can ask around at some of the theaters. Someone will probably know where she's been staying."

He cleared his throat. "Staying? Not living?"

"If she's still working as an assistant, then she'll be on the road, traveling from theater to theater. She won't have a home." Miss Avila extracted her hand from Carter's, and he realized he'd held it far longer than propriety allowed.

"Make your report, detective. Then we can begin looking for Estelle." She tossed the comment over her shoulder as she headed down the hall.

At least he had something hopeful to report now. He'd pray that it would lead to Tad.

Juliet checked on Mary Lincoln and found her sleeping fitfully. Lizzy Keckley sat in a chair at her side, dozing, her head bobbing with her breathing. Lizzy started awake with a jerk. When she saw Juliet, she rose and joined her by the door. "The doctor gave her laudanum to calm her. Is there any word on Tad?"

How much should she share? "Detective Forbes thinks we have some good leads."

The lines creasing Lizzy's face didn't relax. Juliet reached out and squeezed her hand. "We'll find him."

Mary stirred, moaning pitifully.

Lizzy glanced over her shoulder. "You better go before she wakes up."

"But don't you think I should talk to her?"

"No. You go on and find her boy. That's the most helpful thing you could ever do for her."

Juliet gave her hand another squeeze. "We will find him. Tell her that."

Tears welled in Lizzy's eyes, and she nodded.

Juliet slipped from the room, shutting the door gently behind her. She leaned back against it and closed her eyes. "God, if You're there, don't let me be a liar. Please let Tad be all right. Help us find him."

She inhaled a deep breath and pulled away from the support of the door.

Forbes met her at the base of the stairs, his face pale.

"How did it go?"

"About as expected. He doesn't have to order floggings; his eyes make you want to flog yourself when you disappoint him." He accepted his hat from the steward with a nod of thanks. "How is Mrs. Lincoln?"

"Sedated."

The steward opened the door for them, and Forbes ushered her out ahead of him with a hand on the small of her back. A shiver slid up her spine, despite the July heat. "Let's start at Ford's Athenaeum," she said a little too brightly. "It's only about five blocks away."

He helped her back into the carriage, and the ensign pulled down the drive and past the soldiers guarding the Executive Mansion.

At the theater, they walked around to the stage entrance. No one guarded the entryway. Without waiting for the detective, Juliet pushed the door open.

"Wait. Shouldn't you knock?"

"It's not someone's home." Juliet stepped inside, inhaling the familiar smells of grease paint, wood, paste, sweat, and stale flowers. She paused, listening for the sound of human habitation. The murmur of voices came from the stage. She motioned for Forbes to follow her, and he nodded, though his eyes swiveled left and right, as if he expected someone to leap out at him.

They made their way down a narrow hall that opened to reveal a wide area strung across with ropes and divided by an odd collection of set pieces. Juliet brushed past a dusty curtain and stepped onto the stage, where several people sat around a table.

"Good afternoon."

The group turned as one to look at her.

Behind her, the detective's footsteps halted.

A dapper man with a dark mustache and curly hair stood and approached. "Can we help you?" He was joined by a stunning woman wearing an emerald green day dress and an irritated scowl. Juliet knew her. She was Margaret Fanning, a sycophant among those above her in the food chain, a waspish harpy with everyone else. She had actually struck Miss Clara once, when the older woman had dared to challenge her behavior.

"I'm wondering if any of you know where I can find Estelle Bines." Juliet spoke in the most pleasant of tones.

A sudden narrowing of Margaret's eyes informed Juliet that she had been recognized. "Never heard of her." On closer inspection, it was readily apparent that Margaret owed her youthful glow to artifice rather than actual youth.

Juliet affixed a charming smile. "She was a magician's assistant when I knew her a few years ago."

The woman put a hand on her hip. "Well, that's where you went wrong. You won't find two-bit illusionists and their skimpily clad 'assistants' here. Ford's handles high-class theatrical productions and serious artists only."

Juliet cocked her head. "Then what are you doing here?"

Forbes stepped in front of her at the same time the mustached man moved to intercept Margaret.

"I'm Pinkerton agent Carter Forbes." He pulled his identification from his pocket and showed it to the fellow. "I have reason to believe that Miss Bines could help me with an investigation."

The man shrugged. "I'm sorry, Detective. I don't know the woman."

Forbes leaned around him. "Do any of you fine folks know Estelle Bines?"

A chorus of shaking heads was the only response.

"I'm sure you can see your way out, since you managed to see yourselves in," the haughty actress said.

"Perhaps we can show you. I'm sure you'll be on your way out soon enough." Juliet turned on her heel and headed back the way they'd come.

Halfway down the hallway, Forbes touched her upper arm and stopped her. "One of them still might know something."

"Even if they do, they're not going to tell us." Juliet shook her head, unable to believe how stupid she'd been. "Don't worry. There are better people to ask than actresses." She couldn't quite keep the disdain from her voice.

The stage man was at the door this time, and Juliet greeted him with a broad smile. "Howard?"

Wispy patches of white hair orbited his pink scalp like clouds as he turned toward the sound of her voice. "Miss Juliet." His grin revealed nearly toothless gums. "Theater ain't been the same since you and your uncle broke up the act."

"Well, this isn't the same theater, so I guess it couldn't be the same. How did you wind up here?"

"The minstrel show I worked for closed up, and this was the first place willin' to hire an ol' man. Good thing all the young fellers are off fightin', or I wouldn't've been able to find a good place like this'n."

"Do you ever see any of the old circuit crew?"

"Ever so often. But ain't a one can hold a candle to you. There was always something 'bout you that made the crowds look at you and not that trickster uncle o' yours."

"That was merely a flash of ankle and a low bodice. And, believe me, he used it to his advantage." She leaned forward. "He really wasn't all that good a magician."

Howard guffawed. "Don't I know it."

Beside her, she could feel Forbes's assessing gaze. She should probably move this conversation along. He didn't need to learn anything more about her. He already knew more than most anyone. "Howard, I'm looking for Estelle Bines. Any idea where she might be staying?"

Howard pursed his lips. "Now, which one was she?"

"She worked with the Great Norwich. Had bright red hair."

"That's right. She was a nice girl, too." He scratched the stubble on his chin. "Can't say as I've seen her around lately. You sure she's in town?"

"I thought I saw her this morning."

"You might want to try Greene's Amphitheater. She was more of a variety show performer."

"That's a wonderful idea. Thank you."

He took her hand and raised it to his lips. "Come and see me again soon, Miss Juliet. It's good to think about the old days."

She cocked her head and smiled. "Surely not that old!"

"Not for you, but it seems a lifetime ago since I was treadin' the boards and givin' the audience a kick in the pants."

Forbes touched her elbow. "I hate to break up this reunion, but...."

He left the gist of their business unspoken, but Juliet nodded in agreement. They needed to get to the next theater if they were to have any chance of finding Estelle. With a quick hug, she bid Howard adieu, promising to return soon.

Back in the alley, the Pinkerton looked at her with eyebrows raised and lips that made an effort not to smile. "I was afraid if you talked any longer, you'd try to complete another adoption, and we simply don't have time right now."

Juliet laughed. "I suppose not. But don't think I won't come back."

The clink of a kicked bottle sounded from behind a pile of packing crates, and Forbes stepped in front of her, his hand moving to the butt of his revolver. "Who's there?"

A yowling cat sprang out and streaked past them.

Juliet's shoulders relaxed, but Forbes remained alert. "Come out. Now."

A loud sigh drifted around the pile of trash, and then a tall, sandy-haired fellow with a wide mouth stepped out, his hands raised.

Juliet drew back. "I saw you at Cormac's shop. You're a reporter."

"Guilty as charged." He grinned, despite the fact that Forbes's gun remained leveled at his stomach. "Name's Jake Paulson."

"Why are you following us?" Forbes growled.

"I want a story." The reporter lowered his hands, reached inside his vest pocket, and produced a cigarette, which he proceeded to light.

"And why would you think we have a story?"

He raised his eyebrows in derision. "A Pinkerton investigating a murder in Swampoodle? Even the police don't investigate there. And then, the first place you go is the Presidential Mansion? There's got to be a story. Was the old fellow a spy?"

Forbes scowled. "Get out of here. And don't let me catch you following me again."

The reporter shrugged and stuck his hands in his pockets. "It's a free country, Pink." Then he ambled away in the opposite direction from where they were headed.

Forbes shook his head. "That's the last thing we need." He holstered his gun. "Don't let anyone know why we're investigating. As far as the world is concerned, Cormac's murder is enough explanation."

Juliet sniffed. "I did hear you the first three times you issued that warning."

He grinned. "I know. I just can't help myself."

She couldn't help smiling in response. "Shall we head over to Greene's?"

"After you."

As the afternoon dragged on, Juliet's optimism began to wane. They had no luck at Greene's or at the Orpheum or at half a dozen other theaters. Forbes's frustration grew until it hovered around him like an almost visible cloud. Juliet was about to give up when she recognized Betty Moran, an aging chorus girl whose voice was sweet but not very powerful, a fact that had forever condemned her to the background.

Happy to be in the limelight for whatever reason, Betty eagerly told them what little she knew. "I saw Estelle last week. But she's not with the Great What's-His-Name anymore. Poor thing's been having a rough time of it since then. She's living in Hell's Bottom."

Juliet's eyebrows rose. Situated between the Executive Mansion and Swampoodle, Hell's Bottom was essentially lawless. It held several dozen saloons and over a hundred bawdy houses, which had sprung up to cater to the deluge of soldiers in the capital. "You're sure?"

"That's what she said. It's a real shame, ya know. She could'a been a magician on her own, only nobody wants to see a girl magician. They just want to see girls in short skirts." Betty shrugged. "But then, you know that. I could'a said the same about you."

Juliet avoided looking at Forbes. She was determined to get Betty back on track. "Do you know specifically where in Hell's Bottom?"

"Rhode Island." She squinted. "'Round Eleventh, I think."

Juliet took Betty's hand in both of hers and squeezed. "Thank you. You don't know how helpful you've been."

Betty smirked. "Just remember me if you start a new show."

"I will."

Juliet followed Forbes out of the theater.

"Good work, Miss Avila. We may finally be getting somewhere." He considered the lengthening shadows. "It's too late to go there now. Can you accompany me in the morning? I think she'd respond better with you there, and besides, you can make sure I'm talking to the right woman."

It was a wise decision. No one went into Hell's Bottom at night unless he was looking for a fight. Even police officers wouldn't patrol there alone. Juliet had a feeling that a man like Carter Forbes would have risked it on his own, but there was no way he would take a woman with him into such an area after sundown.

"I'll be ready early," she assured him.

"You know me already."

"I know you aren't terribly patient, in any event."

He snorted. "I am an open book." He leaned closer, looking down into her eyes. "And you are deep in thought."

His powers of observation were almost as good as hers. "I was wondering…that is, would—" Juliet stopped. This was a bad idea.

"Yes?" He waited politely.

She forced herself to continue, despite her exceptionally dry throat. "Would you and Emily care to come to dinner?"

His mouth opened, but he didn't say anything.

Juliet rushed on. "It might help Daniel settle in, having a familiar face at the table on his first night. And I imagine Emily doesn't leave the house much."

A slow smile slid across his face, lighting his eyes. "An excellent idea. And you're right about Emily. A night out would do her a world of good."

Juliet smiled, but her joy was quickly dashed when a sandy-haired fellow in a sack suit sauntered by the end of the alley. He tipped his hat to her with a grin. She gasped and clutched Forbes's arm. "That reporter."

The detective's lip curled up in a snarl, and he headed after the man. Juliet followed close on his heels, but when they reached the street, Paulson was nowhere to be seen.

"Enough of this." Forbes snatched off his hat and smacked it against his leg. "I'll have a friend make sure we don't have anyone following us tomorrow. This is one story we can't let out of the bag."

Chapter 10

If there had ever been a more perplexing woman than Miss Avila, Carter certainly hadn't met her. After years of learning what motivated people, unraveling how their minds worked, he believed himself an excellent judge of character. All the facts pointed to one simple conclusion: anyone who pretended to speak to the dead and took advantage of desperate people for financial gain was the lowest form of deceiver. There was no place in his life for such a woman.

Yet here he sat at Miss Avila's table, not only sharing a meal with her family but also enjoying her company immensely. Somehow, she had managed to shake off the gruesome discovery made earlier in the day and was concentrating on those around her. Her cheeks were flushed a rosy red, and she held her hand in front of her mouth, laughing along with everyone else at some joke Artie had told. The only one who didn't join in the merriment was Daniel. He sat hunched over his plate, shoveling food into his mouth, while he kept his eyes up, constantly scanning the area around him.

Leaning over slightly, Carter put his hand on the boy's wrist and whispered close to his ear, "You can slow down, son. The food's not going anywhere."

Daniel looked up with a full mouth and gulped it down in one big swallow. "Sorry, Mr. Carter."

With a wink and a squeeze of his hand, Carter sat back in his chair. Across from him, the older woman named Miss Clara picked up a basket of rolls. "Can I interest you in another, Mr. Forbes?"

He patted his stomach and shook his head. "Thank you, but no. I've already had more than I should."

Miss Clara grinned. "Juliet made them, you know. She's quite a baker."

Beside her, Miss Avila sputtered on the sip of water she'd just taken and shot a look at Miss Clara.

Laughter bubbled up in Carter. "It seems there's no end to Miss Avila's talents."

Seated to his left, Emily bumped her shoulder into his. "Be nice, Carter."

He raised his eyebrows in a question, but before he could open his mouth, Miss Avila spoke up.

"Any culinary skills I may possess are wholly thanks to Miss Clara. Before I met her, I could barely butter a roll, let alone bake one."

Miss Clara's chest puffed out just a bit. "She's exaggerating, of course. But I confess to having taught her everything I know."

"Not everything." Miss Avila laughed. "You never could teach me to sing."

Emily, who'd been following the conversation with rapt attention, rested her fork against the side of her plate. "You're a singer?"

"I was once," Miss Clara said with a sigh, "but that was a long time ago."

"Nonsense. You still have a beautiful voice, when you choose to share it." Miss Avila dabbed at the corners of her mouth with a napkin, then folded her hands on the table in front of her. "Miss

Clara won't tell you this herself, but she was a highly respected opera singer. During the height of her career, she traveled all over Europe. She even appeared before the queen of England."

Emily gasped. "The Queen. How wonderful."

"Yes, it was," Miss Clara said, her tone wistful. "But years of full-out singing, six shows a week with barely a break, took their toll."

"What happened?" Emily asked.

"I woke up one day and realized my voice was no longer the strongest, my face was no longer the prettiest, and I was far from the youngest." Miss Clara's eyes clouded over, and her smile became sad. "The theater is not kind to women past their prime. There came a time when I could no longer book appearances, not even from those who had claimed to love me."

Carter fingered the stem of his water goblet. No one at the table was eating anymore, so involved were they in Miss Clara's tale. Even Daniel was listening, although he kept one arm curled protectively around his plate.

"Fools. All of them," Miss Avila said.

"It was a desperate time of my life. I was reduced to overseeing the chorus girls in variety shows. But then, after—"

At the end of the table, the gentleman they called Professor cleared his throat. Miss Clara looked at him and clamped her lips together. Clearly, the Professor thought it best for her not to reveal too much. *Too much of what?* Carter wondered.

"Things went from bad to worse," Miss Clara continued. "I had no job, no prospects. But then this angel found me."

Miss Avila's cheeks stained crimson as Miss Clara reached out and took her hand. "I'm far from angelic," she muttered.

"Nonsense. She was barely more than a child herself, but she insisted that we would be stronger together. And she was right."

Carter looked at the faces around the table: the Professor, Miss Clara, young Artie, and now Daniel. Why did Miss Avila do it? It would be so much easier for a woman of her unique talents to go it alone. Yet she continued to draw people to her and take them under her wing.

"I really should clear these dishes." Miss Avila popped to her feet, pushing her chair back with just a touch too much force. For someone who made her living putting on shows, she certainly seemed uncomfortable being the center of attention.

The Professor rose slowly, waving his hand in Juliet's general direction. "The boys can take care of the dishes, Miss Juliet. Why don't you two young people take a stroll?" He angled toward Carter. "Aids in digestion, you know."

A moment alone with Miss Avila would be welcome, so that they could discuss the case, of course. But what of his sister?

"Emily, dear," Miss Clara spoke up. "Juliet tells me you're a musician."

Carter felt his sister stiffen at his elbow. Before the attack, Emily had spent almost every waking moment at the piano. But then, the awkwardness of manipulating the foot pedals, added to the pain that came from sitting in one position for too long, had discouraged her to the point that she'd stopped playing. How had Miss Avila even known?

"I used to play." Emily looked at Miss Avila. "But I never told you that."

Carter's heart sank. Was this another manipulation? Another opportunity for Miss Avila to instill in Emily the belief that she had insights from the beyond?

Miss Avila smiled. "When I was at your home, I noticed how worn the piano keys were. I could tell someone who lived there loved to play." She shrugged. "Between you and your brother, you seemed the more likely choice."

Miss Clara stood up and walked around the table. "I would love to hear you play, dear."

Emily glanced at Carter. He nodded in a way he hoped would encourage her. "On one condition," she said to Miss Clara. "I will play, but only if you agree to sing."

"That can most certainly be arranged." With a smile indicating that the conversation had gone precisely in the direction she had hoped, Miss Clara led Emily out of the room. A moment later, the Professor, Artie, and Daniel, their arms laden with dirty dishes, left the room, as well.

Carter looked around and smiled. "It appears we're on our own."

"I promise you, Mr. Forbes, I was not privy to their intentions."

The aghast look on Miss Avila's face sent a chuckle through him. He placed his folded napkin on the table, stood, and walked around the table as he spoke. "I believe you, Miss Avila. But, since we are alone, perhaps that walk would be a good idea. There are some matters I'd like to discuss before our outing tomorrow morning."

She looked up at him as he put his hands on the back of the chair and waited to assist her. Clearly, she was surprised by his show of manners. But it was nothing more than he would do for any woman of good breeding.

And the fact that he thought of her in that way surprised him more than a little.

Juliet took a deep breath, hoping to clear her head. But the warm, moist evening air caught in her throat, bringing on a fit of coughing. Strolling beside her, Carter Forbes patted her back solicitously. Why was the Pinkerton being so nice? True, she'd hoped that by inviting him to her home for a meal, she could prove that she was a decent person with a decent family, despite the abnormalities of her current profession. What she hadn't expected was for her dear family to scheme a way to get the two of them alone, or for the detective to go along with it happily.

"Are you all right, Miss Avila?"

"I'm fine. And please, don't call me Miss Avila."

"Why not?"

She sighed. "Because it's not my real name."

Forbes stopped short, any vestiges of gentility now gone. "Excuse me?"

The name change had been a little lie, and one that would have been easier not to admit. But Juliet had become weary of falsehoods. Her life was so tangled in them, she sometimes forgot what was real and what wasn't. Carter Forbes lived in a world of right and wrong, true and false. If he was to trust her—and she had found that it mattered to her whether he did—she needed to be as forthright with him as possible.

"My real name is Juliet Button."

Forbes frowned. "Why did you change it? Are you in some kind of trouble?"

"Heavens, no." Juliet snorted at the very idea. "I changed it for the stage. Juliet Avila is exotic, mysterious. Juliet Button is the girl who takes in the laundry."

The side of Forbes's mouth quirked, and she could tell he was fighting away a smile. "I appreciate your honesty. And, for what it's worth, I think Juliet Button is a perfectly charming name."

"Thank you." She glanced down at her feet, then continued walking. "But, to keep things simple, please call me Juliet."

He nodded. "As you wish."

They walked in silence. Finally, Juliet chanced a look at him. "Was there something you wanted to discuss? Something about—"

"There was," he said, keeping his voice low. "But I changed my mind."

"Why?"

"Because we're being followed again."

She started to turn, but his hand on her elbow propelled her forward. "Don't look," he said. "I don't want him to know that we know."

The fine hairs on the back of her neck bristled, possibly because of the man following them. It could also be because Forbes had leaned in so close to speak that his warm breath had caressed her ear. Either way, she had to fight to stay focused. "Is it the same reporter?"

"I don't know. Whoever it is, he's given us an opportunity." His hand moved from her elbow down her arm, until his fingers intertwined with hers. "Come with me."

Swallowing her shock, Juliet hurried after him as he quickly changed course and ducked into the park. He wasn't going fast enough to lose whoever followed them, but he certainly was moving with purpose.

"I don't understand," she hissed through her teeth. "What are we doing?"

"We're confusing the issue." They came to a stop by a cluster of trees. Forbes stood in front of her, still holding her hand. "If people continue seeing us together, they'll know you're working with me, and I'm afraid the news about Tad will get out. Or worse."

"What could be worse?"

"You could be in danger. I don't want what happened to Cormac to happen to you or your family."

A tremor shook her body. She'd never considered that the kidnapper might come after her or someone she loved. Panic coiled in her gut. What had she gotten them mixed up in?

Forbes reached out with his other hand, his fingers caressing her jaw, and forced her to look him in the eye. "Juliet, I won't let anyone hurt you. Do you trust me?"

Did she? So few men in her life had proven trustworthy, she'd nearly given up on the gender entirely. Yet this man, whom she barely knew, was different. "Yes, I trust you."

His smile was so kind and warm. "Good. Now, we have to make these people think that you and I are spending time together for an entirely different reason."

As he lowered his head, his face becoming closer to hers, understanding dawned. "You mean...?"

"Yes. They need to believe I'm courting you."

The brush of his lips against hers was soft, quick, barely more than a whisper. But it was enough to wrest the air from her lungs and set her head spinning.

"I...Mr. Forbes, I...." Coherent speech eluded her. For the first time in years, Juliet found herself completely thrown and unable to improvise.

Thankfully, the Pinkerton had taken control. "Juliet, I believe you should start calling me Carter. I've just become your beau."

Chapter 11

Carter seemed to have been forgiven by his sister. Emily wasn't just speaking to him; her cheeks glowed with enthusiasm. "Miss Clara says I have 'wonderful natural talent,' and she would know, wouldn't she? She's performed for all kinds of royal dukes and princes and things, not just Queen Victoria. She played at the biggest houses in London and Vienna and Prague. And when Mendelssohn premiered his last oratorio in London, he insisted that only she could sing the soprano."

Carter braced as the carriage hit a particularly rough patch of road. "She sounds like an exceptional woman."

"Oh, she is. She's marvelous, and—" Emily bit her lip. "She's willing to teach me to sing."

"You want to learn to sing?" Carter was nearly as delighted as Emily. She needed a consuming interest. Something wholesome. And what possible trouble could she get into from taking voice lessons?

"Yes, please. May I?" She clasped her hands together, eyes shining.

"Of course. It will do you good."

"Thank you." She flung her arms around him.

Once home, Emily wandered dreamily off to bed. He hadn't seen her so cheerful in years. Now he owed Juliet and her misfits another debt.

Carter paced his office. What had he been thinking to kiss her? He hadn't been thinking. She had looked so attractive in the moonlight, he hadn't been able to resist. He snorted. But she was too smart; she'd have seen through his excuse in a flash. No one would believe that he was taking a woman he was courting around with him while he pursued an investigation. It was hardly a recipe for romance.

And yet....

He shook his head. Absolutely not. He had to focus. Tad needed him.

Carter couldn't breathe in the stuffy gloom of the house. He went out into the street, taking care to lock the door behind him. A walk—alone, this time—would do him good. Help clear his mind.

Surely, there must be some other avenue of inquiry he could follow, aside from the slim possibility that Estelle Bines knew something of use. He sifted through the bits of information he and Juliet had gathered over the past couple of days. The kidnapping had been meticulously planned, so nothing would have been left to chance.

There had to have been more than one man involved. But how many more? One under the bandstand to pull the lever. One to signal the opportune moment. Would they have risked that no such moment would present itself? No. They would have created some sort of distraction. Nothing too memorable; something just unusual enough to draw everyone's attention for a few moments—a couple of spectators engaged in an altercation, perhaps, or a policeman rousting a pickpocket. A woman fainting from the heat. Any of those things might have done the trick. Carter needed to talk to Lincoln and others who had been there to find out what else they could recall.

A door opened behind Carter's left shoulder, and he half turned at the sudden wash of light and noise. He should have been checking for followers, but there had been no indication that the man—make that men—who had been following him posed any danger. They'd merely wanted information. Come to think of it, knowing they were there could be a boon. He could lay a false trail. He'd have to—

"Carter!"

He whirled to face possible attack.

The man who had called him stopped short, arm still raised, his hail-fellow-well-met smile slipping.

The tension in Carter's shoulder eased, and he sucked in a sharp breath before smiling back. "Sorry, Sean. I've been a bit on edge the past couple of days."

His friend nodded sagely and fell into step beside Carter. "Rumor has it you're up to something right secret."

Carter tried not to be irritated. Pinkertons were nothing if not good at finding out about things. At least Sean didn't seem to know exactly what his assignment consisted of. That was something. "Secret and important and delicate."

"No doubt so important, we lowlier Pinks shouldn't pester the great Carter Forbes while he's working."

"Injured pride doesn't become you, Sean. You know I didn't mean to imply anything of the sort. In fact, I need your help and meant to seek you out in the morning."

Sean raised an eyebrow.

"I've been followed on and off for the past two days. Do you think you could arrange to trail me in the morning and keep an eye out for watchers?"

A wide grin spread across Sean's face. "I'd be delighted."

They discussed the details as they walked, and when they parted, Carter headed for his bed at last. Sean had been remarkably forbearing, not once asking what Carter was investigating. He smothered a yawn and hung his hat on the rack. Once they found Tad, he could share more details with Sean. He deserved that much for his assistance. With his help, Carter might stand a chance of catching the fellow who had been spying on him, and that could give him a real opportunity to identify the kidnapper.

Carter made sure he and Juliet reached Hell's Bottom by seven thirty the next morning. It was the safest time of day, with most of the denizens of the slum sleeping off the excesses of the previous night. Still, he was thankful she'd dressed plainly, with no jewelry, and carried no handbag that would make her a tempting target for a thief. Ensign Morehouse had his rifle across his knees as he drove, and Carter kept two loaded revolvers close at hand.

On either side of the street, the buildings leaned against one another drunkenly. The blind eyes of boarded windows looked over the gaping, toothless mouths of open doors. Carelessly discarded refuse drifted into piles. Several filthy children squatted by one of the larger heaps, picking through it, apparently for something to eat or sell. As the carriage passed, they stared up at it with hard, hostile eyes.

Juliet sat straight-backed next to Carter. She looked ahead, but the redness of her eyes, as well as the way she caught her bottom lip between her teeth, told him she'd seen the children, too, and that the travesty broke her heart. She didn't seem to want him to notice, so he said nothing.

At the corner of Rhode Island and Eleventh, the ensign brought the carriage to a halt. He looked over his shoulder. "You sure you want to walk around here?"

"We've got to find Miss Bines." Carter peered at the ramshackle buildings, then turned to Juliet. "You know her. Does anything look likely?"

Juliet pointed to a three-story tenement. "There. It's the tallest building around. If there's such a thing as status here, Estelle would try to be on top of the heap."

"Then let's go." Carter hopped from the carriage and reached to help her down. He continued holding her hand when he normally would have relinquished it, tucking it into the crook of his arm. "Stay close. Things could turn ugly fast."

"Is this part of our faux courtship?" She looked up at him with an impish smile. She was on to him. But she didn't pull her hand away.

"Better safe than sorry."

They entered the dilapidated tenement by the front door, which sagged on its hinges and had to be scraped across the stoop. The hall stank of overcooked cabbage and stale beer. A rat scrabbled in the corner, dodging the light that streamed through the open door behind them.

Juliet glanced at Carter, looking uncertain but not scared. He gave her a reassuring nod and knocked on the first door.

A frowzy woman with straggly hair and sunken eyes answered. Her tatty dressing gown hung off of one shoulder, and she didn't try to disguise the fact that she wore only a thin undergarment beneath it. "What do you want at the blessed crack of dawn?"

Carter touched the brim of his hat. "Sorry to disturb you, ma'am. We're looking for Estelle Bines."

She looked him up and down. "I don't know nothin'."

Carter produced a 50-cent Postal Currency note and held it up. "I only wish to talk to her."

She eyed the money hungrily. "She in trouble?"

"Not that we know of," Juliet said with gentle diplomacy.

The sound of a female voice drew the woman's avid attention from the money. "What's a piece like you want with Estelle Bines?"

"We're old friends."

The woman sniffed at Juliet. "Sure. And now you're trying to rescue her from a life of sin, no doubt. She don't have time for such like. She's got to support herself." She extended a finger and traced it along Carter's lapel. "But you can try to save my soul any old time."

Carter added a 25-cent currency note to the collection. "Where does she live?"

She plucked the bills from his hand. "Third floor, first door on the right."

"Thank you, ma'am."

She snorted and slammed the door in his face.

Juliet shook her head. "You always bring out the best in people."

"I didn't notice her warming up to you."

"That's because I'm female. She was looking down on me before I could look down on her. I'm sure she thinks I don't understand anything of her life."

Carter paused. "Do you?"

"Enough."

He wanted to ask more about her past, but the clipped note of finality in her answer told him she'd said all she meant to on the subject, at least for the time being. "Be careful. Some of the stairs look like they're about rotted through."

"The whole place could fall down around their ears if they're not careful."

The top floor was hotter than the ground floor, but there was more light, thanks to the fact that a chunk of the roof had caved in. Thin beams of sunlight probed the gloom tentatively, as if not at all sure they'd come to a good neighborhood.

Juliet paused with her hand raised, knuckles almost brushing the door their guide had indicated. "Would you mind if I took the lead in this conversation? Hopefully I can help her accept the idea of a detective at her door."

"All right."

She nodded and tapped lightly.

There was a scuffling sound from inside, followed by a scrabbling noise. A feminine voice sounded. "Who is it?"

"Estelle? It's Juliet Button. We used to know one another in th—"

"I know who you are. What do you want?"

"I'd like to talk to you for a moment."

The door opened just wide enough for an eye to peer through. "Who's he?"

"This is Carter Forbes. He's looking into Cormac's murder. We thought you might be able to help us."

Her eye widened in alarm. "I don't know nothin' 'bout Cormac gettin' himself murdered."

"I saw you outside his shop yesterday morning," Juliet said lightly.

"Lots of people were outside his shop."

"But I know you. And you knew Cormac. When was the last time you saw him?"

"I haven't seen Cormac for weeks, and that's the God's honest truth." She flung the words with such force, it was the first thing she'd said that Carter did believe.

"Estelle, we owe Cormac." Juliet grew stern. "He treated us like kin. Where is your loyalty?"

The door fell open a little as Estelle put her hands over her ears. "I don't know who killed him." She shook her head, eyes shut tight. "I don't know. I don't know."

Juliet reached through the gap to rest a hand on Estelle's arm. She softened her voice. "You may not know for sure, but whom do you suspect?"

Estelle's eyes opened, and she and Juliet stared at one another for a long moment. Juliet didn't remove her hand. "Estelle, it isn't just Cormac. There could be a little boy's life at stake, too."

Tears welled in the redhead's big eyes. "I'm sorry. I don't know anything." She pulled free of Juliet's gentle grasp and then closed the door.

Carter reached inside his pocket, yanked out a scrap of paper and a pencil stub, and scribbled hurriedly. "Miss Bines." He squatted down and slipped the paper underneath the door. "If you change your mind, you can reach me at this address. Call on me anytime, day or night. I can protect you, and I'll do anything I can to help."

There was no sound from inside. At last they turned to leave. The other doors along the hall that had cracked open to allow the occupants a chance to assess the intruders snapped shut.

"I'm sorry." Juliet picked her way around the rubbish on the stairs. "That didn't go as I'd hoped."

"You did very well. I'd bet my next pay packet that she knows something, but she's scared."

Juliet shook her head. "Mortally terrified. Whoever frightened her has done a thorough job of it. I'm glad you didn't take her into custody. She would just stick to her story."

Carter sighed. "I'm not convinced I made the right choice. But you're right, she'd continue to deny all knowledge if I dragged her in, and I don't have anything I can use to prove she's involved in any of it."

They stepped out into the relatively fresh air. The ensign looked grateful to see them and pulled the cart up smartly to what passed for a curb.

Juliet accepted Carter's hand as she climbed into the carriage. "Well, you handled it beautifully. I believe she may come to you."

Carter managed a smile. "I think so, too." He just hoped it would be in time.

Chapter 12

Juliet sat rigidly in the carriage seat, unable to relax. Estelle's fear had been palpable. Perhaps they shouldn't have left her. Then again, they hardly could have stood in that dreadful hall all day. She glanced back at the rotting façade of the tenement. Maybe if she came back without Carter, Estelle would let her in.

A man stepped into the street, and Juliet frowned, sure she'd seen him earlier in the morning. But where? She couldn't quite recall. "Mr. Forbes, I think we're being followed again."

"A man with a brown vest and white shirt? Blond mustache under a round, brimless hat?"

"Yes." Juliet tried to keep the surprise out of her voice. Of course, he would have noticed someone following them before she did. He was always mindful of such a possibility.

"I ought to have told you about him. That's Sean King. He's a Pinkerton, too. I asked him to trail us and see if he could spot who's been following us. I'd introduce you, but I don't want to draw attention to him."

"That is clever. Do you think he'll catch the fellow?"

"I'm hopeful." Carter grinned and propped his feet up on the carriage's facing seat. "Followers never seem to realize they could be followed in turn."

Juliet couldn't quite match his confidence, though she was glad for his sanguine attitude. After all, he was far more experienced in these matters than she. "What is our next step?"

His feet thumped back to the carriage floor. "I need to report to the president and ask him a few questions. It occurred to me last night that there may have been some sort of distraction planned at the time of the kidnapping, to draw attention away during the critical moment."

"Of course." A thrill of appreciation sparked through her. "Look into what they made the audience focus on instead, and you might find a clue solid enough to hold on to."

Carter smiled at her approbation. "I won't find out if I'm right until I talk to a few people."

"What can I do?"

He seemed taken aback. "I don't know if there's anything you can do at the moment."

"Oh. I see." Despite her concern over the idea of being followed, she felt curiously deflated. She wasn't sure if it was because he could think of nothing useful for her to do to aid the investigation, or because she couldn't think of anything herself. "I suppose I shall go home, then."

Though she'd tried to make her voice light, he seemed to sense her disappointment. "If you like, I can come by tonight and share what I've discovered." The words were quick, and he blinked after saying them, as if the offer surprised him as much as it did her.

She wasn't going to let him wriggle free of it, though. "I would like that. You might ask specifically about a red-haired woman at the scene. If Estelle doesn't come forward of her own accord, it might do well to have some means of forcing her cooperation."

"I intend to. Can you think of anything else?"

Juliet shook her head. "I shall be interested to hear what you discover."

His lips quirked ruefully. "Let's hope it's something of use."

Ensign Morehouse pulled up in front of Juliet's home, and Carter scrambled to help her descend. "Tonight?"

She nodded. "Tonight."

She waved as they rattled off, then climbed the front stairs and let herself in. It was just as well that, for the time being, Carter had no further use for her services. Today was a regular sitting day, and she needed the income. Tad might still be missing, but her family needed to eat.

Professor Marvolo and Miss Clara were seated at the kitchen table when she came in. "Would you like some lemonade, dear?"

Juliet dropped into a chair. "I'd love some. It's hot enough to wilt steel." She untied her bonnet and fanned herself with the brim.

Miss Clara slid a tumbler and the pitcher across the table to her. Juliet poured a glass and drank deeply. She smacked her lips. "That's better. Where is Artie?"

"He went out to play this morning and hasn't been back." Miss Clara drained the last of her glass. "I've a feeling he went following after young Daniel, to see what the lad does at the Presidential Mansion."

Juliet shook her head. "Let's hope he doesn't manage to get himself arrested."

The Professor seized the opportunity to address the issue that was obviously uppermost on his mind. "Speaking of law enforcement, what does Mr. Forbes want with us? You did as he requested, and with excellent results. I had thought not to see him again."

"He's in the midst of a tricky investigation, and I have been able to offer some small assistance."

Miss Clara and the Professor traded significant glances.

"What?" Juliet felt like a ship captain facing impending mutiny.

"You're helping him willingly? Not because he has coerced you into something?" The Professor cleared his throat. "He has not, for example, threatened one of us? If he has, we can look after ourselves, even if it means we need to fix a Pinkerton's wagon for him."

"I can assure you that I want to help with this investigation. In fact, I asked to help. You have no reason for concern."

Miss Clara sat a little straighter. "I said as much to the Professor after dinner last night, but he was worried you'd put yourself out on our account."

Juliet stood and kissed the woman's soft, creased forehead. "Of course I would put myself out on your account. I love you both dearly. But I hope your minds will rest easy in this case."

Miss Clara patted Juliet's cheek, her eyes sparkling with mischief. "I wasn't much worried myself. It seemed to me there were more...personal reasons for him to keep coming round."

Juliet's cheeks grew warm as her mind flashed back to the previous evening, standing so close to Carter, with his lips whispering across hers. Time to change the subject. "I must get ready for my sitting. If Artie's not back in time, could you make sure we have billets ready, Professor?"

Short on time, Juliet changed quickly into her lightest dress. Right on schedule, she made her entrance into the séance room. And stopped short.

At the table among her regulars—sweet old ladies and dear Mr. Greenfield—sat the reporter, Paulson. Two seats over was the Pinkerton agent Carter had assigned to follow them. Her thoughts shuddered forward jerkily, like a train running off the tracks. What did it mean? Had the Pinkerton followed the reporter? Should she give him some sort of sign? And what on earth was the reporter doing here, anyway? Maybe the reporter had followed them to Estelle's earlier. Juliet hoped not. Estelle was likely frightened for a reason, and if there was anything worse than a Pinkerton showing up at her door, it was a reporter.

Hoping her hesitation would be taken for a dramatic pause, Juliet managed a smile and breezed into the room. As she went through her normal patter, she tried not to let her gaze linger too long on the Pinkerton. No sense in drawing attention to him if Paulson was unaware that he might have been followed—assuming, of course, that he had been followed. By the same token, Paulson would be surprised if she wasn't intrigued by his presence, since she knew who and what he was.

The whole thing was giving her a headache.

She passed a billet and an envelope to each sitter and asked that everyone write out a question for the spirits. When the sitters had sealed their envelopes, Juliet collected them, stacking them in the center of the table. At least, it looked like she did. She palmed the stack of billets that had been written upon and substituted a pile of blank ones.

She lit a single candle in the center of the table, where its flickering light clearly illumined the gleaming stack of cards, ensuring that no one could tamper with them during the sitting. The Professor came in to draw the curtains, and Juliet discreetly passed the billets off to him. Then she began.

The séance proceeded predictably, with gasps and murmurs from the elderly ladies, each of whom she was able to comfort with pleasing words about the love of their dearly departed. In the middle of rejoicing with Mr. Greenfield over a letter from his son, a warm breath hit Juliet's ear. Startled, she inhaled a sharp gasp, but she quickly recovered and moved on with his wife's message, while trying desperately to listen to the voice whispering in her ear.

"...problem with the billets. You'll have to cover. Professor... explain after." The breath withdrew, and Juliet focused fiercely on making sure she didn't miss another beat, all the while formulating an explanation for the blank cards she would now have to present to the readers.

Normally, the trick was easy to accomplish. Miss Clara would open the envelopes and write messages back to the questioners, usually in the form of a Bible quote or some aphorism.

Then she'd seal the billets in new envelopes, which were smuggled back to Juliet. Through sleight of hand, Juliet would substitute the answered cards for the dummy cards. The sitters were amazed to find that the spirits had magically written responses while the cards had sat undisturbed in the center of the table.

Now, all she had to work with was a stack of blank cards.

She needed a distraction. Something to cut this short. Taking care not to squeeze the hands she held too tightly or to make her voice change, she lifted her legs until her knees pressed against the underside of the table. She lifted them higher, and gradually the table began to tilt. Her muscles ached with the effort, and she was having trouble maintaining the untroubled pace of her discourse.

"The veil closes." With that, she let the table fall to the floor with a loud bang. She slumped to the side, eyes closed, as the sitters yelped, and someone flung open the curtains. One of the ladies called for water, and she heard the Professor enter the room.

Juliet moaned and raised a hand to her forehead. She let her eyes flutter open. A glass of water was pressed on her by the Professor, and she accepted a small sip.

Mrs. Curtis lifted a fluttery palm to her chest. "I've never seen such a manifestation of spirit presence. The whole table floated and then crashed to the ground."

Mr. Greenfield moved close to Juliet. "Are you all right, my dear girl?"

"The veil closed very suddenly. It was as if I were thrust from the other side in an instant. I've never had something like that happen."

"You're all right now, though?" The Pinkerton detective was at her elbow, looking concerned. She wished she could recall his name.

"Yes, I think so." She made a brave attempt to stand, despite the shaking in her hands and legs.

"Oh no, you musn't get up yet. I don't think you've recovered." One of the ladies restrained her with a hand on her shoulder.

"Well, isn't this interesting?"

The gathering parted to reveal the reporter, holding up a handful of opened envelopes. "They're all blank."

A gasp arose, and one of Juliet's regulars raised a hand to her mouth. "That is amazing. The writing must dematerialize as it is translated to the spirit realm. It must have been interrupted in the process."

Juliet nodded. She had just hoped to make everyone forget about the blasted billets, but she wasn't above grasping hold of a great idea when it came by. "The translation process can take some time, as the spiritual material must congeal into the form of new ink."

There was much murmuring as this further proof of the miraculous nature of the spirit world was explored. With tactful evidences of her enfeebled state, she soon had the sitters withdrawing respectfully.

The Pinkerton was one of the first to leave. No doubt, he didn't want to draw Paulson's attention to himself unnecessarily. The reporter was the last to go. He eyed Juliet speculatively.

"Are you sure you don't need something stiffer to drink?"

"No, thank you. I'll be fine." Juliet made an effort at politesse. As long as he was here, perhaps she could learn something from him. "I hope you found the reassurance you sought by your attendance today."

He scratched his ear. "Well, if nothing else, I got some goose pimples. But as I sat here, I started thinking I could do a story about the local spiritualists. I haven't decided yet if it will be an endorsement or an investigative article."

Lemonade curdled in her stomach. "I'm sure that whatever method you choose will prove fascinating to your readers."

He leaned forward. "You could help me decide."

"How is that?" Juliet maintained a wan smile.

"You could share with me what you and Forbes are up to."

Juliet made her smile saccharine. "Mr. Forbes and I are courting."

Paulson raised an eyebrow.

Juliet maintained her insouciance with great difficulty.

At last, the Professor came in, and Paulson looked away to accept his hat. "Thanks." He allowed the Professor to usher him away, but not without sending a parting shot over his shoulder. "I'll be in touch about that article."

Juliet headed to the kitchen. "What was wrong with the billets?"

Miss Clara slid one of the white cards across the table to her. Handwriting slashed across it in dark, bold strokes. *If you value your life, you will stop.*

Juliet stared at it blankly, her mouth dry as ashes.

The Professor entered the room behind her. "Would you care to explain further what it is you've been helping Mr. Forbes with? We deserve to know." He'd never been so stern with her before.

He was right. They deserved answers. How she wished Carter were there. He would know what to say and what to leave out.

"It's a secret. I can't—"

"No secret is more important than your life, young lady." Miss Clara wasn't having any of it. "You can and will tell us, and allow us to help with whatever it is. That is what family is for."

"Yes, family takes care of each other," Juliet conceded, "which is precisely why I can't tell you anything." Miss Clara opened her mouth to object, but Juliet rushed on. "If I'm in danger, then you all are in danger by association. The less you know, the better."

The Professor reached across the table and squeezed Juliet's hand. "My dear, you have always gone out of your way to see to our needs and our safety. I have no doubt you think you're doing the right thing. But, in this case, shielding us from the truth could put us all at risk."

"The truth shall make you free," Miss Clara finished with a sharp nod.

Juliet shut her eyes. Normally, she agreed. Despite the amount of deception required in her profession, she believed in being honest with those closest to her. But she'd promised Carter to keep the details secret. Would he understand if she told them? Did it matter?

Juliet closed her eyes and took a deep breath. She had to tell them something, but she had to honor her promise to Carter, too.

She opened her eyes and exhaled. "A little boy has been kidnapped—I can't say who. But I can tell you that his life is in danger."

"It's Tad Lincoln." The outside door at the end of the kitchen slammed shut as Artie stomped inside, his face as grim as it was dirty. "And I know who done took him."

Chapter 13

All three adults gasped in unison, sounding like a steam engine. Artie wiped the sweat from his brow with the back of his wrist, then grabbed a clean tumbler from the sideboard.

"What makes you think it's the Lincoln boy?" Juliet bit her bottom lip.

"It's all they're talking about at the Presidential Mansion." Artie grabbed the lemonade pitcher and filled his glass nearly to the brim.

Of course. Carter might not want the general public to know about the kidnapping, but there were plenty of people within the Lincolns' inner circle who must know something had happened, even if they weren't sure exactly what. The staff of the Executive Mansion must be buzzing. It might help to know who was talking and what they were saying.

Juliet pulled out the chair beside her. "Tell me what you know."

He shrugged as he dropped onto the hard wooden seat. "I mostly stayed around the stables with Daniel. You'd be amazed how people talk around the help."

Juliet held back a frown. She knew exactly what he meant—most people acted as if their servants were deaf and mute. "You said you knew who kidnapped Tad. What did you hear?"

Artie plunked down his now-empty glass and leaned his elbows on the table, looking from Juliet to Miss Clara to the Professor. "I was hunkered down in one of the stalls. There was a horse with a terrible case of thrush, and Daniel was showing it to me."

Juliet's stomach flipped at the idea of the boys' fascination with an infected hoof. "We can skip over that part."

"All right." He shook his head, clearly of the opinion that she was missing out on the most interesting part of the story. "These two fellas came into the barn. At first, they were talking boring old politics, like everybody else around here. Then one said something about Tad Lincoln."

"Go on."

"Said how 'tragic' it was that the boy'd been kidnapped, but he didn't sound sorry. The other one said it could be just the thing to 'turn the tide of the war.'"

Miss Clara snorted. "Of all the ridiculous things to say. What could the kidnapping of an innocent child have to do with the war?"

Forgetting her manners, Juliet leaned her elbows on the table, too, and talked out the tangle of thoughts in her head. "It doesn't seem like a natural remark."

The Professor held up a finger. "Unless, of course, the speaker had intimate knowledge of the plan and the final objective."

"Or was politically astute. Carter and I have been able to draw similar conclusions without the benefit of being in on the plan."

Artie shook his head, lips pursed. "The way the fella talked, I got the feeling he was in on it."

Juliet's fingers curled into her palms. Artie could simply be seeking attention. Boys his age did that sort of thing. Then again, he had good instincts. He might be on to something. "Would you recognize this man if you saw him again?"

Artie slumped in his chair. "I never saw him. Not his face, anyway. When I looked outside the stall, they were walking away. I only saw their backs."

Fighting back disappointment, Juliet smiled. "That's all right. You've given me something to share with Detective Forbes when he stops by tonight."

"He's coming here again?" the Professor asked.

"Tonight?" Miss Clara looked at the clock on the wall.

"Yes, he's coming by to discuss the status of the case." Juliet turned to Artie and ruffled his hair, pulling a grin from him. "In fact, you and Daniel should talk to him yourselves. I'm sure he'd be very interested in what you have to say."

Professor Marvolo rose slowly to his feet, his rheumy eyes trained on Juliet. "I believe he's interested in more than discussing this case."

Juliet pulled her shoulders back. "What does that mean?"

"It means you need to consider the wisdom of opening your heart to a man like him." With a nod, he shuffled out of the room.

Miss Clara jumped up, wondering aloud what she should make for dinner and whether she'd have time to dress a chicken. As he often did, Artie vanished without a word. And Juliet sat alone at the table, pondering the Professor's words. She was a woman skilled at deception. Carter was a man who lived by the truth. What kind of relationship could possibly develop between them? Friendship, maybe. Perhaps mutual respect. But anything beyond that was an impossibility.

With a sigh, she rose. The sooner they found Tad Lincoln, the sooner they would stop working together, and the sooner she would be able to banish this ridiculous romanticism. And the sooner her family would be out of danger. There wasn't time to wait for Estelle to decide to do the right thing anymore. She looked at the clock. If she hurried, she could make it to Hell's Bottom and back before dark. If she arrived without a Pinkerton in tow, Estelle would surely open up to her.

"Artie!" she called out in a most unladylike fashion as she rushed out the back door. "Run over to the livery and rent a cart!"

Juliet had seriously misjudged how long it would take to harness the horse and drive up to Hell's Bottom. There was such an influx of people in town because of the war that it might have been faster to walk. The sun was a golden orb nestled amongst satiny pillows of pink, orange, and red clouds when Artie pulled the wagon to a stop in front of Estelle's creaky tenement. He stood up to help her down, but she stopped him with a hand to his shoulder.

"You wait here."

"No!" He shook his head so hard that his stringy blond bangs fell into his eyes. "You're not going in that place by yourself."

Juliet looked over her shoulder. She hadn't thought this through very well at all. Truth be told, she didn't want Artie waiting out here by himself, but she didn't want him going inside the building, either. At least in the cart, he could make a run for it, if need be. "I'll be fine. I need you to guard the horse and the cart. If you see anyone who makes you suspicious, I want you to drive off quick as you can."

"Everyone around here is suspicious." He frowned, looking ready for a fight. "I'm not leaving you here."

Juliet looked down the street, as if an answer would present itself from one of the alleys. Not likely. The only thing that might come from that source was trouble. "I won't be long. Drive in a circle around the block until you see me outside again. It's the only way to make sure we'll both get home safely. Do you understand?"

As Juliet stepped out of the carriage, Artie mumbled and nodded his head. She smiled. "I'll be back as quickly as I can."

Her smile vanished as soon as she reached the door. Either the heat of the day had made it swell, or it was heavier than it looked. It required both of her hands wrapped around the knob, and pushing with all her strength, to make it budge. It opened with a terrible screech as the bottom dragged across the ground. So much for slipping in unnoticed.

Down the hall, a door opened just a crack. The woman who'd taken Carter's money that morning stared out at Juliet.

"Get out," the woman hissed.

Juliet stepped toward the door. Now she could see the woman's entire face, with her wide eyes; she could smell the scent of fear clinging to her and snaking through the gap to clutch at Juliet's throat.

"You don't belong here. Get out." She shoved the door shut, and from inside came the sound of something heavy being pushed in front of it.

Juliet made her way up the shadowy staircase. With the sun setting, the light that found an entrance through the hole in the ceiling bathed the walls in an eerie orange glow. Add to that the sweltering heat, and Juliet might have been walking through the bowels of hell itself.

At the third-floor landing, she froze. A door stood open in front of her.

Estelle's door.

Was it fear or good sense that whispered "Run" in her ear? She sucked in a series of quick breaths through her nose. She'd already come this far. Placing one foot carefully in front of the other, she made her way across the rotting floor. The sound of buzzing flies and the familiar, iron-tinged stench of blood assaulted her even before she saw the body.

"Estelle."

Pressing her sleeve against her nose and mouth, she crept into the cramped room and dropped to her knees. If there was any chance she could help.... But one look at the slash across Estelle's neck, and the blood congealed there, told Juliet the woman had been dead for some hours. Still, she placed her fingers beneath Estelle's nose, praying to detect even a whisper of life.

There was none.

A sob tore out of Juliet's throat. Now there was no doubt Estelle had known something about the person behind Tad Lincoln's kidnapping. Juliet lifted her head and drew in a shaky breath. She looked around the dark room, for the first time noticing its state of upheaval. This wasn't the result of slovenly housekeeping. There had been a struggle. From the clothing and undergarments strewn across the floor, it appeared someone might have searched through Estelle's things, as well.

The creak and groan of the floorboards alerted Juliet that someone was behind her. She held her breath. A person who meant no harm would make his presence known.

What could she do? She needed a weapon, but the only thing within reach was her friend's body. Then her eyes fell on the stickpin on Estelle's bodice. The decorative head was broken, and some of the faux jewels were missing from the setting, but that wasn't the part that interested Juliet.

"Poor Estelle." She spoke aloud, leaning forward and changing her breathing to emulate sobs. With her left hand, she reached up, smoothed back Estelle's bright red hair, and then, with two fingers, closed the lids of her eyes. With her body half-concealing Estelle's chest, she carefully moved her right hand to the pin, pulled it out, and palmed it.

She stood up, lifting a silent prayer to heaven. *Lord, help me.*

When she turned, it took no acting skills to display shock as she came face-to-face with the man in the doorway. His hat was pulled down low, and a dirty kerchief covered his face from the nose down, so that all she could see were his eyes. But those were enough to ice her blood.

Beefy hands wrapped around her upper arms. "You should mind your own business."

"I don't want any trouble." *Innocent. Act innocent.* Palms up. Posing no threat. "I was just going to help her, if I could. I'm not going to tell anybody."

The man grunted, his breath hot and foul. "I know who you are. My boss is goin' ta be real happy if I take care of ya for him."

Fear's razor-sharp claws skittered up her spine. She had to get away. Now.

"No!" Her voice rose to a hysterical pitch, and she babbled incoherently, tossing her head from side to side. While the man concentrated on the fit she was throwing, she eased the pin out of her sleeve and plunged it into the underside of the man's arm.

With a bellow of rage, he pushed her away from him. She stumbled backward and hit her head against the doorjamb. Sparks exploded in front of her. The room spun. *No, don't pass out now.*

He grunted and pulled out the pin, cursing when blood oozed from the hole in his shirt.

Juliet pushed herself from the wall, pivoted, and ran for the stairs, holding her skirts high with one hand and balancing against the wall with the other. Gravity pushed her, and she lost control, stumbling down three stairs and collapsing in a heap on the second-floor landing. Heavy footfalls lumbered above her. She rolled over and scrambled to her feet. The man barreled down the stairs faster than she'd expected. There was no way to escape, and, despite all the commotion, no one opened a door to see what was going on. Here she was, in a tenement full of people, and there was no one who would help her.

But they might help themselves.

"Fire!" Juliet screamed, sprinting down the stairs. "The building's on fire!"

Doors cracked open. The orange sunset playing across the walls supported Juliet's claims. Doors flung open, and people poured out into the hallways. Soon, she was surrounded. A quick glance behind revealed that the masked man was caught up in the panicked throng.

Juliet let herself be carried along, bursting out the front door and into the cooling air of evening. She pulled up short at the curb as people ran past her. Where was the cart? Where was Artie?

A hand wrapped around her upper arm. Juliet screamed, trying to yank away, but the fingers gripped tighter. No one so much as glanced in her direction.

She reared back to lash at him. "Let go!"

"Miss Avila, it's me."

At the friendly voice, she stopped fighting and looked at the man who held her. Beneath his brimless hat, his brown eyes reflected concern, and his thick, blond mustache perked up in an encouraging smile.

"Mr. King?"

"Yes." The Pinkerton agent released her arm.

"What are you doing here?"

"Agent Forbes asked me to keep an eye on you and your family. Good thing, too." He frowned. "What possessed you to come here by yourself?"

"I needed to see someone. To ask her...." Juliet's stomach pitched as the gruesome discovery replayed in her mind. "She's dead."

"Who's dead?"

"Estelle Bines. And the man who killed her...he was still up there. He would have killed me, too." Juliet surveyed the crowd surrounding the building. "I don't see him."

"Juliet!" Artie drove up in the cart, giving the Pinkerton agent a good looking over.

"Thank heavens you're all right." She exhaled a sigh of relief, then moved to step up into the cart but teetered on unsteady legs. Agent King reached forward to offer support and helped her up.

The agent looked at Artie. "Take her straight to Detective Forbes's residence."

Juliet shook her head. "He won't be there. He was planning to come to my home this evening to discuss the case."

Agent King smoothed down his mustache. "Fine, then go straight to your home. Tell Detective Forbes that I stayed behind to collect evidence, and ask him to notify the authorities."

"Yes, sir." Artie gave the agent a brisk salute, then slapped the reins against the horse's haunches.

As they moved further out of Hell's Bottom, the reality of what had occurred hit Juliet with the force of a typhoon. Estelle was dead, and Juliet had nearly met the same fate. The trembling began in her legs and worked up through her body, shaking her spine, her shoulders, and her arms, until even her teeth chattered, despite the warmth of the summer evening.

"Miss Juliet, are you all right?"

"I...I...." Her voice quaked so, she couldn't get past the first word. Arms crossed over her chest, she hugged herself and shook her head. "Fine. I'm fine."

For the second time in as many days, Juliet wished she really could communicate with the dead. She could tell Estelle how sorry she was for bringing trouble to her door. She could ask her friend if she knew the man who'd killed her. And maybe, just maybe, she and Carter could find little Tad Lincoln before something equally heinous happened to him.

Carter. She needed to get to him. He'd know what to do. Until then, all Juliet could do was concentrate on not falling apart.

Pray.

The word rang out so loudly in her brain, she jerked her head up and looked to see who'd spoken. Artie had his eyes trained on the road ahead of them, and gave no sign that he'd said anything.

Pray? Would God even hear her? And if He did, would He care? The few prayers she had uttered of late hadn't been granted.

She assumed it was because the Divine One had no interest in any petition her unclean lips might offer.

Perhaps it would do to strike a deal. With her hands clasped in her lap and her head bowed, she moved her lips in a silent plea. *If You lead us to Tad, I'll change my ways. Just please don't let anyone else get hurt.* An image of Carter came to mind, standing in the velvety darkness of the moonlit park. Icy fingers pinched her heart. *Especially not Carter.*

Chapter 14

"You jabbed him with a stickpin?" Carter didn't know whether to commend Juliet for her resourcefulness or chastise her for her foolishness in returning to that pit of depravity alone. What had she been thinking? Really, he should give her a good reprimand to ensure she never did anything so reckless again. But one look at her, hunched in the chair, shaking so hard that the teacup clattered against the saucer in her hand, cooled him down. To unleash his anger now would be like stepping on a baby bird that had just fallen from the nest.

Of course, this baby bird was surrounded by a very protective family of bigger birds. Miss Clara and the Professor stood stern-faced and ramrod straight on either side of the chair, each with a hand on one of Juliet's shoulders.

Artie sat on a hassock by her feet, glaring daggers at Carter, as if daring him to hurt the head of their little clan. Daniel stood off to the side by the fireplace, probably hoping he wouldn't have to choose between his loyalty to Carter and his gratitude to Juliet.

When Carter had first arrived, he'd been hesitant to speak about the case in front of the others. But once Artie told him what he'd overheard at the Executive Mansion, he realized it was a moot point. Everyone in the room already knew about Tad Lincoln. The best he could hope was to contain the damage and pray none of them was prone to gossip. For now, he had yet another murder on his hands.

"Where did you get the pin? Was it your own?"

Juliet looked up at him, her eyes round. "My pin? No." She shook her head slowly. "No, it was Estelle's. I took it from her bodice when I...I...." The rattle of china against china increased.

Averting an accident, Miss Clara reached down and snatched the saucer and cup from Juliet's hands. "Here now, Mr. Forbes, can't this wait until later? Juliet is in no state to answer questions. She needs to rest."

He wished it could wait, but no. He knew from experience that it was best to question a witness several times. Right now, he needed to gather as much information as possible while it was still fresh, before her mind had a chance to jumble and distort the facts. As much as he cared for Juliet—Lord help him, he cared for her more than he should—he had a job to do.

Hunkering down in front of her, he ignored Artie's snort of disgust and took both of her now-empty hands in his. "Juliet." He didn't say another word. Just waited and held her hands until she looked him in the eye. But her glassy, vacant stare told him she was somewhere else entirely.

"Juliet, no one is going to hurt you. You're home, in a safe place, surrounded by people who love you." He rubbed the pads of his thumbs across the backs of her hands. She blinked once, twice. She looked down at his hands holding hers and then back up at his face. At least he had her attention now. "No one can get to you here, Juliet."

What was meant to reassure her had exactly the opposite effect. Her shoulders sagged, and her mouth twisted as she fought off tears. "But they can. They already have." She pulled her hands away and buried her face in them.

"What do you mean?" When no answer seemed forthcoming, he looked at the Professor. "What is she talking about?"

The man frowned, then motioned to Artie. "Go get the billets."

Artie scrambled to his feet and shot out of the room. A moment later, he raced back in, a small stack of paper squares in his hand. He thrust them at Carter. "These are from the sitting this afternoon. I wasn't here, 'cuz I was doing my own detecting in the stable, but I know all about it."

"Slow down." Carter's knees ached, but he wasn't about to move away from Juliet until he knew what was going on. He looked down at the papers in his hand and frowned as he read the one on top.

If you value your life, you will stop.

Carter clenched his jaw, determined not to let his anger show. "Who wrote this?"

Artie opened his mouth to speak, but Carter put a finger to his own lips, signaling for silence. As painful as it would be, Juliet needed to pull herself together and talk through this, before the fear consumed her.

"Juliet." Carter reached up and pulled her hands away from her face. "I need you to focus. Tell me who wrote that note." Her lip quivered, and Carter was afraid she would dissolve into tears again. "You can do this."

She swallowed, then closed her eyes and took a deep breath. When her lids fluttered open, her eyes appeared clearer, and her mouth was set in a determined line. "I can do this," she agreed.

"Very good. Now, who wrote the note?"

"It was one of the people at the sitting this afternoon, but I have no idea which one."

Carter nodded. "You may not know for sure who did it, but at least we have a suspect pool. And it shouldn't be too difficult to narrow it down."

For the first time that evening, she looked hopeful. "You're right."

Carter smiled. This was the Juliet he'd come to know.

It took well over an hour for Juliet to tell Carter all she knew. They went over the details of the sitting and everyone who had been there. Then she told him all she could remember about finding Estelle and the man she'd fought off. By the time Carter was satisfied and left to meet Agent King at Estelle's apartment, Juliet's emotions were stretched tight as piano strings. All she wanted to do was trudge upstairs to her bed. Miss Clara offered to bring up a tray, but Juliet's stomach rolled in disagreement. She wanted only the blissful respite of sleep.

But sleep didn't come easy. She tossed and turned until she tangled herself in the sheets. And when she finally did manage to drift off, it was into a nightmarish world where she was being pursued by a crowd of faceless people, each brandishing a gleaming stickpin.

Things weren't much better in the light of day. Sitting at her dressing table, Juliet frowned into the mirror. Her eyes were still red, the skin around them swollen and raw. How had she let herself become so soft? First she'd missed obvious details about the sitting, and then she'd completely fallen apart. Of course, finding Estelle had been a shock, but it wasn't as though she'd never seen a dead person before.

Once, when she was a girl, she'd curled up in an alleyway, huddled near a steam grate, for warmth. Berta, the elderly woman who'd taken Juliet under her wing, had insisted she take the threadbare blanket they'd salvaged from a rubbish bin. When Juliet awoke, stiff and chilled to the bone, Berta was dead, her skin blue. It was then Juliet knew that she not only had to take care of herself; she also must do whatever she could to help the people she cared for.

A knock sounded outside her room.

"Come in, Miss Clara."

The door opened, and the woman poked her head in. "How are you feeling this morning?"

"Better than yesterday." Juliet smiled.

"Well, you look lovely."

Juliet snorted. "I look a fright."

"Nonsense. That dress is lovely. It complements your skin so well."

"Yes, the pale green really does set off the rosy redness around my eyes."

Miss Clara laughed and stepped behind her. "Silly girl. But, now that you mention it, the shade does seem to tone down the red a bit." She picked up a silver-backed hairbrush and ran it through Juliet's tresses, pulling them into a tidy twist.

"Perhaps I should carry a fan. I could pretend to hide coyly behind it." She held up a hairpin to Miss Clara.

"No need for that." She tucked the pin in, anchoring her creation in place, then reached for another. "I'm sure Mr. Forbes would prefer to see those beautiful eyes of yours, even if they are a little worse for wear."

Juliet jerked to look at Miss Clara and was rewarded by having the business end of the hairpin poke her scalp. "What does he have to do with anything?"

Miss Clara chuckled. "Don't play dumb with me. I've seen the way you look at him. And he looks at you exactly the same."

"Does he?"

"Absolutely." Miss Clara smoothed down Juliet's hair and pulled a stray tendril to curl against her cheek. "I have to admit, I had my doubts at first, him being a Pinkerton and all. But if you're determined to help with this investigation, I'm glad you're with someone like him."

"He is extremely good at his job."

"And he never takes his eyes off of you. I feel certain no harm will come to you with Mr. Forbes around."

Juliet took a deep breath. Miss Clara was right, at least partially. Carter would protect her, physically. But she was afraid her heart was in dire jeopardy, and the longer he was around, the more dangerous it became.

Chapter 15

Carter sat down to a breakfast of eggs and toast. He yearned for bacon, but he hadn't been able to find any for weeks. Hayes placed a newspaper on the table by Carter's left hand and then withdrew. Crunching into a piece of toast slathered in butter and jam, Carter unfolded the paper.

He dropped his toast.

Of all the—! He pushed away from the table and stormed into the hall. Not bothering to pause to put on a jacket, he snatched his hat off the peg and burst out the door, still dressed in shirtsleeves.

The blocks to Juliet's lair passed in a blur as his mind spun. He had believed—hoped—that her gang was trustworthy. He hit the newspaper against his leg. He'd been naive. A fool, taken in by a pretty face. And the country might not be able to withstand his gullibility.

The newspaper crackled as his fingers tightened into a fist.

He bounded up the front steps of Juliet's home two at a time. He pounded twice on the door but did not wait for anyone to answer. Instead he flung it open and marched past a startled Professor, straight back to the kitchen, where he smacked the paper down on the table in front of Juliet.

"Explain."

"And good morning to you, Mr. Forbes," she said coolly. With crinkled brow, she glanced from him to the paper, then picked it up and looked at the headline. She gasped, and her eyes flew to his. "How did they find out?"

"That's what I came to ask you."

She stiffened. "Dozens of people must know by now. Why would you suspect one of us of leaking it?"

"Because this household found out last night, and the news is in the paper today."

She stood. "How dare you? You barge into my home, spouting allegations, when we have done nothing but help you from the day you first arrived, trying to trick me into some admission." Color suffused her face, and her eyes fairly crackled with anger. "I'll tell you, Mr. Detective, you are no better than I am. You manipulate people to get information out of them, but you believe it is justified because you have a good reason."

A hot rush of shame swept up Carter's neck. He opened his mouth to speak, but she was not to be denied.

"Well, I have my reasons, too, and they are just as valid as yours. Now, I would appreciate it if you would leave my home and not return unless you have something civil to say."

Miss Clara calmly set down her mug of tea. "We haven't told a soul, Detective Forbes. Even if we didn't like you, we wouldn't betray our Juliet."

Artie picked up the paper and examined the central column critically. "He don't say where he got his tale. Just a source close to the president."

Carter looked at them all, and a fresh wave of chagrin prickled through him. Juliet had done nothing to indicate that she was untrustworthy, but he had once again made assumptions about her and her family. "I'm sorry." He cleared his throat. "I shouldn't have jumped to conclusions, and I shouldn't have come storming in here with accusations."

Juliet glared at him for a long moment, and then her face softened. "Oh, sit down. Let's talk this through and figure out what to do."

Carter nodded, but instead of sitting, he took the paper from Artie. He hadn't even read the article, he'd been so livid. "Paulson wrote the piece."

"I know that's the man who followed us. But, I assure you, I didn't tell him a thing. You were there."

"But he came to your séance yesterday, and King said he stayed for a while after the others left. To the point King was concerned and almost returned himself." Her eyes narrowed, and Carter held up his hands. "I'm not saying anyone here told him. But could he have overheard something?"

They looked from one person to the next. The Professor had stood silently by the door during the exchange, as if ready to boot Carter out if needed. Now he spoke. "I doubt that is possible. All of the sitters had gone from the house before we discussed the threat."

"Could he have come back in?" Carter asked. "I was able to breeze on in because the door was unlatched."

Juliet shook her head. "That was because Daniel had left for work through that door."

"Do you typically keep the door latched, then?"

"Yes. There are always 'unbelievers' trying to discredit those of my profession."

"Wise. I just don't know where that reporter could have picked up the information."

"The staff at the Executive Mansion all know, Lizzy Keckley knows, and it is likely the president's cabinet knows, not to mention the guards who are supposed to be protecting him. And Mrs. Lincoln's doctor. And others have likely begun to notice that Tad isn't around. It's a wonder it hasn't come out before now."

Carter had to concede the point.

The Professor tapped his chin. "It might have even been the kidnappers. If their plot is meant to destabilize Lincoln's administration, then they cannot stand by and let the investigation continue in secret. Its success depends on people knowing of it."

Juliet poured Carter a mug of coffee, then waved him into a seat. "We can worry about where the information came from later. The most important thing at the moment is to decide what to do about it. There must be some way to counter the claim."

"How? It's true. The only counter would be to make Tad magically reappear. If we could do that, we wouldn't be in this mess."

"I might have an idea." She grinned at him, and his heart soared. He wasn't sure he could attribute it to confidence in her plan, either. No, this giddiness had nothing to do with criminals or conspiracies. This was all about Juliet.

"You can't be serious." Artie's nose positively curled up at the sight of the floppy bow, frilly collar, jacket, and short pants Juliet had laid out.

She looked at the garments. "What? You've worn them for sittings when it was necessary. And his mother has him dress like this."

"But people think I'm a ghost when we do sittings." He crossed his arms over his chest. "I'm not doing it."

"It won't be for long."

His lower lip jutted forward. "I am not wearing that."

When Juliet looked at Carter, there was no ignoring the appeal for help in her eyes. "How about you come to the Executive Mansion with us in your own clothes?" He gave Artie's shoulder a squeeze. "Tad has a couple of uniforms designed to match some of the Union regiments. You could wear one of those instead."

The boy's eyes lit up at that. "Deal."

"Good. Once you're dressed, Miss Juliet can get you looking just like Tad." He cocked a head. "You're the right size, at least."

"Do you think it will work?" Artie asked.

"Absolutely." Carter projected a bit more enthusiasm than he felt, but there was no use giving the lad any reason to doubt his mission. "Miss Juliet has already proven she's a master with her disguises."

She waggled her eyebrows. "The trick is giving people what they expect to see."

"But, under the circumstances, they won't expect to see Tad. They'll scrutinize him closely."

"Yes, but there are other factors that will work in our favor. He hasn't been seen out much since his brother's passing. So, a reasonable facsimile shouldn't arouse suspicion. The most important thing is for the president to treat him as a son." Juliet hoisted her case of stage makeup and wigs.

Carter reached to carry it for her. "Oomph. Are you smuggling gold in here?"

"I wouldn't smuggle gold; I'd spend it."

"And when a revenue officer comes to chat with you about the source of your sudden wealth…?"

Juliet grinned. "I will be very, very grateful to my spirit guides." She offered a two-fingered salute and sashayed out the door, with Artie right on her heels.

Carter stared after her. She was joking. She had to be. Yes, he was pretty sure she was joking.

"Are you coming?"

He found his feet and hurried after her.

Thus far, Juliet had managed to convey a great deal more confidence in her plan than she actually possessed. Still, she couldn't see any other alternatives. At least none she found acceptable. Allowing the president's loose grasp on the warring elements of his coalition to falter was not only politically dangerous; it could spell disaster for the Union.

The Lincolns, especially Mary, were already criticized for sympathizing with their Southern relations. The last thing old Abe needed was to have his judgment called into question, too. There would be no way to win. Some would paint him as selfish, caring for his own son while thousands of other sons perished. Others would claim he had placed his son in danger by heedlessly forcing the rift between North and South. Some might even accuse him of faking the tragedy to gain sympathy.

The trio's earlier banter was gone, stifled under the weight of sun and worry. Even Artie's habitual cheer had withered. He stared out over the field at the incomplete spire of the Washington Monument.

What had she been thinking? How could she ask a little boy to take the place of a child who might even be dead? She shuddered, then reached forward to pat his leg. "You don't have to do this, Artie. No one will think less of you."

He blinked as if roused from some daydream. "What? It's all right. I was just wonderin' if that suit of his is made of wool. It's awful hot for itchy old wool."

Juliet pressed her lips together, so as not to seem to laugh at him. Were all boys so utterly pragmatic?

Carter answered for her. "I'm fairly certain he has a naval uniform you could wear."

Artie swiped at his brow with the back of his hand. "You're not catching me like that. You're talking about a sailor suit. That's for kids."

"But it would be better than a stuffy uniform."

"If them soldiers can handle it, so can I."

"You're sure?"

"I ain't a kid."

The conversation came to an end as they drove into the president's stable yard. Carter hopped down before the ensign could pull the cart to a complete halt. Daniel approached and took hold of the horse's bridle, patting the animal's neck. "You folks are here awful early. I think Mr. Lincoln is still at breakfast." He glanced at them sideways, as if trying to gauge how bad the news they brought might be.

"Has he been given the paper yet?" Carter asked.

Daniel faltered. "I don't know."

Carter sighed. "I hate to disturb him, but we don't have a choice."

He held his hands up to Juliet and swung her down from the cart.

Artie hopped down on his own and winked at Daniel. "You should be salutin' me now. I'm gonna be kinda like a prince."

Juliet shushed him. "It's not the time, Artie."

Carter held a brief conference with Edward the porter. In short order, they found themselves standing before the great man's desk.

His breakfast sat, largely untouched, atop a stack of papers, while he had his head buried in another sheaf.

Carter approached the desk and cleared his throat. "Sir."

Lincoln peered around the papers, then lowered them and removed his spectacles. "Mr. Forbes. You have news?"

"We haven't found Tad, but there is a development. Have you seen the *Intelligencer* this morning?"

The president shook his head warily.

"One of their reporters got hold of the kidnapping story."

Juliet watched Lincoln as his brilliant mind sorted through all the implications in an instant, his eyes registering the resulting dismay.

Carter motioned to Juliet and Artie, who had hung back a step behind him. "Miss Avila has a plan that we believe can help."

The president's eyebrows lifted infinitesimally, and he shifted the power of his gaze to Juliet. She felt herself flush as she moved forward and dipped in a curtsy, with Artie close behind. "Mr.

President." She rested a hand lightly on Artie's shoulder. "I thought that if Artie, here, were to impersonate Tad and appear with you at a few select public appearances, the tales of kidnapping could be put to rest."

"But people must know what Tad looks like."

"Artie would need to dress as Tad, and I shall use stage makeup and a wig to help him look more like your son. As long as no one is permitted to get too close, I believe it will work."

Lincoln turned back to Carter. "Is there any danger to either lad if we do this?"

"Sir." Carter swallowed. "I am very much afraid—"

Juliet took a step forward, so that she stood by Carter's side. "There could be." Lincoln deserved to know the truth, but he also had to understand that this could be their only chance. "However, if we are successful, we will be effectively spiking their guns. The kidnapper may decide he has no reason to hold Tad any longer. He could either release Tad or...."

"Or kill him," Carter finished for her. "He could decide that he can still use Tad for his purposes, by trying to force you to some decision. The trouble is that we don't know who has him, and thus we don't know what strategy will likely be employed."

Lincoln tapped his reading glasses against his chin.

"He's already beginning to grow worried." Carter then filled the president in briefly on Estelle's murder. "We need to continue to keep him off balance, but we do not want him to panic to the point that he moves to cut his losses and run. And now, this story in the paper is another potential clue. The reporter had to have gathered the information somewhere. It could have been the kidnapper who fed it to him."

"Or a thousand other people who wish my administration ill or are just reckless with their gossip." The emotion Juliet had seen in his face earlier was gone, stacked neatly aside, so he could focus on the problem. He was silent a long moment. "Perhaps the fellow has thought of multiple purposes for my boy. If we remove the option of using him to cause a public outcry, then perhaps we could force him to come closer again. In order to manipulate me, he must make his wishes known." He tossed his glasses down on the desk, then stood and started pacing.

Carter nodded. "And any time he attempts contact, he risks exposure."

The president stopped before the window, hands clasped behind his back. "But to trap him, we must anticipate him. How can we do that?"

"Easy." Artie stepped around Juliet, his head up, his shoulders pulled back. "Think like he does."

Chapter 16

Carter thought that putting oneself in the mind of a kidnapper and murderer was disturbing enough for a Pinkerton agent, but it was unthinkable for a father. Nevertheless, President Lincoln insisted on being part of the planning. As he'd said, it was their best way to deduce what the next course of action should be, and the only way he knew to help his son. Juliet had taken Artie to Tad's bedroom to try on a uniform and experiment with the wig.

"Have you considered where we might present our imposter?" Lincoln asked.

Carter nodded. "Obviously, it needs to be someplace public. We need people to see him but not be able to interact with him."

"That could be a challenge. Anyone who knows Tad knows how much he loves to mingle." Lincoln chuckled, but the brief spark of joy in his eyes was quickly extinguished. He pursed his thin lips and pressed on. "I believe I have a solution. When Mrs. Lincoln and I go for carriage rides, Tad enjoys riding his pony beside us." He paused for a moment, cleared his throat, and continued. "He always wears his uniform, as if he's our military escort."

Carter wished they could avoid tainting a happy family memory by making it part of the investigation, but the plan seemed to be the best choice. "You've hit upon the perfect thing, sir. A family carriage ride is casual, so it won't seem as if we're 'presenting' your son. And with Artie riding a pony, it will keep people from getting too close and discovering he's not really Tad. When we—"

A shrill scream split the air, jerking both men's attention to the office door.

"That's Mary." With a speed and agility not often found in a man of his height, Lincoln bolted from his chair and dashed from the room.

Carter followed close behind, muttering under his breath. They had no idea why Mrs. Lincoln was screaming or what the president was running into. Carter should be taking the lead, protecting his commander in chief.

The scream turned to a wail, leading them to the family residence. Lincoln turned a corner, ran into a room, and stopped so short that Carter almost plowed into his back. The scene before them brought an ache to Carter's chest.

The bedroom belonged to a young boy. Mary Lincoln was on her knees beside the bed, hands covering her face, a torrent of grief pouring from her lips. A few feet away was Juliet, also on her knees, her arms wrapped protectively around Artie. Except that, at first glance, he looked nothing like Artie. He was a more than convincing copy of Tad Lincoln.

"Merciful heavens." Lincoln's face paled beneath his beard.

At the sound of her husband's voice, Mary looked up. "Taddie," she said, pointing a shaky finger at Artie. "I thought…thought he was back. He'd come home. But it's not…it's not…." A sob ripped from her, and she screamed to anyone who might help. "Where is my son? I want my son!"

Mr. Lincoln knelt beside her, draping an arm over her shoulder. "We will find him, Mother. And when we do, he will need you to be strong."

Mary clutched the lapels of her husband's jacket and pulled him closer. "Promise me, Mr. Lincoln. Promise you'll get him back."

Carter's spine stiffened. The president was known for his honesty, and he knew as well as anyone that it was impossible to make such a promise. But, as a husband, he would be beyond cruel to dash his wife's hopes. How would he answer?

"I promise, Mother, we shall have him back." He rose to his feet, pulling her up with him. "Before you know it, you'll be scolding him for running through the halls and bringing his goats into the house."

Mary choked back her tears and clung to him, burying her face in his chest. As he led her out of the room, Carter could still hear her pleading.

"I can't lose another child. Not another. Bring him back."

Juliet had seen Artie face down bullies twice his size without so much as a flinch, but the first lady's reaction had left him pale-skinned and trembling.

"I ain't never heard a woman scream like that before," he said, shaking his head. "I didn't mean to upset her."

"*You* didn't upset her, Artie." Juliet put her hands on his shoulders and gently turned him to face her. "She's heartbroken about losing her boy."

Carter rubbed his jaw vigorously. "What in the world happened?"

"I wish I knew. One second, I was putting the final touches on Artie's costume, and the next, there was Mrs. Lincoln, standing in the doorway screaming."

Artie pulled the dark wig from his head, leaving his sandy hair even more mussed than usual. "I'm sorry, Mr. Carter. I guess I looked too much like Tad. I never meant to scare her."

"Juliet's right," Carter said. "You have nothing to be sorry for. We should have warned Mrs. Lincoln about what we were doing, or, at the very least, made sure she stayed in her room."

"Can I put on my own clothes now?" Artie ran his finger under the collar of the wool uniform jacket, tugging it away from his neck.

"Why don't you try on the sailor suit first?" Juliet said.

"We'll give you some privacy." Carter held his hand out and helped Juliet to her feet. Then she followed him into the hall and pulled the door closed behind her.

The deliberately positive attitude Juliet had put on for Artie's benefit fell away as she leaned against the wall to steady herself. "That poor, poor woman. How could I do something to cause her so much pain?"

"Don't you start now."

"But this whole impersonation scheme was my idea."

"An idea that I, and the president of the United States, agreed was our best chance to flush out the kidnappers." Carter's voice was firm but kind. "They are the ones to blame for all the pain, plain and simple."

"You're right, of course. But I can't stop thinking about how I'd feel if Artie was missing. It would tear my heart out, and he's not even my flesh and blood son. How does a mother deal with such anguish?"

His face unreadable, Carter cupped her cheek, brushing away a tear with his thumb. Then a hint of a smile pulled at his lips. "You have a soft heart, Miss Avila."

The use of her professional name—meant to tease, she was sure—instead inflicted a fresh wound. "So many women come to me. Mothers who've lost sons. Wives who've lost husbands. So much loss, but I never truly comprehended the reality of it until now."

A war of emotions played on Carter's face. "It's no secret that I am not an advocate of the work you do. But after seeing you with people, I know you truly do want to help those who walk through your door."

Carter pulled her to him. The warmth of his arms wrapping around her provided a bit of comfort in the midst of the turmoil. Somehow, he had put aside her questionable deeds and looked instead at the woman she was.

But who was she, really? In the past, she'd been able to justify the deception; now she wondered how she could continue. She took money from people who were so desperate for comfort, they chose to believe she could commune with the dead. Juliet thought of all the charlatans doing the same kind of work—people like Lord Shelston, who strung their victims along until they had no money left, then discarded them. She used to tell herself she was better than that, because she cared about her clients and sought to provide them with some relief to ease their sorrow. In actuality, she was just as much a fraud as any other huckster.

She needed to change. But if she did, how would she provide for her family? Fear sat like a boulder crushing her chest as the memory of life on the streets filled her mind. If she were alone, she could manage. But what of the rest of them? The Professor and Miss Clara wouldn't last a day. With a sigh, she straightened her spine, pushing away from Carter's chest and out of the shelter of his arms. This was no time to wrestle with a private dilemma. There were more important matters at hand.

She took a deep breath and looked him in the eye. "As unpleasant as the incident with Mary Lincoln was, we know one thing. Artie can pass for Tad."

"Particularly if we keep him at a distance from others." Carter lowered his head slightly, concern creasing his brow. "Does that mean you're still with us?"

She nodded sharply. "I'm with you." For a moment, the cultured guise of Miss Avila fell away, and she was once more the street urchin Juliet Button. "Let's flush out the monster."

Chapter 17

The president reentered the room as Juliet was pinning up Artie's sleeves. She stood at his entrance, unsure of the proper etiquette.

Carter stood, as well.

Lincoln waved them both back down. "I cannot ask it of her." He slumped into a cane-back chair. "She is too fragile. We will have to think of something else."

Juliet's eyes felt hot and itchy. She was fresh out of ideas.

Carter shrugged, as if he didn't see the problem. "That shouldn't matter."

"It would be a change in the routine," Lincoln explained. "If Mary weren't to go, as well, it could do more harm than staying quietly at home. People would know something wasn't right."

"Yes sir, but Mrs. Lincoln has been in mourning for Willie. She often wears a veil. Make the veil thick enough, and even I could pass for her, if need be." Carter put an arm around Juliet's shoulder. "And we have an actress here who can make people believe she's an eighty-four-year-old lady or a six-hundred-year-old Indian chief."

Lincoln looked to Juliet. "Do you think you could manage to look like Mrs. Lincoln?"

Juliet considered his question for all of two seconds, then nodded. "Easily."

"What would you need?" Carter asked.

"Not much. One of Mrs. Lincoln's gowns and a suitable hat and veil."

"Lizzy is with her now. Once she's gotten her to sleep, I'll send her to you."

With the plan back on track, Lincoln seemed to have gained heart. Juliet noticed, however, that he avoided looking at Artie. She couldn't blame him. Having the boy there must be excruciating, knowing he was not his son, yet having him look so much like him. *God, please let all this work. We must find the lad.*

Carter seemed to sense the president's tension. He put a hand on his arm. "Sir, this will work."

"I hope so, Forbes. I do hope so." Lincoln shook his head, and then a smile lightened the gloom on his features. "If people do not believe it is Tad and Mary, tomorrow's papers will be full of tales of my 'secret' family. The opposition will have a field day." He turned and left the room. His shoulders still drooped, but his chin was high, as if he meant to do everything he could to get Tad back, even if he held little hope of their being successful.

Juliet dabbed at her face and neck with her black-edged handkerchief. Between the summer humidity, the heavily padded black gown, and her own nervousness, she feared she might faint during the ride. She hadn't had a bout of stage fright this bad since her debut as her uncle's assistant when she was twelve.

She tucked the handkerchief in her sleeve, then lowered the veil into place. A critical appraisal in the looking glass, and then she nodded. She would do, with her dark hair pulled into a neat chignon, such as Mary frequently wore, and her torso padded to fit Mary's bodice. With the heavy veil in place, no one was likely to question her identity. The biggest trick was mimicking Mary's mannerisms. If she got those wrong, people might see through the disguise. She practiced the first lady's posture and gestures for several moments before the mirror.

Finally, she could not deny even to herself that she was simply delaying. It was time to put the plan into practice. She smiled grimly beneath the veil. With the help of the president and a Pinkerton detective, she was about to pull off the biggest hoax of her career.

Carter and Artie jumped to their feet as Juliet stepped out from the one room they had been sure Mary Lincoln would not enter: Willie's bedroom.

"I'm ready."

"I'll get the president."

Stares followed as one staff member after another caught sight of them and paused to gape.

Of course, there was no way they'd be able to completely fool those who lived and worked in the Executive Mansion and knew Tad was truly gone. But they were not the ones this little exercise was meant to reassure. It was intended to reassure average citizens, discredit Paulson's report, and, hopefully, lure the kidnapper into action. Juliet breathed another prayer that the plan would work.

President Lincoln's face looked hollowed out by overwork and grief, but when he saw them, a faint glimmer of humor crept into his eyes. "I'd believe it myself if I didn't know better."

He plucked his top hat from the corner rack and plopped it on his head, then offered Juliet his arm and Artie his hand. "Let's shake the hornet's nest."

Juliet wasn't entirely certain she liked the image. They were all liable to get stung.

The usual hubbub in the stable yard died away at the appearance of the First Family. Daniel had saddled Tad's pony, and the carriage was ready, as well. Sweat trickled down Juliet's spine as the president handed her up into the conveyance.

Artie mounted the pony with Daniel's help.

Good gracious, she'd never thought to ask whether Artie had ever ridden. He didn't look the least bit intimidated. In fact, he glanced at her most solicitously, almost as if she were his mother, and he was worried for her. Impulsively, Juliet reached a hand toward Artie, and he nudged his mount close so he could grasp it.

"Thank you, Ar—Tad. You are very brave to do this."

"Aww, anybody tries to kidnap me will get a black eye for his trouble."

Lincoln let out a bark of laughter. "I believe you mean it."

"'Course I do."

"And I believe you'd do it."

Daniel hopped up into the driver's seat, and they set off.

Juliet couldn't help looking back to make sure Carter had found a horse, too. Sure enough, he rode at a discreet distance behind them. His presence comforted her, and she settled back against the leather upholstery of the state carriage.

Might as well try to make things feel as normal as possible. "What do you and Mrs. Lincoln typically talk about during these rides?"

The president looked mildly surprised. "I don't think we've talked much about anything the last few months. There was a time when we would recount the boys' antics, or she'd tell me about the latest dress she was having made. I suppose it was the normal discourse of a man and wife."

"I imagine the war has changed things. It must be difficult to be unable to share all your burdens."

He gave her his full attention. "You are uncannily perceptive, Miss Avila. It must be a great help to you in your line of work. I understand you have worked on the stage."

Juliet stifled a sigh. She couldn't lie to him. Couldn't bring herself to offer anything but complete honesty. "Since I was a child."

"Mr. Forbes mentioned that you had even worked as a magician's assistant?"

She smiled, though he probably couldn't see it through the veil. "My uncle was the Great Harrison."

"Harrison? Did he come out to Springfield?"

"Once, I think. We made a loop up to Chicago and out to St. Louis, but he decided he preferred the Eastern theaters he was more familiar with. Especially in winter. He liked to head south." She could have bitten her tongue off. Nothing like telling the commander in chief of the North that she might have Southern sympathies.

But Mr. Lincoln didn't seem to think anything of her faux pas. "The weather out on the grasslands can get mighty nasty come winter. Of course, at the moment, a blizzard doesn't sound so bad." He drew a handkerchief from his pocket and mopped at his face. "I now remember seeing your uncle's show, and I recall his cunning assistant. At the time, it seemed to me that you did most of the tricks while he distracted people with his patter. As I recall it, you were quite good."

That was it. There would be no lines of wealthy clients seeking out the woman who gave séances at the Executive Mansion. The president of the United States trusted her. How could she possibly return to her deceptive ways and give another sitting in Washington? Oddly, the notion didn't carry with it the bone-deep sense of dread it once had. Perhaps...perhaps, if she could trust God to find Tad and solve this crisis, she could trust Him with her daily cares, too.

The president must have taken her silence for consent. "No need to be shy on my account, Miss Avila. I never did like false modesty. Never liked a braggart, either. I suppose it's a fine line to walk."

"I thank you for the compliment, sir. Most people never noticed."

"That's because most people don't mind being led around by the nose." He gestured with his chin at a group of soldiers clustered on the walk. The men were looking from the newspaper one of them carried to the president's carriage and Tad's pony, and back again. "I believe you have achieved another successful illusion."

Juliet had been trying to ignore their audience, as she thought Mary would have done. But as they neared the group of soldiers, one of the men stepped forward.

"Three cheers for the president."

"Hip hip hooray! Hip hip hooray! Hip hip hooray!"

"Three cheers for Tad."

"Hip hip hooray! Hip hip hooray! Hip hip hooray!"

Lincoln tapped Daniel on the shoulder, and he slowed the carriage. The president waved at the soldiers, utterly at ease with these men. "Don't you boys have a latrine to dig somewhere?"

The men guffawed.

"We're finished with latrines. Now we're moving on to the dirty work of wiping up some Johnny Rebs." At this jest, the men roared and jostled one another in the ribs.

The highest ranked among them, a corporal, slapped the newspaper he held with the back of his hand. "We're sure glad this blamed paper is only fit for latrine duty, Mr. President. We pray God keeps His hand on your family."

Lincoln cleared his throat. "I thank you kindly, boys. My family and I pray for our soldiers every day, too." He tapped Daniel's back, and they drove on.

He no longer seemed in much of a mood to talk.

Juliet found she didn't really care to chat, either. Now that her attention had been focused on the passersby, she couldn't seem to ignore them any longer. There were so many people on the street. Since the start of the war, Washington had swollen with people. There weren't just soldiers; there were all the people necessary to support the army, not to mention all the people hoping to make money off the soldiers and the war effort.

Now, every one of the strangers they passed posed a threat. She could see news of the president's carriage ride sweep before them up the street as people paused to turn. Most seemed friendly enough. More than once, spontaneous applause broke out among the populace.

Juliet caught Tad's name on the lips of the crowd more times than she could count. But, despite the evident goodwill of most of the people they passed, there were enough stony gazes and pugnacious jaw lines to raise her hackles.

This must be what it was like for Carter, day in and day out. Ever vigilant. Seeing threats everywhere. Always expecting something awful to happen. Her stomach did a flip at the thought of something terrible happening right then and there. She wanted to tell Artie to ride closer. To tell Daniel to drive faster. To forbid the president to embark on another of these foolish expeditions ever again.

But she couldn't do any of those things. All she could do was pray.

Carter took what felt like his first breath in an hour as they pulled back into the long, looping drive that led up to the steps of the Executive Mansion. He was pretty sure the ruse had succeeded. He had heard several outraged remarks from people who condemned the *Daily National Intelligencer*'s shoddy reporting practices. He hoped complaints rolled in and Paulson got a wigging from his editor.

Speaking of Paulson, it was high time Carter paid the reporter a visit. The fellow could have valuable information.

As the president, Juliet, and Artie entered the Executive Mansion, Carter left his horse with the stable hands and had Ensign Morehouse get the cart hitched up. The ensign nodded dully, and it occurred to him that the young man wanted more to do than play coachman. He should find some way to make the fellow more useful. The problem was that he wasn't sure he could trust him.

But you can trust Juliet Button?

He snorted at the realization that he did indeed trust Juliet. He trusted her, and he owed her for the way he had treated her. She'd been gracious in forgiving him, but somehow he would find a way to make it up to her.

She descended the front steps in a remarkably short amount of time, given how long it had taken her to achieve the transformation into the first lady. But her face was flushed.

Carter stepped forward to meet her. "Are you all right?"

"Just hot." She drew a fan from her handbag and swished it in front of her face, sighing slightly. "That was miserable. I don't know how you do your job. I think I would go mad."

Well, this was new. "You've been helping me do my job for several days now. Is the strain becoming too great?"

"No, not that. I'm talking about the guarding part. So many people, and no telling if any of them poses a real threat. I would shoot on sight and ask questions later."

"The thought has occurred to me a time or two. While it might solve some problems, it would create a whole new set."

She laughed as he helped her into the cart. "I sent Artie on home."

"Good. I think it's time we find Paulson and put a few questions to him."

"Do you think he really knows anything of use?"

"I'm not sure, but I can't pass up the possibility."

They tried the *Intelligencer* offices first, and a harried clerk drenched in sweat sent them to a café down the street, where he thought the reporter might be getting some lunch.

Paulson was indeed at the café, surrounded by compatriots whom he was regaling with the tale of his fine reporting. Carter claimed the table next to Paulson's and ordered glasses of iced lemonade for himself and Juliet. They both needed it.

She looked at him, waiting for his cue, but he was content for the moment. He'd get unguarded information from the fellow by listening in on his friendly boasting, which he could then use later during a direct interrogation.

"So, after the Fourth of July parade, there was all this consternation...Joe, that means people were distressed"—his colleagues laughed at Joe's expense—"and I started nosing around, trying to find out what was going on. But nobody was saying a thing, even though I could see Mary Lincoln practically being carried back inside."

The lemonades arrived, and Carter took a long swig. The blend of tartness and sweetness puckered his lips, but the coolness made him sigh with relief.

Juliet closed her eyes as she drained her drink. "That is so good." She wiped the condensation from the glass with her handkerchief and then passed the damp cloth over her cheeks.

Carter tore his eyes from her motions as she trailed the fabric over her neck. He signaled the waiter for two more lemonades. "Do you want something to eat?"

"Not unless they have ice cream."

He raised an eyebrow at the waiter, who shook his head. "Just the lemonades, then."

The waiter hurried off, and Carter realized he'd allowed himself to become distracted.

"At that point, I figured this Pinkerton must know something about what was going on," Paulson continued. "He's had briefings at the Executive Mansion every day. But now he's at some old carpenter's workshop looking into his murder. That's when I knew it was something big. Something really big."

"Yeah, but how did you know the Pink was on to something big? He could have been investigating government fraud or a dozen other things old McClellan's got them working on."

"Ah, but that was the beauty." Paulson shrugged. "It didn't really matter what he was investigating. Soon as I knew the fellow was a Pinkerton, just about anything he was looking into was probably newsworthy, be it spies or fraud or what have you. But even I didn't expect it would be this big."

"So, you started following him, and this gal he's going around with. Is she a Pink, too?"

"Not that I can tell. I haven't quite figured out the connection. But that's not really germane to this discussion. They go to some very interesting places—not the kind of places you'd take your ma to—some of the worst parts of town, looking for an actress named Estelle Bines."

"What does she got to do with anything?"

"I haven't figured that out yet, either. But what I do know is that she got her throat cut, too."

Murmurs went around the table.

One of the reporters, a fellow with a broad face and slicked-back yellow hair, refused to be impressed. "You don't seem to know much of anything, for sure. How'd you make the link to the kidnapping?"

Paulson sniffed and swiped the back of his hand under his nose. "I talked to people."

"So you got a tip?" The guy shrugged dismissively. "Anybody can write a story when someone feeds it to him."

"It wasn't just that," Paulson insisted. "You have to know who to talk to. What questions to ask." He leaned back in his seat. "And besides, if it's so easy, how come you haven't come up with any big stories?"

Carter finished off his second glass of lemonade and stood. "I'm afraid your 'big story' hasn't come to much either, Mr. Paulson."

The reporter and his friends turned as one to face Carter.

"Well, well, if it isn't the Pinkerton I was just mentioning. And his lovely…companion."

Juliet's smile looked brittle enough to splinter. "Mr. Paulson."

"What's that you were saying about his story?" the yellow-haired fellow asked.

"I hate to break it to Mr. Paulson, here, but Tad Lincoln was seen by hundreds of people just this afternoon, on a customary ride with his parents."

Paulson looked genuinely confused. "What?"

Carter twisted his lips in a mock pout. "I guess your source wasn't all that trustworthy."

"I'm afraid the other papers are going to have a grand old time rubbing the *Intelligencer*'s nose in this," Juliet said sweetly.

Paulson swallowed. His friends proved to be of the fair-weather variety, melting away faster than the ice in Carter's glass. They either had no desire to associate with someone who might find himself unemployed very soon, or else they were racing to their own papers to write articles condemning the *Intelligencer*.

"Might we join you?" Carter claimed the now-empty seat next to Paulson.

The reporter still looked dazed.

"So, Paulson, where did you get the story?"

The question seemed to shake the reporter awake. "Sorry, I can't reveal my sources."

"Oh, come on. The fellow hasn't done you any favors, believe me."

"No." Paulson shook his head. "I don't think he was lying." His eyes narrowed. "What's going on here? You really saw Tad today?"

"As I said, hundreds of people did. He went riding with his folks, as usual."

"But where's he been? The Presidential Mansion's been buzzing with talk."

"Then why didn't one of the other papers pick up the story, too?" asked Juliet.

"I don't know." Paulson appeared to be struggling to put the pieces together. "But if he's not really missing, why are you here asking about my source?"

That was an excellent question. Carter shrugged, trying to play it casual, but knowing he was a poor actor compared to Juliet. "We came in for refreshment and overheard your conversation."

Paulson shook his head. "I don't think so."

Carter tried another tack. "You must know the president wouldn't like someone spreading such rumors. Even when proven untrue, it's not good for morale. Now, who sold you that crazy story?"

"Uh-uh. You can ask all day, Pink, but I'm not talking. What's it matter if it's all a load of bunkum, anyway?" Paulson got to his feet and left the café without paying for his lunch.

Carter wished he could arrest him and clap him in irons until he coughed up the name. But he could turn the tables on the little weasel by following *him* for a change. He noted the way Paulson turned as he left. Not going back to the office, then.

He popped a piece of potato from Paulson's plate into his mouth. Then, after leaving enough money on the table to cover Paulson's bill and theirs, he stood and motioned to the door.

"All right, Juliet. Let's go see what he's up to."

Chapter 18

Carter and Juliet had followed the reporter from the café, keeping a cautious distance. When Juliet placed her hand in the crook of Carter's arm, he smiled down at her, reminding himself that she was merely keeping up the pretense of courting.

For the longest time, Paulson seemed to wander aimlessly, strolling along the sidewalk with no apparent purpose. But when Lafayette Square Park came into view, Carter's hopes rose. Maybe they had prompted him to return to the spot where Tad had been kidnapped. Suppose the reporter had been involved? Perhaps he'd come back to make sure he hadn't left any evidence behind. Or maybe he was meeting an accomplice.

Juliet's fingers tightened on his arm, and he knew she was thinking the same thing. They stopped beneath a tree, using its thick trunk and deep shade as cover, and watched as Paulson approached a woman with dark hair and a dress that appeared freshly laundered yet was threadbare. He produced something from his pocket and handed it to her. Carter held his breath. Was this some kind of payment for the information she'd given him? Was he passing her a message?

But then, the woman turned slightly, and Carter could see the basket hanging from her arm. Paulson dropped a few coins in her palm, and she handed him a small bag. He then strolled to a nearby bench, plopped himself down, and began tossing stale bits of bread to the birds.

Other than the fact that Paulson appeared to be aiming for the pigeons, since he laughed every time he hit one, nothing seemed amiss. No one joined him on the bench; no one approached him. At last, he stood, crumpled the empty bag, and dropped it on the ground. Then he turned toward the spot where Carter and Juliet stood, gave a two-fingered salute from the brim of his hat, and strode out of the park, whistling to himself.

Carter had underestimated the reporter. There was no way Paulson would lead them anywhere important. But then again, Carter hadn't truly wanted him to go anywhere significant. Not while Juliet was with him. He searched the park until he found Sean, a hundred paces or so away, to all appearances absorbed in a newspaper.

"Well, that was cheeky." Juliet huffed. "I say we go after him anyway. See how he likes being followed about all the time."

Carter led her toward Sean. "I've got a better idea."

She looked up at him, eyes wide with expectation. Carter did not look at Sean as they passed, but he did give him a new assignment. "Follow the reporter. Now that we're off his scent, he'll loosen up. See you at the Round Robin tonight."

Sean cleared his throat and rattled his newspaper.

Carter strolled on past with Juliet. He didn't have to caution her not to look back, as he would have with most women—and most untrained men, for that matter.

"I suppose Mr. King will be less conspicuous, but now what do we do?" she asked.

"I'm calling in the reserves. I telegraphed Allan Pinkerton this morning, and he agrees. The thing to do now is make sure we have men watching the Presidential Mansion and the Soldiers' Home, so that if anyone attempts to deliver a ransom demand, we'll be able to follow him back to his lair. With luck, he will lead us to Tad and the ringleader."

He decided not to mention all the things that could go wrong. She would be able to think of them on her own, if she wanted to.

It would be good to have more men on the ground. But the responsibility for Tad's rescue would still lie primarily with him.

"Will you have men to do anything but watch the president's house?"

Carter looked at her out of the corner of his eye. "Did you have something particular in mind?"

A sharp smile quirked her lips. "There's the small matter of Estelle's death. You haven't told me if you were able to find any sort of clue in her apartment."

Carter pursed his lips. "I didn't discuss it with you because I had hoped to spare you the potential heartache of reliving what happened."

She tightened her hold on his arm, and they stopped to face one another. "It will cause me a great deal more anguish if her murder goes unpunished."

A part of Carter shrank from inflicting any further suffering on her by involving her in the ongoing investigation. And she would suffer—he knew that much about her now. Her empathy made her take to heart the pain of others. And her compassion made it impossible for her to stay detached. He could understand. He often felt the same way. "All right. There wasn't a lot that seemed as if it might mean something."

"Did she have any stage props or costumes?"

"A few. I counted twelve packs of playing cards. Some costumes. There were a few things I didn't recognize. She had some rings, some sort of sticky wax, and several long pieces of stretchable cord. More important was what I didn't find. There wasn't a single thing in the room that linked her to another person. No notes, no pictures, no address book, no calling cards."

Juliet walked along silently, her lower lip caught between her teeth, as she considered. "Did you find her scrapbook?"

Carter shook his head. "I didn't see anything like that."

Once more, Juliet stopped. "She had one, filled with playbills and reviews. It was among her most precious possessions. It was the closest thing she'd have had to a diary. If we find it, it could tell us who she'd been working with most recently. Maybe they would know more about her associates."

There was still enough daylight left to make it there and back again before dark. As much as he disliked the idea, it appeared they were once more on their way to Hell's Bottom.

Juliet's pulse fluttered in her temples, and she attempted to slow her breathing, as they stopped in front of Estelle's tenement. Nausea roiled in her stomach, and she tried to breathe through her nose. How had she ever managed to live in such places?

Though she was fairly confident she hadn't allowed her distress to show, Carter searched her face, apparently to gauge how she was feeling. Juliet faked a bright smile, and he gave an infinitesimal nod, then led the way. Halfway up to the third floor, they came upon a drunk, passed out across the stairs. Carter nudged him out of their way and took her hand, drawing her close behind him. It was a liberty, but Juliet had no intention of pulling free.

At the top of the stairs, she paused. The sound of children's voices came from Estelle's apartment, and a moment later, an infantile wail pierced the thin walls. Juliet exchanged a questioning look with Carter as he rapped his knuckles on the door.

A young girl, perhaps eight years old, opened the door, but only a foot. Carter bent down. "Is your mother here, darling?"

Juliet looked through the opening. The room beyond was almost entirely empty. Estelle's jumble of mementos and cheap furnishings was gone.

The child's only response was to shake her head.

"This was my friend's apartment," Juliet said gently. "Did you just move in?"

"She's murdered," said the girl, her grip loosening ever so slightly from the doorknob.

"I know. It was a terrible thing. I want to find who did it."

"Why?"

"So they can be punished. And so they don't kill someone else."

"I didn't do it."

Juliet nodded gravely. "I know you didn't. Do you know what happened to her things? Was there anything here when you moved in?"

"Like what?" The baby continued to howl with rage, but the little girl ignored it with practiced equanimity.

"Any of Estelle's things."

"You could ask the landlord, Mr. Guffey."

Juliet's hopes spiraled toward the ground like a bird shot from the sky. If Estelle's belongings had gone to a landlord avaricious enough to have already rented out her apartment, no doubt he would have sold off everything of value and disposed of the rest.

Desperate, she continued on. "We're looking for a scrapbook. It's full of a lot of colorful handbills and pictures."

Something in the little girl's eyes flickered, but she maintained a stoic gaze. "I don't know what they done with all her stuff."

This required finesse. Juliet shot a warning look at Carter to make sure he didn't interrupt. "Are you sure you didn't see a book like I described? I ask only because it's very important, and I'm offering a reward."

"A reward?"

"Yes. The reward is a whole dollar, and…." Her fingers delved through her purse quickly. "These." She pulled out a bag of lemon drops and opened it so that the girl could see what was inside.

The child swallowed, her eyes going big. "All of them is part of the reward?"

Juliet nodded.

A toddler of about two waddled to the girl and clung, swaying, to her skirts. She picked the tot up absently, patting its back. "Do you want the book to take away?"

Aha! She did have it. Juliet nodded. "I'm afraid so, but what if I promised to bring it back to you when I'm done looking through it?"

"How do I know I can trust you?" Given her living conditions, the question was entirely reasonable.

Juliet thought. "How about this? I will give you the money and candy to rent the book from you for a week. I shall also give you my address, and you can fetch it if I don't come back."

The girl pursed her lips.

"And if I don't return it on time, I shall owe you another dollar."

"And more candy?"

"Yes, and another bag of candy."

It was clearly a bargain the girl could not pass up, but she still heaved a sigh. "Stay here."

They did as instructed, and the girl went to the single closet near the entrance. She opened the door and got down on her knees. A moment later, she emerged with the scrapbook hugged tight against her bony chest. "You won't muss it, will you?"

"No, I promise to be very careful," Juliet said.

"'Cause it's the most beautiful thing I ever saw, and it's all mine. I found it in that closet, shoved down in a crack in the plaster."

Juliet looked at the battered scrapbook and crouched until she was on eye level with the child. "I will take good care of it and return it to you. I promise."

With this reassurance, the girl breathed deep. "All right." She relinquished the book, and Juliet handed her the candy and a dollar coin. Then she told the child her address.

The baby had cried itself to sleep by the time they left, Juliet hugging the scrapbook nearly as tightly as the little girl had.

"Do you really think there might be something of value in there?" Carter looked at the book dubiously.

"Why not? It's meant to be a record of her achievements, if not her entire life."

"Surely she wouldn't be silly enough to chronicle a kidnapping plan."

Juliet sighed, unsure how to articulate her thoughts. "I think the man who killed her was the one behind the kidnapping. I knew her, and she wasn't a criminal, so the man who convinced her to participate in the abduction must have meant a great deal to her. But a part of her must have known he wasn't entirely trustworthy, and what would she do? She wouldn't tell anyone. It would be something she likely didn't even fully acknowledge to herself."

"You think she left a clue of some kind?"

Juliet nodded. "I do. It's likely oblique, but if there was a romance with this man, she would want to record some trace of that, too. It would have been her best hope of getting out of this death trap of tenement existence. So, either way, I think there might be some hint of who he was."

Carter nodded, an appreciative light dawning in his eyes. "You may be right."

Juliet could see his fingers starting to itch to hold the book, and as soon as they were settled in the carriage, she opened it. They paged through to the end, but nothing obvious stuck out to either one of them.

He looked deflated as they pulled up in front of her house.

"Never fear. I'll go through it again. I'm convinced there's something here, but I never thought it would be blatant."

He nodded, but she could see he'd dismissed the scrapbook as a potential source of information. "My men will be gathering at headquarters to get their orders, and I need to talk to Sean."

"Of course. Shall I see you tomorrow?"

"Oh, yes. Mr. Lincoln will want to keep up the illusion that all is fine. We'll need you and Artie both."

"We'll be ready at noon." Juliet climbed down before Carter could walk around the carriage. She was unaccountably disappointed. No, not unaccountably—not if she was honest. She was disappointed that he hadn't expressed a desire to see her again for some more personal reason. Once again, she reminded herself that it was foolish to hope for such a thing from him. They were like chalk and cheese. Incompatible. And that was all there was to it.

Vaguely, she could hear Carter ordering the ensign to stay and guard her and her family. Gratitude felt heavy in her heart, and she could not offer any thanks but a smile.

She looked down at the scrapbook again. Somehow, she was certain there was a clue inside. And she would find it and teach Detective Forbes not to underestimate her.

After escorting Juliet home, Carter made his way back to his own house, all the while going over the facts he knew. They didn't amount to much, and what they had discovered didn't point anywhere specific. The only thing their investigation had seemed to accomplish was making the perpetrator desperate enough to cover his tracks by killing people. Meanwhile, they were no closer to finding Tad.

Pulling his front door shut behind him, Carter let out an exasperated sigh. This case had more holes than a woolen jacket in a moth-infested closet. He took off his hat and hung it forcefully on the coat tree. He needed insight. He needed revelation. He needed—

"Joy to the world, the Lord is come!"

What on earth? Carter looked at the closed door of the parlor, thinking of something other than the kidnapping for the first time that day. Someone was singing. Someone who sounded a lot like his sister.

Carter slowly opened the door, careful not to make a sound, and poked his head inside. There, at the piano, sat Miss Clara, plunking out a tune and nodding her head in time to the music. Emily stood beside her, eyes closed and hands clasped together at her chest, singing with a strength Carter hadn't known she possessed.

"Bravo!" He barreled into the room, applauding fervently.

Emily's eyes snapped open, and her voice stilled. But her cheeks were flush with excitement.

"Carter. You're home."

"Apparently, I was gone so long, the season changed from summer to winter." He had to raise his voice to be heard over Miss Clara's persistent playing.

Emily put her hand on Miss Clara's shoulder. The older woman lifted her hands from the piano keys and turned around. "Why, Mr. Forbes, what a pleasure to see you."

"It's a pleasant surprise to find both you and Christmas in our home."

Miss Clara chuckled and swiped the air with one hand. "'Joy to the World' is a wonderful song for warming up. It travels up and down a scale, you know."

Carter hadn't known, but they could be singing bawdy drinking songs, for all he cared. It would be worth it to see life come back to Emily's eyes the way it had. "Your teaching methods obviously work. Emily, I had no idea you had such a beautiful voice."

"Thank you, Carter." She tilted her head abashedly. "But it surely wasn't beautiful to start with."

"Now, child, that's not true," Miss Clara scolded. She looked at Carter and nodded in a knowing way. "The moment this one opened her mouth, I knew there was a great soprano hiding inside.

All she needed was someone to lure her out and polish off the rough edges."

Emily laughed. "And, my heavens, there has been a great deal of polishing."

Carter had missed something. "Isn't this your first lesson?"

"Oh, no. We've met several times." Emily's smile slipped, replaced with a look of concern. "You said it was all right, remember?"

Carter erased the frown from his own face. "Of course I remember. And it's more than all right. I'm thrilled with your progress." He smiled at Miss Clara. "You are welcome to bring music into our house any time."

Miss Clara blushed and turned back to Emily. "In that case, let us proceed while your vocal cords are still limber."

She began to play a tune Carter didn't recognize. With a surge of affection, he went to Emily, drew her into a hug, and kissed her forehead. "Enjoy yourself, little one."

Normally, the old endearment would earn him a protestation that she was a grown woman, at the very least a scowl. But today, she hugged him back and then smiled as he walked out the door.

The stairway up to his room felt longer and steeper than ever before, each step bringing a new question to his mind. How could he have missed what was going on in his own house? He'd been so caught up in his work, he hadn't seen the transformation in his sister. And what of the kidnapping? Only once in his career had a case gone unsolved. The thought of Sarah DeKlerk, the lovely young woman found strangled to death in her family's garden, soured his stomach. He'd been so sure he had his man on that one. Carter had chased him for years, all across the country, only to discover he'd been wrong. Now the trail had gone cold, and he had little hope of ever finding Sarah's killer.

Guilt weighed heavily on him as he closed himself in his room and collapsed on the bed. This couldn't be a repeat of the DeKlerk case. He would not allow another criminal to slip through his fingers, another family to have to live without justice. He was a Pinkerton agent. It was his job to be observant, to uncover the facts. But what few facts he did have had mostly been procured with the help of a woman who lived by the art of deception.

He swallowed, his tie suddenly feeling too tight, cutting off his air supply. He tugged it from his neck and hurled it across the room. Images of Juliet filled his mind, bringing both peace and turmoil. She was a beautiful woman with a kind heart, yet she lived a life of lies. How could he have fallen in love with such a woman?

The realization was like a fist to the gut. He loved her. With a groan, he sat up, scrubbing his face with his hands. Love would only complicate things, especially loving Juliet.

"Dear God in heaven, help me." He raised his gaze to the ceiling, and a bit of calm settled inside him. He took a deep breath, let it out, and closed his eyes. God was with him, he knew that. He would help them.

Besides, things couldn't get much worse.

Chapter 19

The boy was sleeping, or he was playing possum under the covers. Either way, the silence was so wonderful, the man didn't bother checking to discover which was true.

Tad Lincoln had turned out to be a spitfire. The medicines he'd procured at Estelle's insistence for the boy's breathing problems had done the trick, but with Tad's return to health had come a stubborn belligerence he found most annoying. What a shame he'd needed to eliminate Estelle. The boy had been easier to control when she'd been around.

There was a knock at the cabin door. He pulled his gun and aimed it until he heard another two knocks exactly five seconds later. That was the signal. Still, he didn't holster his weapon until the door opened and he saw the brute standing in the doorway.

"I got the supplies." Victor held up a stack of paper-wrapped parcels. The fellow was slow in the brains department, but he could usually be counted on to follow orders.

He nodded. "Very good." The stunt Forbes had pulled yesterday was foolish, parading around an imposter meant to look like Tad. They needed to know he would not be deterred from his mission. "You will stay here tonight and watch the boy."

Victor looked with distaste at the lump beneath the blanket. "Be nice if he slept till morning. Little cur bit me yesterday."

"Keep your hands to yourself, and that won't happen again."

"Pardon my sayin', sir, but he ain't movin'." He scratched his head with one hand and pointed at the mattress with the other. "You sure he's still alive?"

He wrinkled his forehead in a frown. The boy's death would be inconvenient but not entirely bad. At least it would eliminate the necessity of one of them being tied to this godforsaken cabin at all times. He walked across the room, knelt down beside the straw tick, and pulled back the blanket.

A growl rumbled in his throat. "For the love of—" He yanked the blanket away, revealing a bunched-up pillow and a pile of dirt. "How did this happen?" He muttered a curse as he inspected the area for any clues. Cold air whispered across his hand, coming from the edge of the tick. When he pulled it away from the wall, he cursed again. Somehow, the boy had made a hole in the rotting wood. An adult could never get through it, but a child as slight of frame as Tad could easily use it to escape.

"He had to be working on this for days. What were you doing when you were supposed to be watching him?"

"We watched him. Mostly." Victor looked away.

He held up his hand, not wanting to hear any more. "How it happened doesn't matter now. We need to see to the task at hand."

"Right." Victor's eyes remained blank. He had no idea what to do.

"Go find him, you idiot!" His roared command ripped through the hot, musty air.

"Where should I look?"

He paced the cabin, scratching his chin. The boy had proven himself resourceful, and there was no way to know how big a head start he'd gotten. If he made it through the woods, there was one place he was sure to go.

"Everywhere between here and the Executive Mansion." He leveled a finger of warning at the big man. "Do not come back here without him."

The candle on Juliet's table guttered and spat. She rubbed her eyes. It was no use. She had pored over the scrapbook for hours, but nothing seemed the least bit unusual or out of place. Estelle's stage appearances had been spaced further and further apart, until there was nothing more recent than a minor role in a play that was still running.

Maybe she shouldn't be so literal. The value of the book might simply be in the fact that she now knew where to ask questions about Estelle. Laying aside the nagging sense that she had missed something important, Juliet changed into a dress more suitable for the theater.

A knock sounded at the door as she pinned up her hair. Miss Clara poked her head in. "Is everything all right? We missed you at supper."

"I'm sorry. I was caught up in this scrapbook of Estelle's." She turned to face her friend. "Perhaps you and the Professor would like to go through it?"

Miss Clara moved to the bed and picked up the scrapbook. "I can't tell you how many of these I've seen over the years. Come to think of it, I believe you were the only young performer I knew who didn't keep a book like this."

Juliet shrugged and turned back to the looking glass. "I suppose I had no reason to cling to that life, since I didn't choose it to begin with."

Miss Clara nodded. "What were you looking for?"

It took Juliet a moment to realize that she was asking about the scrapbook rather than posing a larger, existential question about life. Though, on reflection, the answer felt much the same. "I don't know."

Miss Clara opened the scrapbook and began to flip the pages.

Juliet rushed to fill the silence. "I was hoping there would be a clue about the kidnappers. She was never interested in politics, so it seemed that whoever manipulated her into taking part must have played off of her affections."

Miss Clara smoothed out the rumpled corner of a page and nodded. "She was a silly girl, easily led. But essentially kind-hearted, I think."

Juliet secured the last pin and turned away from the mirror. "You will look, then?"

"Of course, child. I want to catch her killer, too, especially if he's threatened you." She kissed Juliet's forehead. "Now then, where are you off to?"

"The only thing I discovered was that Estelle had a small part in a play that's still showing. I'm going to inquire if anyone saw her beau or knew anything of her personal life."

"But what if he's part of the company? That could be dangerous."

"It will be fine. Ensign Morehouse can drive me."

Miss Clara gave her the look of a woman who'd heard thousands upon thousands of whoppers from accomplished actresses. "Where's Detective Forbes?"

Though she had considered trying to track him down herself, Juliet now turned recalcitrant. "I don't know, but he doesn't need to come. I will just be asking a few questions. I won't be doing anything dangerous."

"There is nothing more dangerous than playing with fire." Miss Clara heaved a sigh and smoothed the front of her dress. "If you won't get the detective to accompany you, I must go myself."

"That's not necessary."

"I think it is, and what harm will it do for me to be there?"

Juliet had no intention of testing what harm could come from putting Miss Clara in a vulnerable position. She held the older woman at arm's length. "If I promise to find Carter and take him with me, will you be satisfied?"

A broad grin brightened Miss Clara's face. "Carter, is it?"

Juliet cocked her head. "Are you truly concerned, or are you trying to play matchmaker?"

Miss Clara's eyes went wide with feigned innocence. "Are the two mutually exclusive?"

Juliet pursed her lips and cast her gaze to the heavens. "It is a fantasy. We are too different. But, if it will make you content, I believe he mentioned being at the bar at the Willard this evening. I will ask him to accompany me to the theater."

"Excellent."

"It's no wonder you gave up chaperoning young women. You can't have been good at it if you are encouraging me to find a man in a bar and ask him to take me to a theater."

Miss Clara patted her cheek. "I trust you, my dear, which is more than I could have said for most of my charges." She opened a drawer and pulled out Juliet's single set of opera gloves. "Here you are. Before you go, will you be holding your sitting tomorrow?"

Juliet focused on fitting her fingers into the satin gloves. "I'm afraid I need to cancel. I shall be playing Mrs. Lincoln again." She managed a bright smile and did not mention that the idea of holding another séance made her feel queasy. "Would you send notes to the sitters first thing?"

"You know I will, dear. That's why I asked."

Juliet held her arms out for inspection.

Miss Clara made a circle in the air with her finger, and Juliet spun obediently. "You look lovely."

Juliet kissed the older woman's cheek. "Don't worry about the sittings. I will make sure we have enough money to survive."

"I'm not worried, not about money, anyway. Go find that little boy and bring him home safe."

Carter put his head closer to Sean's and lowered his voice. "He didn't spot you?"

"Give me a little credit."

Carter raised both hands and smiled. "All right. I had to ask. Did you find out anything?"

"He wandered half of Washington talking to clerks in a dozen different offices."

"Government offices?"

Sean nodded once. "Some, but also a couple of insurance offices and a telegraph office. Then he went to the depot."

"What did he do there?"

"Nothing I could see. Wandered about a bit, like he was waiting for a train to come in, but when it came, he didn't meet anyone or pick up a package. I didn't see him talk to a soul."

"Where was the train from?"

"Philadelphia."

Carter couldn't think of any particular tactical or political significance that Philadelphia held at the moment. He pushed away his full glass. "Could he have passed a message off to someone?"

"Anything's possible, but I had a good view of him and didn't notice a thing."

Tracing a wet ring on the table, Carter thought furiously. "And what of the government offices?"

"Army victualers, the patent office, the post office, a couple of senators' aides, and he hung around the stables at the Executive Mansion, where he struck up several conversations, though people didn't seem to want to talk to him much."

"What do you think he's up to?"

Sean shrugged. "He's a reporter. It's likely the men he went to see were sources who feed him information from time to time. If his story on Tad went sour, he'd be desperate to either find more on it or get a lead on a different story in order to keep on his boss's good side."

"And the train station?"

"Maybe the person he intended to meet missed the train. Things like that do happen."

"True. But what if that wasn't the case?"

"Then his behavior was extremely suspicious." Sean raised his glass.

Carter nodded. "Stick with him, will you? See what else he gets up to?"

"Sure."

Carter looked up and saw a vision in pale green silk standing near the doorway. He tossed down enough money to pay for Sean's drink, too, and stood. "Excuse me."

Sean followed the direction of his gaze and offered a knowing wink. "Have fun."

Carter wanted to explain that it wasn't like that, but Sean was busy draining his untouched glass.

Carter practically had to fight his way to Juliet's side.

She smiled brightly. "There you are. I was hoping I had remembered correctly."

He took her elbow and tried to gain some distance from her admirers, a difficult feat, since the hotel's lobby was apparently six feet deep in them. "What are you doing here?"

"Do you recall Ford's Athenaeum?"

"What does—"

"Estelle had a small part in the play we saw them practicing. I'd be willing to bet she talked to someone there about her life."

In spite of himself, his pulse quickened, beyond the accelerated rate caused by her appearance in the hotel. "Let's go ask a few questions."

"Precisely." She placed her hand delicately on the crook of his elbow as they walked. "Miss Clara insisted that I should involve you."

Carter looked askance at her. "Quite right of her. Is there some reason you would not want me involved?"

"No, it's just that...." She glanced back at the gleaming windows of the Willard Hotel.

"Many entirely respectable ladies have stayed at the Willard with their families." He had meant to be reassuring, but the words came out stiff and too formal.

She didn't respond.

The carriage ride to Ford's Athenaeum took only a few minutes. Once again, Juliet led him to the stage entrance.

Howard sat at his place inside the door. "Miss Juliet! It's good to see you so soon again."

"Hello, Howard. I'm afraid I have some bad news."

"'Bout Estelle?"

"Yes. She was killed."

Howard shook his head, his white hair puffed around his pate like clouds hugging a mountain peak. "I sure am sorry to hear that."

"Now, why is it that no one would admit that she had a part in the new show here?"

He sighed. "Nobody wants to get involved with the Pinks. And, honest to goodness, nobody knows nothing. She was a nice little girl, but not too bright. And she hadn't been 'round long."

Carter stepped up just behind Juliet's left shoulder. "Did she ever mention a new beau?"

"Mention?" Howard snorted. "That's all she talked about."

"Did she give you a name?"

Howard thought a moment, then shook his head. "I don't think so. Leastways not that I recall."

"Did she describe him?"

"Ad nauseam." He rolled his eyes. "But with the usual folderol these girls talk about. He had an 'air of mystery.'" He fluttered his hands around his face in imitation of girlish excitement.

"Anything more concrete?"

"I think she said he had wavy hair. Had a good, solid job. And, of course, to hear her tell it, he was handsome. He bought her some nice things."

"Like what?"

"There was a pin that she liked to wear. Some ribbons, I think, and some sort of perfume. But I kind of got the sense that there was trouble the last time I saw her."

"What kind of trouble?"

"I dunno. She wasn't happy. He wouldn't let her go out with any of the other girls after a show, I guess. One of the girls told her she should come out anyway; he didn't have to know. But she said he 'saw everything.'"

"What did she mean by that? Did he know people here whom she feared would tell tales?"

Howard shrugged.

"Did you ever see this beau of hers?"

"Not a once, and that's unusual. Mostly they're trying to cajole their way in and watch the shows for free. Or else making sure there's no other fellows hanging around their young lady. But not him."

"And when did you last see Estelle?"

"Maybe a week before you came looking. They'd already replaced her in the show when she didn't turn up for rehearsals. So, if they told you she wasn't in the show, they weren't lying to you or nothing."

Carter didn't bother arguing. He glanced at Juliet and raised his eyebrows to see if she had any questions to add. She gave her head a slight shake.

"Thank you, Howard. I'll be back to see you soon. Hopefully under happier circumstances."

Carter led the way deeper into the theater. He would interview every one of the players, even if it took all evening. Juliet had been right. They were closing in on the kidnapper.

Chapter 20

Juliet poked her head out from beneath her pillow and squinted at the hazy light of early morning. Why did the sun have to rise so early in July? It was already hot enough to melt tar. She pulled her hair away from her neck, then covered her mouth with the back of her hand and yawned hugely. It had been a late night, and she and Carter had gained little. Everyone at the theater had heard Estelle speak of her beau. No one had heard a name. No one had ever seen him. Most of the cast had come to the conclusion that there was no beau outside Estelle's imagination.

It seemed to Juliet that the man must have forbidden Estelle to tell anyone his name, which meant his plans had been nefarious from the beginning. Rubbing grit from her eyes, Juliet sat up.

They had to put an end to this.

She shrugged into her lightest wrapper and hurried downstairs. The only thing she could think to do was pore over Estelle's scrapbook again. She could not let go of the idea that it contained some clue of significance. It was likely a ridiculous notion, but she was out of any better ideas, for the moment.

Despite the early hour, the Professor was dressed and ensconced on the settee, with the scrapbook open and held up close so he could read it. Magnifying glass in hand, he glanced around the book's bulk. "Ah, Juliet. Come in. I imagine you were looking for this?"

"I can't help but feel there is a clue in there."

"It would not surprise me. Performers love to read about themselves. She had no diary, I suppose?"

"Not that I'm aware of."

"No. That would have been too much to hope for." He held the book out to her.

Juliet accepted it and settled down beside him. There was nothing to indicate that Estelle's relationship with the kidnapper had been longstanding. She really should come up with a name for him rather than just calling him "the kidnapper" all the time. "Mr. Greyback" would do. Actually, there was nothing to support the existence of Mr. Greyback, except for the tales Estelle had told to her comrades at the theater. But it fit. He fit. There must be a Mr. Greyback.

Juliet flipped to the back of the scrapbook and stared at the most recent playbill. Estelle's name was a tiny smudge at the bottom. It was all that remained of her.

She rubbed a finger across the name, and the cheap ink smeared further. Appalled, she pulled back, as if the act had been the equivalent of erasing Estelle. Tears sprang, hot and stinging, to her eyes.

Even mostly blind, the Professor was perceptive. He put an arm around her shoulder and drew her close. "She was involved with this man before you knew anything of the plots. Her death wasn't your fault."

"How can you be sure?" Juliet pulled free of his gentle touch. "I think our questioning made him doubt her commitment. He killed her to keep her from talking to us."

"If he questioned her loyalty, nothing could have saved her, but for her to be completely honest and seek your young fellow's protection. Your finding her gave her a way out. It didn't seal her fate."

Juliet tried to let the words soak in and alleviate the bloodguilt she felt, but she couldn't release her self-reproach so easily.

Artie came in, yawning and scratching under one arm. "Do I have to be Tad again today?"

Juliet glanced at the clock. "Yes, and we should probably get going."

He stuck out his tongue. "That wig is awful hot."

"And well I know it. But at least you don't have to wear padding."

Artie brightened, seemingly at the prospect of someone else being more miserable than he. "Aw, I guess it's for a good cause."

Her tears dispelled by Artie's unabashed Artieness, Juliet stood. "I'll give you money for an ice cream this afternoon."

"Two, so I can treat a friend?" His quick response pulled another smile out of her.

"Okay, two. But I'm not treating the whole neighborhood."

"Fair enough."

Juliet headed to the kitchen to make breakfast. Carter would be by for them soon. Maybe he would want to take another look through the scrapbook. He might be able to find the clue she had missed.

"There now, you look perfect." Juliet gave Artie's wig a final tweak and held him at arm's length, inspecting her work.

This time, Mary Lincoln was secured in her bedroom, with an attendant inside and a guard posted outside the closed door.

Carter stepped into the room. "How is it coming?"

"Artie's ready." She patted the boy on the back.

"Can I wait for you in the stable?" Artie looked from one to the other, his eyes imploring. "I brought an apple for Tad's pony."

Juliet smiled. He'd quickly formed an attachment to the animal. "You may go down and give him the apple. Don't set to talking to anyone but Daniel, and don't break character. We don't want them to suspect any more than they already do. We'll be down in a moment with the president."

A huge grin split Artie's face. "Ah, Papa. He's good to me."

"Don't be disrespectful!" she called after his retreating figure, then laughed at the sound of him pounding down the stairs.

Carter chuckled. "He knows how to make himself at home."

"I just hope he doesn't get so used to pomp and circumstance that he begins to despise our house."

"I doubt that would happen. He seems sensible."

Carter changed the subject to one that was obviously on his mind. His eyes lit up—positively twinkled, in fact—as he talked about Emily's singing lessons. Not for the first time, Juliet noticed how his smile transformed his face, and the easy way his laugh slipped out when he was relaxed. If they'd met under different circumstances—if she weren't a spiritualist, nor he a detective, and there'd been no kidnapping.... If they were just two people, enjoying the discovery of one other....

The moment slipped through her fingers too quickly, and Juliet moved toward the door. "I should get into costume. The president will be ready to go soon." She tried to keep her voice light.

"Of course."

She was almost out of the room when Carter's voice called her back. "Juliet."

She stopped and turned. "Yes?"

"I...." He glanced past her, then returned his eyes to hers. "I wanted to thank you again for all you've done."

Juliet forced her lips into a smile. "You can thank me after we've caught the kidnappers."

"Mr. Carter!"

Juliet turned at the sound of shoes thumping up the staircase. Daniel appeared. A cut beside his eye bled freely, and his lip was split and swollen. "They took him! They took him!" the boy shouted hysterically.

Carter grasped Daniel by the shoulders and shook him, just enough to make the lad's unfocused gaze sharpen. "Who was taken?"

He began to tremble. "A-Artie. They took Artie."

Juliet's breath caught in a gasp. Her eyesight narrowed to a pinprick. She felt for the wall.

She heard two sets of footsteps start down the stairs. Blinking furiously, she stumbled down after them.

Carter slung his arm over the boy's shoulders as they descended. "Do you know who they were?"

Daniel shook his head, his breath still loud and ragged.

"How many were there?"

"Two, I think."

Juliet staggered as she followed them out through the front door. They went down the steps and started across the expansive lawn to the stable yard.

"Okay now." Carter squeezed Daniel's shoulder. "Tell me exactly what happened."

"I was talking to Artie in the stables. This fellow—" Daniel came to a dead stop, gulping and squeezing his eyes shut tight, as though trying to hold back tears.

"It's all right, Daniel." Juliet ran to his side and took his hand gently in hers. "None of this was your fault. Just tell us what happened."

Daniel looked at her and gave a somber nod. "A fellow came up to Artie and snatched him by the scruff of the neck."

"What did he look like?" Carter asked.

"Big and mean. Brown eyes, brown hair, with a beard. Wearing a brown vest over a red checkered shirt."

"Good." Carter's nod encouraged him to keep going.

"Then something hit the side of my head. I whirled around, and somebody punched me twice. I fell down, and before I could holler or get up, they were gone. Then I ran to get you."

"Can you describe the second man?"

"No, I'm sorry, Mr. Carter." Daniel shook his head. This time, he was unable to hold back the tears. "I couldn't see nothin'. I'm sorry. I'm sorry."

Carter hugged him to his side. "You did well, Daniel. Did you see which way they went?"

Daniel jerked his thumb toward the left. "They had a carriage waiting. A closed coach. Black, but the driver's seat was green, I think. Looked hired. Only one horse, a bay mare."

"Excellent." Carter turned to fling orders to the men who had gathered around at the scent of a disturbance. They shouted and began scurrying about the yard. Carter looked from Daniel to Juliet, his lips pressed into a grim line. "I'll find him."

He snatched the reins of the nearest saddled horse, mounted, and took off at a gallop. Juliet didn't stop to think; she simply reacted. Pushing aside the secretary of state as he prepared to mount a magnificent stallion, she put her foot, instead, into the groom's hands. An instant later, she had mounted and was turning the beast to follow Carter down the drive.

Her heart pounded in her ears, matching the beat of the stallion's flying hooves. Hot grit scoured her face, and she squinted and hunched low over the horse's neck, urging him on. In her head, she was screaming for Artie, but she could not say a word. There was nothing in the world but this mad chase.

She galloped full tilt out into the street, cutting off an oncoming team of horses and setting them to rearing. Carter was only a dozen yards in front of her now, and she followed him tenaciously, weaving through the infernal Washington traffic, pushing aside any thoughts of the mayhem she must have left in her wake.

Nothing mattered but finding Artie. Her eyes ached with straining for a closed cart. She glanced left and right. What if they had gone down a side street?

Down the avenue she raced, further and further from the heart of Washington. Why was this happening? Why would anyone take Artie? Had they thought they were getting Tad? But he had already been taken. Surely—there! There, just ahead. A black carriage sat abandoned at the side of the street. Carter pulled his mount to a stop beside it.

So did Juliet. He looked at her twice, as if just realizing she'd been following him. Ignoring his surprise, she pointed at the carriage. "It's got a green seat."

A sharp yelp sounded from a side street behind them, and she tugged on the reins, pulling the stallion around. At the far end of the alley, two men wearing bandanas over their faces had just mounted up. They each held the form of a small boy on the saddle in front of them.

What was going on?

Spotting Carter and Juliet, the men turned their horses around and spurred them into a gallop.

Juliet dug her heels into the stallion's sides. Carter followed suit, pulling up hard by her right side. They careened out of the alley and made a sharp turn onto a larger street. The men were straight ahead.

On they raced until Washington was a memory, the wide, congested streets giving way to narrow, less populated ones. Beneath her, the horse's sides heaved. She leaned forward, shouting encouragement and trying to dodge the sweat and spittle that flew back at her face.

Please, God, she begged silently. *Please let us catch them.*

"Ya!" Juliet kicked her heels into the horse one more time. It lurched forward with a new surge of energy. They were gaining on the criminals. She was getting closer to Artie.

One of the men looked over his shoulder, his eyes narrowing in a scowl. A moment later, he pulled a pistol from beneath his coat, turned awkwardly in the saddle, and aimed.

The shot thundered. As the bullet flew past, the crack reverberated through Juliet's skull. Her horse screamed and reared.

She reached forward, trying to grab the horse's mane, saddle, anything. But her fingers remained empty as she became airborne. The world spun.

She landed hard. Crushing, blinding pain pounced on her.

She couldn't breathe.

She writhed, mouth gaping, avid for air.

"Juliet!" Carter knelt beside her and took her head in his hands. She stopped thrashing. And then, with an indrawn moan, air filled her lungs. She coughed and sucked in another lungful. Coughed some more.

Carter sighed heavily. "Thank God you weren't hit."

She closed her eyes against a pain far larger and more immediate than that of being thrown from a horse. "They got away, didn't they?"

Chapter 21

Carter smoothed the hair from Juliet's temple. What had she been thinking, chasing after a suspect? She was going to be the death of him. But for now, he needed to keep her calm. "Yes, they got away. For the time being. But they've made mistakes, left clues. We *will* catch them."

His reassurances seemed to matter little. Tears slid silently down her cheeks, and she curled on her side, away from him. He could only guess at her pain.

"Juliet, can you stand?"

No response.

"Where does it hurt?"

Nothing.

"Juliet, it's not all over. I have to get men to help in the search, but I can't leave you like this." A drop of blood seeped from a scratch on her cheek, and he wiped it away with his fingertips.

She flinched away from his hand and shuddered. "We have to get help."

Carter took her hand. "Can you sit up?"

She made a motion as if to rise and drew in a hissing breath. He put a hand under her side and helped her. "This corset of yours probably saved you from a broken rib." A flush burned his face.

Had he really just spoken of her undergarments? But she made no comment.

She was shaky enough that he was reluctant to let her go. Luckily the stallion hadn't gone far. Carter propped her against a rain barrel and brought the horse over to her.

"Do you think you can ride?"

"I have to."

"No, you don't. I can get help from one of the nearby houses and leave you with them."

"Too long." She moved away from the barrel and lurched toward the animal. "I'll need your help, though."

Carter nodded. He put his hands around her waist and lifted her bodily onto the horse. She cried out, and he wondered if he hadn't been too optimistic about her lack of broken ribs. "Are you all right?"

"I'm fine. Thank you."

She looked far from fine. Her complexion was ashen, her cheek smeared with blood, her hair disarranged. But her jaw was set in an expression of bulldog determination.

Carter collected his mount, and they headed back toward town. Every few hundred feet, he glanced over, and she seemed to have grown paler. He rode close by her side. If she would just fall the right way, he could catch her. But she hung on with grim tenacity, even as she sagged lower in the saddle.

"What will we do?" Her question shocked him for a minute. She had seemed only partially conscious.

She deserved an answer. "First, I will set men to scouring the countryside. We've a description of at least one of the kidnappers. And although I couldn't see his face or hair, the second fellow wasn't as tall as the first, maybe five feet ten inches. Strong build. Wearing a gray suit and waistcoat. He looked more like a businessman or a city fellow."

She nodded. "I think he might have had red hair."

"Like the reporter?"

She nodded again.

"Then I'll send men after the reporter."

"Good." The word was little more than a gasp.

"We'll also work on tracing the carriage. I think Daniel was right that it was rented. We should be able to get more details about the fellow from that."

"Why two boys?"

"What?"

"They both had boys with them." Juliet straightened a little and touched the side of her head. "The only thing I can think is that Tad escaped, and they hoped to catch him before he could make it to safety. They saw Artie and grabbed him, but then maybe they spotted the real Tad on their way back through town and stopped to get him, too."

Carter nodded. "Since we were right behind them, they didn't have time to figure out which was the real Tad and which was the imposter, so they took them both."

"Will they kill him?" Juliet asked in a whisper-thin voice. "Artie, I mean, when they figure out he's not Tad?"

Carter couldn't answer.

A groan erupted from her. "God, please don't let him die."

"We'll do everything we can to get him back."

She did not respond.

They turned onto Pennsylvania Avenue. The abandoned carriage was ahead of them, a team of men swarming over it like ants. The officers spotted Carter and hailed him. He raised a hand in greeting, meanwhile scanning the crowd until he found the face he was looking for.

"Morehouse." He waved the ensign over. "Miss Avila has been injured. Please find a wagon and escort her home, then fetch the doctor."

"Carter, no." Juliet started to shake her head, then swayed and clutched the saddle pommel with white fingers. "I need to help find Artie."

Morehouse frowned. "Artie?"

"Yes. Now there are two boys missing." Carter turned his attention to Juliet. "You won't be of any help to Artie in your condition. Go home and get some rest. I will do everything in my power to find Artie and Tad. You have my word."

Juliet opened her mouth to argue, but then she crumpled low in the saddle, as if her spine could no longer hold her upright. Jumping down from his mount, Carter was able to grab her and guide her gently to the ground.

She looked up, beseeching him with pain-glazed eyes. "Find them, Carter. Please."

The ensign stepped forward. "I'll take care of her."

Carter wished he could stay with Juliet and make sure she was all right, but he'd made her a promise, and the only way he could see it through was to do his job. As soon as the ensign had her settled in a borrowed carriage, Carter turned to his men and began issuing orders to anyone within shouting distance.

Two boys were counting on him to find them. Two families relied on the promises he'd made. He couldn't let them down. He had to get Artie and Tad back. God help him.

God help them all.

It was all Juliet could do to hold herself upright on the ride home. Every bump and rut in the road jarred the cart and rattled her body. The usually taciturn ensign kept up a steady stream of chatter, no doubt meant to distract her from her troubles, but she wished the fellow would be silent.

"I know you're worried, miss. But Agent Forbes doesn't let a thing by him. He'll get the boys back."

"Of course." She pressed her fingertips against her right temple.

"I'm sure he has lots of leads already, doesn't he?"

She made a sound that was meant to be affirmative. "Not as many as he'd like. But yes, he has leads."

"The way I understand it, your help has been invaluable. You should be proud of yourself."

Something in the tone of the ensign's voice made her glance his way. He was looking at her, his face blank. She was certain he wasn't nearly as impressed with her assistance on the case as he wanted her to believe. No doubt he was tired of being told to drive her about, and now to be her nursemaid.

"I'm just doing what I can. Anyone else would do the same."

A laugh rumbled in the man's throat. "Don't know about that, miss. I can't think of many souls who'd thrust themselves into the middle of an investigation the way you have."

She wasn't convinced it was a compliment.

Finally, he pulled onto her street and stopped in front of her home. She tried to exit the carriage on her own, but a wave of dizziness overtook her.

"You just wait until I come around to help you."

For once, she didn't argue, and when the ensign offered his hand in assistance, she was glad to take it. Thankfully, he didn't wrap his arm around her waist the way Carter had. His hand remained firmly beneath her elbow as he walked her slowly up the front steps.

The Professor opened the door, his expression quickly changing from welcoming to worried. "What happened?"

"I fell off a horse."

The Professor looked from her to the ensign, waiting for more details. Morehouse shook his head. "It's a complicated story. Right now, we need to get her inside."

"Of course." He stood aside, ushering them in. Then he moved beside Juliet and helped her to the sofa in the sitting room.

Once she was settled, Ensign Morehouse stepped back. "Agent Forbes ordered me to fetch a doctor. Will you be all right with her until I return?"

"Of course." The Professor shooed him away with one hand. "Please hurry."

Now that she was home, in a place where she should feel safe and protected, illogical panic descended on Juliet. She shut her eyes, forcing herself to breathe steadily, focusing on the sound of the ensign walking from the room, the closing of the front door. Piano music played in the distance, accompanied by a sweet, clear soprano. Miss Clara must be giving Emily a lesson. Life went on, just like any other day. They had no idea.

Juliet's breath caught in her chest, and a sob tore from her lips. Hands enfolded hers, and she looked into the eyes of the Professor, who was now kneeling beside her.

"They have Artie."

That one admission unleashed a torrent of grief. Sounds that Juliet didn't recognize poured from her lips—they were not words, but neither were they mere sobs. More like the "wailing and gnashing of teeth" spoken of in the Bible. Now she understood how Mrs. Lincoln had felt when her son was taken.

The door to the music room opened, and Miss Clara flew in, followed closely by Emily Forbes.

"What in the world is going on?" Miss Clara hurried to the sofa and knelt beside the Professor. "What happened?"

He shook his head. "I don't know for sure. But someone has Artie. And I'd be willing to bet it's the same person who has Tad Lincoln."

"Dear Lord in heaven." Miss Clara reached out and stroked Juliet's cheek and forehead, smoothing back her hair and cooing soothingly. "Peace, child. Artie is a resourceful young man. The Lord will bring him back to us. I know He will."

Her words broke through Juliet's pain. Yes, Artie was resourceful. He'd endured more in his young life than most adults. He would get through this, and they would find him.

Miss Clara turned to the Professor. "Was she beaten?"

"Thrown from a horse. The ensign went to get the doctor."

Emily gasped, and from the panic in her eyes, Juliet knew what she was thinking. "Carter is fine," she said. "He's looking for the boys. We—" She pulled in a breath. "I'm sorry. I'm so thirsty."

The Professor jumped up and left the room. Miss Clara continued to pat her hand and murmur prayers over her. Juliet looked at Emily. "I heard you singing. Beautiful."

The young woman smiled shyly. "Thank you."

"Please, sing now."

Emily looked at Miss Clara, who smiled and nodded. "What a wonderful idea. Music to soothe and uplift us. Emily, what about 'Amazing Grace'?"

As an answer, Emily closed her eyes, drew in a breath, and began to sing.

Amazing grace! how sweet the sound
That saved a wretch like me!
I once was lost, but now am found,
Was blind, but now I see.

Emily continued, her voice, sweet and pure, filling the room. But Juliet held on to the words of the first verse. Artie was lost, but he would be found. He had to be.

Juliet must have drifted to sleep, because she found herself opening her eyes, unaware of how much time had passed. A doctor was now in the room, asking everyone to leave so he could examine the patient. Carter's friend Sean also stood over her, his face etched with lines of concern.

As they filed out, Sean stopped and pointed at a small table in the corner. "What's that?"

Juliet squinted at the worn leather cover. "It's a scrapbook. We found it in Es—in a suspect's apartment."

"You think it holds a clue to the kidnappers?"

"It might. So far, it's yielded nothing." Juliet pulled in a labored breath. "But I'm hopeful."

"Perhaps I might find something you missed." He picked up the book and tucked it under his arm.

"No!" Juliet's refusal came out more sharply than intended.

Sean's eyebrows lowered into a frown. "Miss Avila, this book is evidence in a murder investigation and a kidnapping. It should be somewhere secure."

"Carter entrusted the book to me," Juliet said. "I will relinquish it to no one but him."

The Professor walked up to Sean, putting a firm hand on his shoulder. "Correct me if I'm wrong, Mr. King, but isn't Agent Forbes your superior? He left the book in Juliet's care. I believe that indicates his belief that this house is secure enough."

For a brief moment, Juliet caught a flash of something new cross Sean's face. Something dark. Apparently, he was no happier being forced to work with a person of Juliet's station than the ensign was. With a tight smile, he handed the book to the Professor. "You make a good point, sir." He turned to Juliet and gave a slight bow. "I hope you're back on your feet soon, miss."

The detective left, and the doctor looked at the Professor. "I'd like to examine my patient now."

Before he could leave, Juliet called out to the Professor, "Keep a close eye on that book."

He nodded and opened his mouth, as if to say something, but then he closed it again and left the room, clutching the scrapbook to his chest.

Juliet sighed. Every instinct told her there had to be a clue in that book. If there wasn't, then she couldn't even trust herself anymore.

The doctor knelt in front of her and handed her a glass. She drank it down, wincing at the bitterness. She handed it back to him and put her feet on the floor. She couldn't play the invalid when Artie needed her. "Thank you for the draught, Doctor. I'm going to be just fine. There are no broken bones or anything. So, if you would please give me a clean bill of health, you may be on your way."

"I'm afraid it's not going to be that easy, young lady."

"I really am perfectly well."

He snorted. "You look like you've been in a brawl, and you need some rest."

"What I need is to find my son." Her vision was growing fuzzy. She blinked to clear it.

"Miss Avila, I'm afraid you're going to rest, whether you want to or not." His voice sounded far away and oddly muffled.

Juliet squinted at him, trying to bring him into focus. She moved to stand but found the room spinning around her. A hand gripped her arm.

"Whoa, there. Careful. You're going to sleep now. When you wake up, you'll feel worse. But then you'll start feeling better."

"No!" Her mouth felt like it had been filled with glue. She struggled to articulate her thoughts. "I can't. The horses got away. Artie is Tad. Need help."

"Come, now. Let's sit for a moment so you can collect your thoughts."

Juliet nodded. She was feeling strange. A thought bobbed to the surface of her consciousness. "You drugged me."

"Only for your own good." He drew a blanket over her.

Unable to move, Juliet could do nothing but cry. "But he needs me."

"You will do more for him when you are better."

Her mind seemed to detach from her body. She couldn't speak any longer; the words were too difficult to form. But, as darkness edged in on her, she wished she had asked the Professor what he had meant to say. It might have been important.

Chapter 22

Carter closed one fist over the other and relished the crack of his knuckles. With any luck, he'd be doing the same to Paulson's nose in a few minutes. The fury that had been seething inside him since he saw Juliet thrown from her horse needed an outlet.

He pushed past a flunky guarding the door of the *Daily National Intelligencer* and surveyed the anthill of chaos inside. Seconds later, he pinned his gaze on a man in a frock coat who seemed to loom above the figures hunched at desks and the mail boys racing frantically through the room. That was an editor, if ever he'd seen one.

Carter strode forward through the aisle formed by two rows of desks. He did not veer left or right in order to make way for anyone. In his wake, the clamor quieted as heads turned to follow his progress.

The presumptive editor went into an office. Before he closed the door, Carter caught it. A few of the clerks made sounds of distress, but Carter slammed the door on them. The editor turned with a frosty expression, then pulled back warily when he realized the intruder wasn't one of his minions.

"Where's Jake Paulson?" Carter demanded.

"Who are you, sir? And how dare you come barging into my office in this manner?"

"I am either your friend or your enemy. It all depends on whether you cooperate. But believe me when I tell you that you do not want me for an enemy." Carter plunked his Pinkerton identification down on the desk, behind which the editor had sought refuge.

"I don't take kindly to threats."

"I don't take kindly to stalling. Paulson is a wanted man."

The editor's mouth twitched. "Wanted for what?"

Carter tamped down the inclination to throttle the man. "I don't think you understand how this works. I ask the questions. You answer them."

"No, my dear man, I don't—"

The door burst open, and a couple of tough-looking characters in bowlers and plaid shirts piled in. They were definitely not reporters. "Is this fellow causing trouble, boss?"

Carter turned toward them, widening his stance and clenching his fists.

The editor raised a hand as he sat in his chair. "On the contrary, he's brought me a story."

Carter didn't bother to correct him. "I just need to know where Jake Paulson is."

"Jake is no longer employed by the *Intelligencer*. But, do tell me, are the forces of law and order arrayed against him because of his recent article?"

Carter pocketed his identification.

The editor leaned back in his chair. "Maybe there was more to that blasted story than I thought."

Carter turned to leave but found his way barred by the two *Intelligencer* thugs, standing shoulder to shoulder in the doorway.

"Someone made us look foolish, but maybe it wasn't Paulson after all."

Carter smiled at the two innocent lambs now before him. Though they didn't know it, they had all of three seconds to get out of his way.

The editor continued to muse. "Could be President Lincoln's trying to pull the wool over the eyes of the people. What could he be trying to hush up, I wonder?"

Carter didn't answer but moved toward the door, braced for a fight. To his immense disappointment, the men looked over his shoulder, then shifted to allow him to pass.

The editor's voice caroled out from his office. "Thank you for bringing this matter to my attention, detective."

Carter didn't turn around or slow his pace.

Back on the street, he sped around the corner into the alley and pressed himself up against the building. Sure enough, half a minute later, the two toughs darted down the street, looking left and right for him.

Giving them time to pass, Carter let his head fall back against the wall. He had to get his anger under control. That hadn't been the smartest move. He should have quietly gossiped with the clerks, maybe slid them a coin or two. He would have gotten more for less.

Maybe it wasn't too late. When he was sure the would-be followers were well off the scent, he emerged from the alley and hurried across the street, to the little café where he and Juliet had encountered Paulson before.

It was between the lunch and dinner hours, and there weren't many customers inside. Carter examined the lot carefully. There, at the back. Focusing intently on his bowl of soup. Surely, that was one of the men Paulson had been regaling the previous afternoon.

Carter approached, settled in a chair, and placed his hat on the table.

Spoon halfway to his mouth, the reporter looked up.

Carter offered him a broad grin. "I think we met yesterday, though we weren't introduced."

The reporter lowered his spoon into the bowl and wiped his nose with the back of his hand. "I remember. What do you want?"

"I'm looking for Paulson." Carter studied the man's wary expression. What would be the best way to play this? From what he'd seen of Paulson, the man was a braggart and a bully. He decided to be straight with the reporter. "I'm afraid he's wanted for questioning."

The reporter's eyebrows went up. But then he raised his spoon to his mouth and slurped. "Couldn't happen to a nicer guy."

"Do you know where he is?"

"We aren't exactly friends."

"Understandable." Carter took care to keep his face pleasant.

"You're not going away until I tell you something, are you?"

"Nope."

The man sighed. "I think I have his address here somewhere."

"I know where he lives. What watering places does he frequent?"

The reporter dropped his spoon into the bowl, sending soup splashing on the table. "I told you, we aren't friends. How should I know?"

"Are you going to tell me the two of you never went for a drink after work?" Carter raised an eyebrow. "Every reporter I've known is always angling for a story. And if he can get a lead from another reporter through careless talk, then so much the better."

The reporter's lip curled, as if he smelled something rotten. "Jake was always trying to pull those tricks. It even worked on me once." He shook his head. "But just once. I guess you could try the Eagle. He goes there most often, but he gets around. Trying to chat up sources."

Carter nodded. "Thanks." He plunked a dime on the table. "The soup's on me."

Outside again, Carter once more looked about for the *Intelligencer* thugs. They were nowhere in sight. He headed to Paulson's house. It wasn't likely he was home at this time of day, but now that he was out of a job, it was possible. Though, if Carter were an out-of-work reporter, he'd be drumming up a juicy story that would get him hired on at another paper.

Paulson's landlady grew hospitable as soon as Carter introduced her to a couple of silver coins. By her report, Paulson had packed up and moved out the previous day. He hadn't lived there long. She could think of no friends who'd come to see him, nor of any young lady he'd mentioned fancying. But he had liked to take an evening pint at the Eagle when he could. She had no idea where he might be staying now, as he had not left a forwarding address. She was most clear on the fact that he hadn't found fault with the room or her cooking.

Carter filed away the information. It all fit. Paulson was a lone wolf. He knew a lot of people, but no one well. He moved lodgings frequently. In short, he acted just like one would expect a Southern spy to act.

Carter headed to the Eagle. The barkeep hadn't seen Paulson in a couple of days. The fellow figured he'd be by pretty soon. He usually came in after the supper hour.

Perfect. If Paulson hadn't left Washington, he'd get some answers from him. Carter had time to check in with his men and report to the president. Then he would come back here. He had managed to tamp down his anger for now so that he could focus. He needed to keep doing that, at least until he found Paulson. Then he could let him know what he thought of a man who kidnapped children and shot at women. The moment couldn't come soon enough.

The evening was sultry and languid, the kind of night to spend sitting on a porch sipping lemonade with a beautiful girl. Carter's thoughts strayed to Juliet. God grant that she would be okay. He pulled up hard on the reins of his anger. Not yet.

Someone hissed, and Carter turned. Sean motioned to him from the shadows. Excellent. That meant Paulson was here.

Carter crossed to him. In the dim light, Sean looked worse for wear and bone-tired. "What's wrong? Paulson's in there, isn't he?"

"Yeah, he's in there." Sean rubbed the back of his neck. "I'm afraid he shook me for a while today. I didn't catch up to him until he came in here, about twenty minutes ago."

Carter clenched his teeth, though he'd been expecting the admission. If Sean had realized there was a kidnapping in progress, he would have put a stop to it, and Artie and Tad would both be safe. This raised the question of whether Paulson had been toying with them all along. But Sean was good. He'd never been spotted before. Then again, a spy would be on his guard.

Carter sighed. He was going in circles. Just like he had been with this whole investigation.

No more. It was time to put an end to all this.

"C'mon, Sean. This fellow has to be the kidnapper. Let's take him in."

"What happened? How do you know?"

"He kidnapped another boy today."

"Why?"

Carter sighed. "It's a long story."

Sean clapped a hand on his shoulder. "Sounds like a story that can wait. Let's finish this."

Carter nodded. Then, shoulder to shoulder with Sean, he marched into the Eagle.

The bartender Carter had spoken to earlier that day saw them enter. He nudged a customer at the bar and gave a jerk of his chin. The fellow turned around. Sure enough, it was Paulson.

He met Carter's eye for an instant. Then he jumped up as if electrocuted and darted toward a door at the rear of the building. Carter took off after him. He shoved his way through the standing crowd, a savage yell ripping from his throat.

The door led to a kitchen, which, in turn, opened into a rubbish-strewn alley. Hearing footsteps retreating to his left, he chased the noise. His legs pumped, his arms churned, his whole being concentrated on the fleeing form of Jake Paulson.

Paulson knocked over a stack of empty crates, sending them crashing into Carter's path. He leaped. His heel caught the edge of one, and he almost went down. Staggering, he planted a hand against the wall and then pushed off again. He careened around the corner and kept going.

Thirty feet.

Ten.

With a final burst of speed, he lowered his head, ramming into Paulson and taking him down in a bone-jarring impact.

"All right. All right!" Paulson put his hands up. "I give up."

No! He couldn't give up. Carter had scores to settle with this man. He got hold of Paulson's collar and pulled him to his feet. Sean arrived, panting, and holding his pistol.

"Where are Tad and Artie?" Carter demanded.

Paulson's brow furrowed. "I don—"

Carter slammed him back into the nearest wall. "Do not trifle with me! Where are the boys?"

Paulson blinked his eyes frenetically. "I—you told me he wasn't kidnapped."

Disgust for the worm made Carter's fingers flex. "No more games. Tell me where the boys are."

Paulson was sniveling. "I don't know. I don—"

"Why did you run?"

"I heard you had it in for me."

Carter's hands were nearly shaking from the effort of restraining himself. Again he slammed the reporter against the wall. "You heard right. Now, you tell me where the boys are, or I will…God help me, I will shoot you."

Paulson grew pale. "I swear. I swear I don't know where they are. I don't even know who they are. I mean, I know Tad, but—"

Sean stepped up beside Carter and struck the butt of his pistol against Paulson's temple. The man crumpled.

Carter stared at the trickle of blood seeping from a cut on Paulson's forehead and felt sick to his stomach. What was he doing? What would he have done if Sean hadn't intervened? He pushed back his nausea and looked at his friend. "Why did you do that?"

Sean shook his head. "He's lying, and he'll keep on lying, unless we put the fear of God in him. Let's take him to the Old Capitol. A night in a cell will loosen his tongue. Especially if there's a hanging in the yard for him to watch." He looked at Carter, his eyes hard as bedrock. "Trust me."

"All right," Carter answered dully.

Between them, they got Paulson up. They dragged him to the nearest livery, where they rented a horse. Carter checked to make sure Paulson was still breathing as they draped him over the horse's back.

The walk to the Old Capitol Prison went by in dazed silence. Carter couldn't believe himself. Since when was he the kind of man who beat confessions out of subjects? Who threatened to shoot them?

God forgive him.

Sean looked at him as they reached the drive leading to the prison. "You're awful quiet, Carter. Especially for a man who just solved the biggest case of his career."

"It's not solved. I don't have the boys."

"A matter of time. Don't worry."

Carter nodded.

"Listen, why don't you leave this fellow to me? I'll make sure he's introduced to the warden."

Carter opened his mouth to protest.

"No offense, Carter, but you're pretty overwrought about this. It might be better for someone who's not so attached to take a crack at him."

Sean was right. Carter swallowed his pride. "Fine." He licked his lips. "If you get any information, send a runner for me."

"I will."

Carter left them at the gate. He'd promised Juliet he would report on the day's progress. He hadn't anticipated having to tell her that he still didn't know where the boys were.

Chapter 23

The doctor had been right. Juliet felt infinitely worse when she woke the next morning. At least, she thought it was the next morning. The sun streamed through the sheer window coverings, and the sound of birdsong outside, normally uplifting, now grated on her nerves. How long had she been asleep? She pushed up slowly on one elbow, the mattress giving beneath her. How had she gotten upstairs?

She peeled away the blankets, her movements slow and deliberate, as if pressing through thick mud. She put one leg over the side of the mattress, then the other, then clutched the edge while she waited for the room to cease spinning.

"You're awake." Miss Clara sounded chipper as she carried a laden tray into the room.

Juliet squinted at her through one eye, keeping the other shut tight against the throbbing behind her forehead. "I suppose I am."

Miss Clara set the tray on the small table beneath the window, then sat on the bed beside her, touching her cheek with the back of one hand. "How do you feel, dear?"

"As if I've been dragged down Pennsylvania Avenue behind a stagecoach."

"Well, you were thrown from a horse."

At the mention of the accident, every harrowing, terrifying moment of the previous day rushed back, sucking the air from Juliet's lungs. "Artie." She gasped and tried to rise from the bed, but Miss Clara held her back.

"Now don't you move so fast. Your body has been through a traumatic experience. You need to get your bearings and try to eat something. Do you think you can manage tea and toast?"

"There's no time to nibble at toast. Artie and Tad are out there now, and I have to help find them."

This time, when Juliet attempted to stand, she met no resistance from Miss Clara. Instead, her own body revolted. Her stomach lurched, the room tilted, and black spots filled her vision. She felt Miss Clara's hands on her arm and back, guiding her down to the stability of the mattress.

"There now, breathe slowly." Miss Clara patted her knee, then moved to the tray and brought back a cup of tea and a plate of toast. "If you sit quietly and get some food inside you, I'll tell you what Agent Forbes said when he was here last night."

"Carter was here?"

Miss Clara shook her head. "No answers until you take a bite."

It was extortion, but Juliet was in no condition to argue. Instead, she took a piece of toast and gingerly bit off one corner. When she got ahold of that doctor, she was going to give him a piece of her mind. Whatever he had given her was worse than falling from the horse. She could only hope the effects would wear off soon.

"Good girl." Miss Clara nodded her approval.

"Please." Juliet spoke around the sawdust-like toast in her mouth. "Carter?"

"He returned last evening, very concerned about you. In fact, when he saw you huddled on that short couch, he insisted on carrying you upstairs. I stayed with you the entire time, of course."

There was no fear of impropriety with Miss Clara around. Juliet took a sip of tea and then nodded for her to continue.

"He wanted you to know that he made an arrest. That reporter who wrote the story about Tad."

"Jake Paulson?"

"Yes, that's the name he said."

Juliet's pulse surged with hope. "Did he find the boys?"

Miss Clara shook her head. "I'm sorry, child, but no. He said he's hopeful, and he'll come back today with more information." She put her hand on Juliet's shoulder, discouraging her from making another attempt to leave. "Until then, you are to stay here. He was quite insistent on that count. Said it would only slow him down if he had to worry about you, too."

An argument started to form, but her mind was still so foggy, it wouldn't take cohesive shape. Juliet sighed. "You're right. But I'd like to go to the parlor and wait there." She smiled sweetly and fluttered her eyelashes. "If you help me navigate the stairs, I'll eat more toast."

Miss Clara laughed. "Don't think you can manipulate me with your charms. I'll help you downstairs, and you'll eat, but neither is dependent on the other."

That was enough for Juliet. She wanted to be available the moment Carter walked into her home. Until then, perhaps she would take another look at Estelle's scrapbook, if only to make herself feel as though she was helping.

Emily would not stop talking.

Since she'd begun taking singing lessons, Carter's sister had blossomed. She was more open, more full of life, than she had ever been since the accident. Normally, he was thrilled with the change. But this morning, he simply wanted silence.

He nodded every now and then while slathering apple butter on a biscuit, but his mind was elsewhere. If Sean had gotten anywhere with Paulson last night, he would have sent a runner. That told Carter they were no closer to finding the boys. Still, he was anxious to get to the jail and take another crack at the reporter. He was calmer now, in control of his emotions. Perhaps, if he appealed to Paulson's sense of decency…no. A man who used innocent children as political pawns had no decency. Common sense, then. The man was a reporter—he was used to dealing with facts. Carter would present him with the facts that his plan had been thwarted and that it would go better for him if he gave up the children. Then—

"Carter!"

Emily's bark of reproach cut into his thoughts. "Yes?"

"You haven't heard a word I've said."

"Why would you say that?"

She scowled. "Because you've been buttering what's left of that biscuit for the last five minutes."

He looked down at the mess of crumbs around his plate. Muttering to himself, he set down the biscuit and wiped his hands on a napkin. "I'm sorry, Emily. I can't get this case off my mind."

Her face softened. "You're doing all you can, Carter."

That was exactly what worried him. "What if that's not enough? What if I don't find those boys?"

"You will." Emily rose and made her way to Carter's side of the table. She threw her arms around his shoulders and hugged him. "You will find them. I know it."

Carter chuckled as her grip around him tightened. "For a little slip of a thing, you certainly are strong." He patted her arm. "Now turn me loose. I have a job to do."

Emily kissed his cheek and pulled away, smiling. "I pray for you and Juliet every day."

The fact that Emily was finally willing to talk to God again was perhaps the biggest miracle of all. It was as though the discovery of song had proven that her life was not as empty as she'd thought, and that, perhaps, God could be trusted, after all.

How interesting that she said she prayed for both him and Juliet. Carter wondered what that meant, exactly. Did she pray for them individually, or as a couple? Before he could ruminate further, a knock at the front door drew his attention. When he looked back at Emily, she was singing softly to herself as she cleared her breakfast dishes from the table.

Carter hurried to the front door and found a runner waiting for him. The gangly lad appeared to be all of sixteen, and he crushed the brim of his hat nervously in his hands.

"Sir. I'm here about Agent King."

Finally, there was news. "Excellent. Did he get any information out of the suspect?"

The young man swallowed, his Adam's apple bobbing like a cork in a barrel. "I don't know, sir. My orders were to tell you to come to the jail immediately."

This was not good. "What's happened?"

"There was an incident...a shooting." The frustration Carter felt must have shown, because the runner hurried on. "That's all I know, I swear."

Browbeating the messenger would only waste time. "Get back to the prison. I'll be right behind you."

"Yes, sir." The fellow gave an awkward salute, stumbled backward a few steps, then ran off, away from the house.

Carter had Red saddled and ready to go in record time and was soon making his way to the prison as quickly as was safe on the crowded streets. A shooting. Who had been shot? The runner would have been sent to Carter only if it involved the Lincoln case, which meant that either Paulson or King was involved. But how?

Who'd shot whom? No matter how the possibilities played out in his head, the results were unacceptable.

When the prison was finally within sight, Carter saw a sheet-covered body being loaded onto a medical wagon. His heart sank. Someone was dead.

Red had barely come to a stop when Carter dismounted and handed the reins to the first officer he saw. As he ran to the front door, several men left the building. One of them was Sean, his hair mussed, a bruise on his right cheek, and blood on his white shirt-front. When he saw Carter, his face paled.

"Are you all right?" Carter asked.

Sean nodded. "I wasn't hurt." He raised his hands, and now Carter saw the blood on them. "I'm so sorry."

"What happened?" In his heart, Carter already knew, but he had to hear the words.

"I worked on Paulson last night, but I didn't get anywhere. I came back early to question him. He was slumped in his cell, and I thought he'd fainted, so I.... He got the jump on me. Made a run for it. I had to stop him."

"You shot him," Carter stated flatly.

"I tried to stop the bleeding." He looked down at his hands, his head shaking back and forth. "I knew we needed him. I tried so hard." When Sean looked back up at Carter, his eyes blazed. "Nothing would have happened if he hadn't tried to run."

Carter clasped Sean's shoulder. "Have the doctor look at you, and get cleaned up."

Without another word, Carter continued up the stairs and entered the jail. He'd speak to the other prisoners, to the warden, to anyone who might have any information. If Paulson had talked in his sleep, Carter wanted to know what he'd said. But the plain, simple truth weighed him down like a yoke of granite.

Paulson was dead. And Carter feared their last chance of finding Artie and Tad might have died with him.

Chapter 24

Juliet paged idly through Estelle's scrapbook. She had managed to get her clothes on, though she felt scandalously underdressed without a corset. But her ribs were too sore. Now she obeyed Miss Clara by resting on the settee, all the while keeping a covert gaze out the parlor's bay window. Carter had come by last night, but he should be back today. He had to be back.

She realized her leg was bobbing up and down in a mad rhythm, and she made an effort to control it. Fifteen minutes. If he wasn't back in fifteen minutes, she would go searching herself.

Now, to plot her escape from Miss Clara's watchful eye. She would need laudanum….

Her hand froze on the book. Why would there be a smudge like that in the middle of the page? It wasn't where a finger would naturally touch in the process of leafing through. Juliet squinted, trying to decipher the word beneath the smear.

We.

Well, that was hardly illuminating. Why couldn't it have been a name? She turned back to the beginning and searched through the other handbills. Nothing.

She flipped through the last few playbills. There was another word.

Never.

She found one more smudged word on the last page. *Sleep.*

Despite the heat, her skin felt suddenly clammy. "We Never Sleep" was the slogan of the Pinkerton Agency. And Howard at the Athenaeum had quoted Estelle as saying that her beau "saw everything." Could that have been an oblique hint?

Could the man behind all this be a Pinkerton agent?

The scrapbook slipped from her numb fingers and crashed to the ground, knocking loose a few of the pages.

Miss Clara hurried to gather them up. "I think you should head back to bed, dear. You need rest." The words were indistinct, like a bee's buzzing.

Juliet shook her head and waved a hand, shooing away the annoyance. Her mind spun. Where better for a spy to be placed than among the Pinkertons? A position of trust that could ensure double harm. Such a man could gather information on the Union's plans and pass it along to Southern generals. He could also pass false information back that would have the Union forces bumbling and flat-footed when the time for battle arrived.

A man like that, who could befriend and then betray people and take children hostage, had to be completely ruthless. There was no telling what lengths he might go to in order to protect his secrets.

Gritting her teeth against the dizziness, Juliet stood. Carter needed to know. He needed to know right now.

Miss Clara stood in front of her, her forehead creased with deep lines of worry.

"I'm sorry, Miss Clara. I have to go. I have to warn him."

"Who, dear?" The older woman put a hand under Juliet's elbow. "Who do you need to warn?"

"Carter. There's a spy. He could be in danger."

"We know, dear. He's being very careful." Miss Clara smoothed a wisp of hair away from Juliet's forehead. "He's a Pinkerton, don't forget. He's trained to deal with danger."

As quickly as she had stood, Juliet sat back down. Carter was a Pinkerton. He was in charge of the investigation. What better position could there be from which to make sure the mystery was never solved?

Could Carter be the spy?

Miss Clara waved a vial of smelling salts under Juliet's nose, and she shied away from the pungent scent.

"Miss Clara, please. I'm fine. Truly. Just thinking."

Miss Clara sat beside her. "Child, you gave me a start. What is all this?"

Juliet shook her head. Her thoughts spun and slid, colliding into one another and whirling away again, staying just outside her grasp. As the man in charge, Carter could direct progress away from uncovering anything of worth. And those people who seemed as if they might offer information of value ended up dead. Carter had known the potential significance of both Cormac and Estelle. He easily could have gone back and knocked them off, to make sure they didn't talk.

But then again, Estelle had given no sign of knowing him. And if he was concerned about what would be discovered, why not kill Juliet rather than his accomplices?

There was a knock at the front door. A moment later, the Professor showed Carter in. He wore his hangdog expression like an ill-fitting garment. She knew instantly that he had no news about Artie. She scrutinized his face for anything else she might be able to discern. Reading people was what she did. If she couldn't trust her instincts in this regard, then she really was a sham.

His eyes studied her almost as intently, taking in the bruises and scrapes. His fingers closed convulsively around the rim of his bowler. "Juliet, I'm sorry, but I have some bad news."

Her stomach heaved, and she clenched her jaw. It was worse than she thought. The room narrowed to a tiny point of focus that included only Carter's face.

"Jake Paulson was killed last night in an escape attempt. We didn't get any information out of him before he died."

The weight on her chest lifted slightly, and she struggled to find her tongue. "So, there's no word on the boys?" That meant there was still a chance they were alive.

"No." He crossed the room in three long strides and took her hand in his. "I'm so sorry, Juliet. I'm doing everything I can. I've got men working on this around the clock. We will find the kidnappers."

Their eyes locked. In his, she read sincerity, compassion, and concern. Trusting people didn't come naturally to her, but she had come to trust Carter. She didn't believe he'd had anything to do with the kidnappings. The realization swept over her, as soothing as chamomile tea, and her thoughts cleared. "I've found something you should see."

He frowned as she reached for the scrapbook. Miss Clara made to stand.

"Professor, Miss Clara, I'd like you to hear this, as well. I know you love Artie, too, and I think we're going to need your help."

Juliet opened the scrapbook to the page with the first smudged word and showed them what she'd found.

Carter's face paled, his skin suddenly looking as if it had been pulled taut over his cheekbones. "Who?" He whispered the word so quietly, he was almost speaking to himself.

The Professor pulled out his thick reading spectacles and magnifying glass and reached for the scrapbook. "Perhaps this will help." He flipped to one of the earlier pages, one that showed, among the accolades for the play, an artist's sketch along the right-hand side of two men and a woman—the hero, heroine, and villain of the play. He pointed to one of the men. "Yes, right here. I may be wrong, but it seemed to me that this picture has been altered."

They all leaned in close. Juliet squinted. Sure enough, on close examination, it looked as though someone had taken a pen and added a full mustache to the last man's face, squared off his chin, and given him a bowler. She had been so caught up in examining the words for a message, she had hardly glanced at the pictures.

"Estelle must have wanted to make him look like her beau." Juliet's nose nearly touched the page. "Is it just me, or does it look like—"

"Sean." Carter looked as if he'd been whacked with a sledgehammer.

Juliet reached for his hand, hoping to comfort him, but another thought occurred to her. "Last night, he saw the scrapbook. He wanted to take it away after I told him it was from a suspect's apartment."

Carter frowned. "He could have been trying to help."

"He told me it was evidence in a murder case. But how could he know that unless he knew where it had come from? And how could he know where it had come from unless he had seen it before?"

Carter breathed deep. "I'll meet with him and see what he has to say." Hope flared in his eyes. "Maybe he has a logical explanation."

"If there is one spy among the Pinkertons, there could be more," Professor Marvolo said.

Juliet nodded. "If he doesn't know he's a suspect, he might lead us to the boys."

Still looking stricken, Carter shook his head. "He knows me too well. He'd spot me, and if I can't trust any of my other men…."

"You can trust us," Juliet said. "You know we want Artie back, and we wouldn't do anything to jeopardize his safety."

"But you don't know how to trail a man."

"Don't be too sure about that. I used to be able to follow a mark halfway across an unfamiliar city without him ever growing wise." Juliet offered a roguish grin.

Carter managed a thin smile in return. "I'm not sure that's the ringing endorsement you might think it is. Besides, you're injured."

"I'll be fine. Consider the black eye part of the costume. I will blend right in among the ragamuffins and street urchins. Surely you know his address? And doesn't he usually check in at the Pinkerton headquarters in the evening? I could follow him from there, too."

"I can keep an eye on his lodgings," Miss Clara said. "I can disguise myself as a blind beggar. In fact, I've got an old dress I just put in the rag bin to cut up for polishing cloths. That would be perfect." She bustled out of the room, apparently taking for granted that Carter would capitulate.

Professor Marvolo stood. "Direct me toward his favorite tavern, and I can watch for him there. Between the three of us, we ought to be able to keep track of him."

"The four of us," Carter said.

Juliet frowned. "But you were right. He would recognize you."

"Not after you're done making me anew. I've seen the transformations you have achieved." He still looked pained.

"Then, you do believe he could be the culprit?" Juliet asked quietly. It must be a blow to think he'd been betrayed by someone he'd long considered a friend.

He raked a hand through his hair. "I don't want to think it." He sighed. "But the theory does make some sense. Sean has known about many of the developments in the case. And he was on the scene for some of the events. At my direction, no less."

His face looked gray at the idea, and Juliet again reached for his hand.

"Even if the possibility is remote, a traitor among the Pinkertons would be disastrous. I have no choice but to check it out." His hands clenched into fists. "And if he has betrayed us, he will pay."

Carter stared at his reflection in the looking glass, unable to quite believe his eyes.

"Well, what do you think?" Hands on her hips, Juliet stood back, looking him up and down.

"I hope it isn't prophetic."

She had turned him into a balding man with only a fringe of stringy, gray-brown hair. And, as if that weren't enough, she'd given him a paunch that made him look a good forty pounds heavier than he was. She'd even painted a gold crown on one of his front teeth. The artful application of stage makeup made him look at least fifty. Wearing a frock coat worn shiny at the elbows and carrying a walking stick, he looked like one of thousands of slightly shady businessmen in the capital.

She grinned at him in response. "It's important to concentrate on the way you move, as well, and how you hold yourself. Those things can give you away as easily as if you were to walk up and introduce yourself, if someone knows you well."

"So what should I do?"

"Hunch your shoulders a bit and shorten your stride. The walking stick will help, too. Make sure you use it and don't just tuck it under your arm." She removed her apron and draped it over the back of a chair. "I'll be back shortly."

Carter nodded, still staring at himself in the glass. There was more to this disguise stuff than he'd thought. He practiced walking and standing differently. It was harder than it looked. Every time he thought he had it down, he found himself lapsing into his usual, long-limbed gait.

The door opened, and a scruffy boy of about seventeen swaggered in, gnawing on an apple. Carter whirled to face the lad.

Mouth still full, the boy gave him a cheeky grin and a wink.

The boy had velvety dark eyes with long lashes. He looked again. "Juliet?"

She swallowed. "In the flesh."

He still couldn't believe it. "I never would have recognized you, except for your eyes."

Evidently taking this as criticism, she frowned and approached the glass. "Hm. I see what you mean."

He couldn't take his gaze off of her. Free of corsets and hoops, she was agile and even more graceful. He cleared his throat and focused on her face.

With a small brush, she made her eyebrows thicker and darker. A few more deft strokes with a different color emphasized lines beneath and above her eyes, making them look sulky and hooded.

"There." She examined herself critically in the glass. "Now what do you think?"

"I think you look like the kind of young scamp I would feel compelled to arrest on sight, just on principle."

She grinned. "Perfect."

They all convened in the parlor. Carter cleared his throat. "I cannot stress enough that if your theory is right, Sean is dangerous. Do not try to apprehend him on your own. Simply watch him and discover what you can. We will all report back here. Does everyone understand?"

Miss Clara and Professor Marvolo nodded dutifully. Juliet examined her fingernails, newly encrusted in dirt.

Carter narrowed his eyes. "Juliet."

"Yes?"

"Promise me you will not try to take him down on your own."

"I promise not to tangle with him, unless there is no alternative."

"That's not good enough."

"It will have to be." Her eyes bored into him. "If I find him about to hurt the boys, I will intervene."

Miss Clara straightened, appearing taller. "That goes for me, as well."

"And for me," said the Professor.

Carter held back a growl. What had he started? Pinkertons at least knew how to take direction. "Promise to try."

"I promise." Juliet smiled gently. "I don't want to do anything but get the boys back, and I won't take any unnecessary risks."

Knowing that their definitions of "unnecessary risks" might be vastly different, Carter also knew it was the best assurance he was likely to get. He sighed. "Just be careful."

They all nodded solemnly.

Carter put on the porkpie hat Juliet had supplied him and followed them out the back door. This was either the best plan he'd ever been a part of, or it was the worst. He'd find out soon enough.

Chapter 25

Pinkerton Agent Sean King puffed out his chest as he removed the stopper from a crystal decanter and poured himself a snifter of brandy. Swirling the warm, brown liquid in the glass, he remembered the exact moment Paulson had put it all together. Standing outside the man's jail cell, Sean had said just enough to nudge the reporter from dot to dot, until Paulson had gasped his epiphany. "You."

Sean shook his head. Such smug satisfaction from the reporter, until the moment Sean had taken the key from his pocket and opened the cell door. Then the reporter had blanched, realizing there was only one logical reason for the Pinkerton to have shared so much with him. Paulson had realized he would never have a chance to repeat what he'd heard.

Just as Sean had hoped, the reporter had decided his only chance was to make a run for it. They'd scuffled, enough to put both of them in a state of disarray, and to provide evidence of a fight. Then, he'd done what he had to.

Sean gulped the brandy, savoring the burn as it coursed down his throat. It was a day for celebration. As far as anyone else was concerned, Tad Lincoln's kidnapper had been killed during an escape attempt. And he had Carter to thank for making it all possible.

He stared at the portrait of his father, which dominated the wall above the mantel. Father would be proud of his progress thus far, but he would also be quick to remind him there was more work to be done. Sean was not going to stand by and let the tyrant Lincoln destroy the Southern way of life. He smacked his glass down on the table. The man had already stolen too much.

Now there was twice as much work, since that imbecilic Victor had grabbed the wrong boy. They had come close to disaster when Carter had chased them down yesterday. Sean had desperately feared he'd been recognized, which was why he'd gone to Juliet's house first. Her lack of reservations about his presence had told him he was safe.

Sean's eyes stung with exhaustion, but he rubbed them and stood. In the rush and confusion yesterday, he hadn't had time to accompany Victor to the hideout, so he'd had to postpone taking care of the little imposter. He set his jaw. Some jobs were unpleasant but necessary. "No time like the present."

He grabbed his bowler and strode outside. Finding a blind beggar camped on his step, he nudged her aside with his foot. She rattled her cup at him and spat. What a blight they were. It would be so simple to knock the concrete urn from its spot atop the brick column, right onto the woman's head.

He'd be doing the general public a favor.

"Boss."

The sound of Victor's voice froze Sean in his tracks. The brute was hurrying up the sidewalk, his frown so deep, his bushy eyebrows had merged into one.

When Victor reached him, Sean grabbed his arm and pulled him toward the house. "What are you doing here?" he hissed under his breath. "I told you not to leave those boys alone."

"I know, sir. But that new one, I got him to talk. Said he knows something important that's going to happen tonight, but it won't do you no good unless he can tell you right away."

Sean released his grip. "What is happening tonight?"

Victor shook his head. "Little wretch wouldn't tell me. Said he'll only talk to you. Kept saying he needed to work out his cut."

"His cut?" Sean barked out a laugh. "Once a crook, always a crook. Forbes thinks he can trust those people, but the little urchin is ready to turn and work for whoever will pay him the most."

Victor's face was blank. Apparently, Sean had voiced his suspicions in words too big for him to comprehend. "People don't change."

Understanding dawned on Victor's face. "True, true."

Sean sighed. "I hope you tied up those boys good and tight before you left them."

"I tied 'em up good, but I didn't leave 'em." Victor stuck out his jaw. "You told me not to leave 'em, so I didn't."

The ground felt slightly shaky beneath Sean's feet. He wouldn't have. "Where are they?"

Victor looked over his shoulder. "In the back of the wagon."

Sean cursed. Thankfully, a heavy piece of canvas covered the back and was tied down on the sides. At least the oaf had done that much right.

Sean looked up one side of the street and down the other, checking for witnesses, but even the beggar woman had moved away. What had she overheard? Unless she was deaf and dumb, as well as blind, she could be a problem.

He couldn't keep the boys at his home, but the city was crawling with other Pinkertons, all concerned with the whereabouts of the president's son and on the lookout for anything unusual. He needed to take them somewhere close.

A plan began to spin in his mind. The capture of Paulson had essentially diverted suspicion away from other suspects—and he wanted to keep it that way. Wherever he took the boys needed to be a place that no one would seriously consider.

And he knew just the spot.

The costume was unbearably hot. To disguise her female figure, Juliet had not only bound her breasts, but she also wore several layers of clothing. With her hair piled atop her head beneath a worn cap, and with the layers of makeup caking her face, she felt as if she was suffocating. Her worry over the fate of Artie and Tad didn't help matters any.

Despite the heat, she couldn't stop moving. Since Sean was more familiar with her, she had agreed to the wisdom of Miss Clara being the one to assume a post just outside Sean's home. Once Juliet had guided her "blind" friend down the street and settled her safely, she'd sauntered down the block with the easy gait of a young man free of care. Then she'd doubled around and come up behind the row houses.

Through a gap in the heavy window coverings, she caught a glimpse of movement. He was inside. She itched to burst in and demand he take her to Artie and Tad. But doing that would be not only dangerous but foolish, too. The man was a Pinkerton agent, trained in subduing suspects, either through brute force or a well-aimed bullet. Juliet's tricks were no match for either.

As she stood there, she occasionally picked through a garbage pail. If anyone happened to see her, she would appear to be just another hungry street urchin. It occurred to her that Sean's own refuse might reveal a clue, but several minutes of surreptitious digging revealed only that the man enjoyed his brandy.

More movement inside caught her attention, followed by the sound of a door slamming. He was leaving the house.

Juliet's heart raced as she hurried back down the alley. This could be it. He could be going to wherever he held the boys. She darted around the corner to the sidewalk and ran straight into a Union officer.

"Where are you off to in such a hurry, lad?"

Keeping her eyes down, she rubbed the toe of one worn shoe into the ground. "Going to fetch my ma. Pardon my clumsiness, sir."

"You wouldn't have been rummaging through the garbage, eh?" His voice was hard and serious.

This was exactly the kind of unexpected interference that could destroy a well-laid plan. Telling the truth, or a version of it, was really the only way out. "Yes, sir, I was. Food is scarce 'round our place." She reached into the pocket of her trousers and pulled out the half-eaten apple she'd placed there earlier. Time within the confines of hot wool had already turned it brown, making it look like something one would find in the trash.

"I see."

The soldier's voice softened, and Juliet dared a quick peek at him. He felt sympathy, but he still had a job to do. She turned her pants' pockets inside out to prove she'd stolen nothing of importance, then held out the apple. "Sorry, sir. I beg for mercy."

The man didn't take the apple. Instead, he reached inside his own pocket. "There's something you need more than mercy."

He was going to arrest her. He was reaching for his handcuffs. Juliet swallowed down her fear. If she made a run for it, she might be able to get away.

Before she could make her move, the man reached for her other hand. Instinctively, she pulled back.

"Open your hand, boy. I'm not going to hurt you."

She did as directed and was shocked when two shiny quarters dropped into her palm.

"I know it's not much, but it will help."

Only one word came to Juliet's mind. "Why?"

"My son is about your age, off fighting to hold the Union together. I'd like to think if he needed help, someone would offer it to him."

In the midst of the turmoil of her situation, a warm peace spread through her. The officer had said she needed something more than mercy, yet that was exactly what he'd given her. Mercy and kindness.

"Thank you, sir."

The officer cleared his throat and motioned down the street. "Off with you now. And stay out of the trash bins. Some folks don't take kindly to it."

He didn't need to tell her twice. She hurried past him and up the street, tamping down her desire to run at top speed. She couldn't lose Sean, not now. Not when it seemed they were so close to finding the boys.

Juliet nearly endured her second collision of the day, with Miss Clara, who had completely dropped her ruse as a blind woman and now ran in her direction.

"Miss Clara, stop. What's wrong?"

"They're here." She pointed behind her. "The boys. Hurry."

Miss Clara hurried back from where she'd come, with Juliet hot on her heels. They were just in time to see the wagon moving down the street.

"I should have stayed with them," Miss Clara wailed. "I tried to untie the canvas, but it was so tight, I loosened only one knot. That's why I ran to find you. And now they're gone. What have I done?"

A fist tightened in Juliet's stomach as she watched the wagon move away. But then, she saw something that gave her hope. "I think you may have saved them."

"What?"

"Look."

A small hand poked out from under the canvas and dropped what appeared to be a wig.

Miss Clara gasped. "It's Artie. He's leaving a trail."

Leave it to the clever little scamp. However he'd been restrained, he'd gotten at least partially free. And though he couldn't get to the knots on the outside of the wagon, Miss Clara had made it possible for him to send this message.

"I'm going to follow them. You find Carter."

She didn't wait for Miss Clara to agree or argue. She simply ran after the wagon, achingly aware that two lives depended on her success.

Chapter 26

Carter adjusted his fake paunch for the millionth time. How had he ever let himself be talked into this ridiculous scheme? That picture in the scrapbook didn't prove anything. It could have been any one of a hundred men. There had been a resemblance to Sean, but that was all. And this—he looked down at his getup—was a kind of betrayal. He should just find Sean and ask him about Estelle, not skulk after him like he would stalk some common criminal.

Resolved to pursue a more honorable course, Carter dropped a couple of coins on the counter and stood. The barmaid didn't offer him so much as a second glance, much less call out a cheery farewell, as such women usually did when he departed.

The clues Juliet had found might point to a Pink, but they could just as easily have been the product of an overworked imagination. He should have examined that scrapbook more carefully. What if she had missed other vitals bits of the puzzle?

He tried hard to imagine what those might be, but his creativity failed him. He wouldn't know until he had a good look through that infernal book.

Hand on the door, he paused. Why had he been so quick to trust Juliet's deductions? She didn't have any experience with detecting, but she'd practically been leading him around by the nose through this entire investigation.

The answer was there, just beneath the surface, where he had refused to examine it too closely until now. Though he'd tried at times to set his feelings aside, he loved her.

He loved a charlatan and a cheat. He loved her quick wits. He loved her capable hands. He loved her daring and her dash. And if he loved her, shouldn't he give her the benefit of the doubt? He had trusted her other assertions and had been proven correct to do so. Why should he stop now?

Gah! There was no easy answer. No convenient black-and-white to latch on to. There was only what his head shouted and what his heart whispered.

The door swung open, and he pulled back to allow the new arrival entry. Miss Clara smacked into him, eyes wide, breath coming in heaving gasps.

Carter grabbed her shoulders to steady her. "What is it?"

She swallowed. "King." Gasp. "Has the boys."

His fingers tightened on her shoulders. "It really was Sean?" She winced, and he released her. "Pardon me."

She nodded. "I'm sorry. I know he was your friend. Juliet's gone after them."

Carter took her hand and yanked open the door. "Show me."

She pulled free. "I'll just slow you down."

Carter was practically vibrating with the need to move, but he had to get the story from Miss Clara first.

"At least walk with me."

She nodded, and they headed down the street. "A man with a wagon came to speak to King. He let on that the boys were tied up in the wagon. I was able to loosen the edge of the tarp that covered them. And as he drove away, Artie was tossing out bits and pieces like he was Hansel."

"And Juliet?"

"She went haring after them."

"She's going to get herself killed." Fear, bright and hard, lit Miss Clara's eyes, and Carter wished he'd bitten his tongue. He tried to repair the damage. "She's smart. She'll be all right. She won't take any chances."

"She will if she thinks she must. They were headed west, away from King's lodgings. Now go. Find Juliet and the boys and bring them home safe."

He squeezed her hand and took off, running flat out, peeling away at the disguise as he went. He discarded the huge jacket and ripped the padding from underneath his shirt, determined not to let anything slow him down.

Before rounding the corner, he heard Miss Clara call out, "I'll be praying."

It was a good thing. They were going to need it.

Juliet dug her fingers into her ribs to hold off the pain and kept running. Where was all the traffic that should be congesting the streets and slowing King and his henchman to a crawl?

They turned a corner some two blocks ahead of her. With her breath coming in huffing gasps, she redoubled her pace. She could not lose them.

Head down, she careened around the corner. An oyster seller's cart blocked the walk, and Juliet barreled into it. She bounced off and sprawled in the street. The cart's owner, a burly man in a grimy apron, loomed over her, a shucking knife raised in his enormous fist.

Juliet scrambled to her feet. She craned her neck, trying to see around his bulk. Where had the wagon gone?

"Trying to steal from me?"

"No." Where was the wagon?

"I'll teach you a lesson." The man lunged for her.

"No!" Juliet skipped back two steps and dodged around him. She ran into the middle of the street and continued the way the wagon must have gone. Where was it?

It had vanished, as if it had been part of a magic show. The oyster vendor shouted imprecations after her. She glanced back and saw a policeman approaching the man to see what the trouble was about.

Time to do a vanishing act of her own. But she didn't know which way to go. She paused at the next crossroads. "God, guide me. Help me to know which way to turn."

A child's laugh fluted from the side street, and she turned toward it, spying two little girls playing with a length of gold braid, which they rested on their heads like pigtails.

Juliet ran to them. "Where did you get that?"

The girls backed away, clutching their treasure protectively. "We didn't steal it."

There was no time for this. "No, I'm sure you found it. But can you show me where?"

"We found it in the road." They pointed a bit farther down the side street.

"Wonderful. Did a wagon go by, too?"

They nodded.

From behind, a policeman's whistle sounded.

Juliet began running again.

Her eyes scoured the road for any other clue Artie might have tossed out. There, to the left, just after the turn, a handkerchief lay in the road. It could be anyone's. There was no time to debate. She had to act. She swerved down the new path.

And then, there it was, not 200 yards in front of her. The wagon had slowed. Grateful, Juliet slowed to an amble, as well, so as not to overtake them. She glanced around, taking stock of the neighborhood. Brick row houses lined both sides of the street, standing as smug and freshly scrubbed as star pupils in grammar school. Definitely not the kind of place one would expect a kidnapper to hold two boys.

They couldn't be more than a half mile from the Presidential Mansion. The wagon made its way down an alley to the lane behind the homes. If he meant to take the boys inside one of the houses, that made sense. He wouldn't want witnesses.

Juliet moved down the alley and then crept up behind the wagon, which had stopped in back of one of the homes. A conveniently placed rain barrel provided cover, and she crouched low. King went to the door and fussed with the lock for a moment. She pulled back as he turned, but he was so intent on his task, he didn't even glance her way as he hauled a wriggling, kicking form from the bottom of the wagon.

Juliet's breath caught in her throat. *Tad.*

King's thug hauled out a second form, which writhed like a whirlwind in his arms. *Artie.*

Juliet tensed, ready to spring from her hiding place, but she couldn't think of a way to free both boys. Pulse hammering in her ears and muscles bunched to leap, she nevertheless stayed where she was.

The boys were hustled inside, and the door closed. Juliet scrambled from her place and scuttled to the stoop. She tried the door handle, but it was locked. She peeked in the nearest window and saw the kitchen. No fire lit the hearth or made the stove glow, which explained why the window was closed tight in the middle of July. She tried to raise the sash, but it was locked.

She slipped to the other side of the door, where another window beckoned invitingly. It was securely locked, as well. Swallowing a groan of frustration, she glanced around, then backed out into the alley, craning her neck to get a better look at the house.

Maybe, if she could make it atop the wagon, she could climb up to the roof of the stable, and then, if she reached, she could get one of the second-story windows open. If it was unlocked.

It was a chance. She climbed up into the wagon and reached for the edge of the stable roof. Her ribs ached, and a moan escaped through clenched teeth as she hooked her elbows over the lip of the roof and began hauling herself up.

A hard hand gripped her ankle and pulled her, tumbling, back into the wagon, where her fall was mercifully broken by the thick tarp and what looked like a wool blanket. "What're you doing, boy?"

Stunned, Juliet scrambled to the ground, arms wrapped protectively around her chest. She squinted up at the policeman glaring down at her.

"C'mon, you." He grabbed hold of her collar.

"Please, no." She tried to wriggle free. "The men in there kidnapped two young boys. They're in there now."

The policeman shook his head. "You'll have to do better than that. Those are Allan Pinkerton's lodgings. The founder of the Pinkerton Agency. Not exactly the kind of fellow you'd think might kidnap anyone. He's not even home."

Juliet stilled in her attempts to break free. It made a diabolical sort of sense. Even in a city crawling with agents hunting for Tad, no Pinkerton would look for him at the boss's house. "You don't understand. If Mr. Pinkerton's gone, then what is to prevent someone from using his apartments for evil?"

The officer yanked her so close, she was scarcely an inch from his face. "Me." He began hauling her away.

She dug her heels into the ground and grabbed hold of the wagon. She couldn't think beyond the certain knowledge that she could not leave the boys. If she left, she might never find Artie again.

The officer was growing angrier. He wrapped his arms around her and lifted her completely off the ground. Pain sliced through her ribs. Wrestling her away, he dragged her down the alley and around to the street.

"What's all this, then?"

Carter! Juliet twisted in the officer's grasp. "Carter, it's me. The boys are just there." She indicated the direction by pointing with her chin.

The officer boxed her ear, setting her ear ringing.

Carter moved like lightning and pulled Juliet free of the man's grasp. Holding her protectively against his chest, he put out a hand to ward off the man's efforts to regain his prize. "Officer, I am Pinkerton agent Carter Forbes."

The man stopped his onslaught.

Carter fumbled in his pocket and pulled out his credentials.

The policeman examined the papers, looking from the documents to Carter's face and back again. Even though he'd succeeded in shedding most of the disguise, including tearing the bald cap from his head, he still looked a fright. With his shirt untucked, his too-big pants, and bits of adhesive gum clinging to his face around the hairline, it was no wonder the officer had his doubts. "You're really a Pinkerton?"

"Yes. And this young…person is helping me in a critical investigation."

"The lad tried to tell me some cock-and-bull story about Allan Pinkerton kidnapping someone."

"No," Juliet cut in. "They're just in his house."

Carter looked down at her. "I half suspected it when the trail led down this street. They're in there now?"

Juliet nodded.

"Then we're going to get them out." He turned to the policeman. "Officer, if you could round up all the men you can, we could sure use your help."

"I don't know. I mean, are you thinking of leading an assault on Mr. Pinkerton's house? My sergeant—"

Carter moved close to the man and looked him in the eye. "Officer, Tad Lincoln is being held in that house. You go get your sergeant and anyone else you can find. You have ten minutes. Or I will personally see you in the Old Capitol this very night."

"Yes, sir." The officer stopped just short of saluting, turned on his heel, and hurried away.

When the man was halfway down the block, Carter looked at Juliet. "Let's go get the boys."

Chapter 27

Juliet frowned. "I already tried the downstairs doors and windows, and they're locked tight. An upstairs window is our best bet."

"Blast it, Juliet. You're still on the mend from falling off that horse." Concern etched his face. A moment later, he brightened. "And besides"—he delved into his pocket—"that's not necessarily the only way in." With a triumphant lift of his eyebrows, he pulled out a pair of lock picks.

Juliet sucked a breath through her teeth and looked both ways down the street, lest another policeman be lurking nearby. "Where did you get those?"

"You know what they are?"

"Yes, I know what they are. I picked the lock at Cormac's house, remember? Where did *you* get such a thing?"

He looked smug. "From a friend. I have hidden depths."

"Do you know how to use them?"

There was an infinitesimal pause before he replied. "Yes."

She raised an eyebrow. "In theory or in practice?"

"My friend explained it all to me."

She shook her head. "I know how to pick a lock."

He mimicked her movement. "No. You're not going in first. It's too dangerous."

"What is 'too dangerous' is sitting around debating while the boys are in that house with a vicious murderer." Juliet laid her hand on his arm. "It will be easy for me to pick the lock. I'll be quicker and quieter. It has to be me. Then you can go in."

She knew she'd made her case when a little growl rumbled in his throat. "All right. But don't forget, I go in first."

"What are you going to do?"

"I'm not sure yet. But I will be when the time comes."

She smiled. "I know you will. We're going to get the boys out of there."

He handed over the lock picks, and Juliet turned, ready to sneak back down the alley. Carter arrested her with a touch on her shoulder. "Be careful." His voice was raspy with worry, his gaze intense.

"I promise."

Without another word, he pulled her close, bent his head down, and kissed her. She melted against his chest, drawing strength from him for just a moment. With an effort of will, she pulled away. Her hand shook as she picked a small piece of the torn skullcap from his hair. "It's a good thing no one was around to see that. We're not dressed for it."

Carter looked down at her ragamuffin apparel and shook his head ruefully. "I'll get it right next time." His eyes were dark with concern. "Promise me there will be a next time. They won't hesitate to kill you if they see you."

"I'll be careful." She reached up and caressed his jaw, and he covered her hand with his. "I promise."

He didn't look convinced, but he released her hand when she pulled away.

Keeping to the shadows, Juliet hurried down the lane, trying to look as if she belonged in the neighborhood. Her disguise had been necessary, but it would have been easier if she were dressed as herself. No one would challenge her then.

Carter was close enough behind her that she could practically feel his breath on her neck. When she reached the door, she glanced over her shoulder. "Keep an eye out for anyone coming."

He nodded, thrust his hands into his pockets, and turned his back to her.

Juliet slid the first pick into the lock. With no way to know if someone was on the other side of the door, silence was even more important than usual. Now for the second pick. She inserted it and jiggled it softly, exploring the lock's inner workings. She closed her eyes, willing the picks to become extensions of her hands.

There. The last tumbler clicked. She moistened her lips and withdrew the picks. Very slowly she turned the knob.

It was time to rescue the boys.

Never in a million years would Carter have believed he'd have cause to break into the home of Allan Pinkerton. Everything about this plan, from the disguises to Juliet cracking the back door like it was a safe, smacked of the absurd. Carter prayed that none of the multitude of things that could go wrong would.

He turned at the sound of a tiny click. Juliet's fingers were wrapped around the knob, turning slowly. He covered her hand and shook his head in silent reproach. She stepped back, and he took over the delicate job. As the door glided open on silent hinges, Carter thanked his boss's penchant for keeping everything in perfect order.

Gun at the ready, Carter peeked his head around the door. No shots rang out. One potential catastrophe avoided.

The door opened into a back service area attached to the kitchen. Normally, the room would have been occupied by the staff. But the house was only a seasonal residence, cared for by temporary workers, all of whom had been discharged when Mr. Pinkerton had left town for his extended assignment. Now there was only a man who checked on the place a couple of times a week. Just one more reason Sean would see this as a deviously good place to hide. At least for a short time.

Which did not bode well for the boys.

Carter crept through the kitchen and down the hall. The sound of voices grew louder. He paused and heard feet shuffling above.

Drat. He would have to negotiate the stairs. The middle of the tread was too liable to squeak, so he tentatively placed a foot on the outside edge of the first step. Breathing a prayer, he let the wood take his weight.

The voices upstairs became more distinct.

A child's wail. "Don't tell them nothing, or you're a traitor, too!" There was a scuffle, the sound of scraping wood, and a high-pitched yelp.

"Leave the kid alone, and I'll tell you about the plans." There was no mistaking the voice or the implication. Artie was standing up for Tad, but what story was he spinning?

More rustling. "Tell me, and it better be good, or Mr. Lincoln, here, gets worse than a smack on the mouth." The voice was unmistakably Sean's.

There was no room for doubt now.

Jaw set, Carter eased onto the landing. The first door in the hall stood ajar. The gap wasn't wide, but it was enough for him to see into the bedroom.

Sheets covered most of the furniture, and the boys, both bound, lay side by side on the bed.

Sean hovered over Artie, the boy's shirtfront bunched in his fist, and pulled him close enough to growl in his face. "The only reason you're alive is because I'm interested in the information you claim to have, but I'm getting bored. Tell me or I'll shoot you now."

Artie didn't blink. "That would be a real waste, see, 'cause I can tell you what I know now, and you'd be happy. But if you let me go,

I can get lots more information for you. You'd have someone who can get into the president's office and find out anything you want to know."

Sean barked out a laugh. "Sure. And there's no way you would ever betray me to Forbes, right?"

It took every ounce of Carter's control and training not to burst into the room and defend the boys. But revealing himself now would be foolish. There were two of them, and he should wait for reinforcements.

He felt a presence at his back and spun. Juliet stood there, motioning for him to do something now to free the boys. Heartbeat thundering in his ears, Carter let out a breath. She was *not* the reinforcement he'd hoped for. He bared his teeth and jerked his head toward the stairs, signaling her to flee.

She ignored him and jutted her chin at the door. He turned in time to hear the heavy tread of a big man's feet.

There was no time to get out of sight. Gun drawn, he moved even closer to the door. The footsteps drew nearer.

Carter counted the steps.

Nearer.

Now!

He barreled forward, slamming the door inward and sending Sean's thug staggering back. Carter followed through the door and kicked out, knocking a gun from the man's hand. It fell with a heavy thud to the floorboards a second before its owner.

Carter leveled his gun at the man he used to call friend. "It's over, Sean."

Sean's eyes were black with anger. "You never could mind your own business, Forbes." A mirthless chuckle rumbled in his throat. "I guess that's what makes you such a good Pink. But it's also what's going to get you killed."

"Carter, look out!"

Juliet plowed into the small of his back, and he stumbled forward, just as a gunshot ripped through the room. Carter regained his balance and slid to the side in time to see the thug on one knee, holding the gun he must have had hidden on his person. Across the room, Sean had taken advantage of the moment of confusion and drawn his gun, which he now aimed at Carter.

A sharp gasp from Juliet drew the attention of everyone in the room. She stood in the doorway, one hand clutching the frame, the other pressed against the front of her shirt, just below her left shoulder. Blood oozed between her fingers. Then, as if time had slowed, she crumpled to the floor. Artie cried out, his face contorted, as he strained against his bonds.

In that moment, Carter knew, Sean believed he had the upper hand. Indeed, Carter Forbes, the man, wanted to run to Juliet's side. But Carter Forbes, the Pinkerton agent, stood his ground, his mind working quickly and efficiently. He had one chance to save not only Juliet, but the boys and himself, as well.

Carter stared at Sean, then lifted his lips in a slow grin as he holstered his gun. "That couldn't have worked out better if we'd planned it."

Pain seared through Juliet, stealing her breath and making her vision jittery. Her legs refused to hold her upright, and she sagged to the floor.

She had to get up. Had to move. Artie needed her. Carter needed her.

But her body wouldn't cooperate.

Carter holstered his weapon and held his hands wide in a gesture of friendship. Dazed, she blinked. She was seeing things.

Her ears were ringing, but it sounded like he chuckled. "Too bad you didn't come to me in the first place, Sean. Maybe then I could have avoided participating in this ridiculous charade."

The words made no sense. Artie began yelling, and Sean jerked a chin at his lackey, who struggled to his feet and stuffed a gag in the boy's mouth. Anger bubbled through Juliet, and she managed to lift up her head and shoulders for a brief moment before she lost the battle against gravity and fell back to the floor. From there, she could see most of what was happening, the men towering and tilted at a crazy angle. She was audience to whatever they chose to do to the boys, but she couldn't do anything to stop it. Her head lolled to the side, frustration squeezing her heart like a vise. And then she saw something truly interesting. The gun Carter had kicked away from Sean's man lay tantalizingly close. Only three or four feet from her.

Sean waved his gun toward Carter. "What are you getting at?"

"Come on, Sean. You must have figured out that you and I are on the same side."

"You expect me to believe you're a Southern sympathizer?"

"Think about it. Why else would I involve a fraudulent medium and her band of misfits in such a sensitive investigation?"

"You were setting her up." A hint of admiration colored Sean's words as he lowered his gun to his side.

No. This was wrong. Juliet looked back at Carter, waiting for him to deny the accusation, but he didn't so much as glance in her direction. "You have to admit, it would have been perfect. She was so eager to assist, and Mary Lincoln just wouldn't stop until the woman was foisted upon me. No matter how things turned out, I could blame her ineptitude for leading me astray. I never actually thought she'd be smart enough to figure anything out."

An entirely new kind of pain blossomed in Juliet's chest and spread fiery tentacles in all directions. She closed her eyes against the hot sting of tears.

She had trusted him.

She was a fool.

It would be a relief to give up and sink into the blissful ignorance of unconsciousness, but she couldn't. The boys were still in danger. Rallying her ebbing strength, she cautiously slid a hand toward the gun on the floor.

Sean shook his head. "I was sure you were out for blood. I wish I'd known before I had to silence a valuable operative."

"Estelle? She was weak. She'd have caused trouble eventually."

Sean snickered. "True, but she was accommodating."

"Forget about Estelle. Just think what could be accomplished if we joined forces. We might not be able to win it for the South, but we could sure lose it for the North."

Sean took his eyes off Carter, and Juliet froze. But he wasn't looking at her. He had shifted his attention to the boys.

"We need to get out of here before someone investigates the gunshot. First we need to get rid of these brats. They've become far more trouble than they're worth."

"Good point." Carter drew his gun.

"You and Victor take care of them," Sean said. "I'll finish off the medium."

"Oh, please, let me have that honor." Carter moved toward Juliet until he was standing between her and Sean. "I've been itching to do this."

The well of anguish in Juliet's heart was so deep and hard, she couldn't breathe.

Carter looked down at her, gun raised. Then he winked.

Her fingers closed over the butt of the pistol in a flash of clarity. She raised it and fired.

Carter spun, and another shot tore through the room.

The recoil thrust the gun from Juliet's grasp. The world went blindingly white. Her vision switched from white to gray, fading slowly, until there was nothing but black silence.

Chapter 28

Carter cradled Juliet close, protecting her from the feet of the policemen and Pinkertons who filled the room. Where was the doctor?

One of the officers cut the boys free, and in an instant, Artie was by their side.

The lad grabbed hold of her hand. Tears cut tracks through the grime on his cheeks. "Juliet! Juliet, wake up. Can you hear me?"

Her eyelids fluttered.

Artie grew more shrill. Carter put a hand on the boy's shoulder. "She's not mortally wounded. She's in shock. This is the body's way of protecting itself."

Artie looked up at him with enormous, hope-filled eyes. "You're sure?"

Carter nodded, hoping to heaven he was right. If he lost her now, he didn't know if he could survive.

Suspicion entered the boy's eyes. "I don't know. You lie pretty good."

Carter tried to look offended. "I didn't lie. I was being strategic in the midst of a crisis."

Juliet stirred, brushing his arm in a feeble attempt at a swat. "I believed you."

Her voice was weak and thick with pain, but it was the sweetest sound he'd ever heard.

Beside him, Artie's concern had transformed into a magnificently joyful grin. It matched Carter's own idiotically happy smile. "You're okay?"

"Right as rain." She grimaced.

Tad joined their little knot. "You were awfully brave."

She looked deep into Carter's eyes, and though her gaze was still glazed with pain, a smile flitted across her lips. Then her eyes drifted closed again.

A doctor arrived at last, and after he got Carter's assistance in moving Juliet to a bed, he shooed Carter, Artie, and Tad away so he could examine her.

The three of them stood awkwardly in the hall, looking from one to the other. "You've been fantastically brave, both of you." Carter put an arm around each boy's shoulders. "Let's see how you two are doing."

He took them both down to the kitchen and settled them in at the table. Pawing through the cupboards, he managed to find a cache of clean linen napkins. After pumping some water, he tended to the boys, cleaning the grime from their faces and dressing their cuts and bruises. All the while he asked questions, drawing out the story of what had happened while Sean had them prisoner.

As he smoothed the cloth over Tad's face, the little boy's eyes welled with tears. "I almost got away, and that's when they got Artie, too. He was only captured 'cause of me." His distress made his lisp more pronounced.

Carter met his gaze directly. "Tad, you did exactly right by trying to escape. That's what soldiers are supposed to do, and I can't imagine any officer or enlisted man being braver and stronger than you have been."

Tad sniffled and wiped his nose with the back of his hand. Carter handed him a dry napkin.

There was a commotion and a shout from the front of the house. "Tad?"

"Papa!" The little boy sprang to his feet and took off running.

Carter and Artie followed.

The tall, gangly form of the president of the United States was backlit by the sun filling the doorframe. His son raced to him and leaped into his arms.

Lincoln dropped to one knee and pulled the boy close, as if he never meant to let go. "Oh, Tadpole, my boy. My precious boy." Tad wept on his shoulder as he stroked his hair and held him.

Carter's heart swelled. "Thank You, God." The murmur was quiet, but Artie heard him.

"Amen." The boy was equally fervent. Casually, Artie leaned against Carter. He draped his arm over the boy's shoulder and together they watched the reunion of father and son.

Lincoln at last regained his feet. Keeping a protective arm around Tad, he extended his free hand to Carter. "Detective Forbes, you have my wholehearted gratitude."

"I'm just glad they're both safe, sir."

Tad looked up at his father. "His friend got hurt."

The president looked back at Carter inquiringly.

"Miss Avila was shot. The doctor is with her now."

Grave lines of care etched Lincoln's face. "She's a gallant young woman."

"Don't you worry 'bout Juliet. She's tougher than hardtack." Artie straightened away from Carter. "She'll pull through, you wait and see. Carter said her body's in shock."

Mr. Lincoln nodded seriously. "You will let us know how she does?"

Carter returned the nod. "Yes, sir."

"Now, if you'll excuse us, I need to get Tad home to his mother." Holding tight to his son, as if the lad might disappear should he let go, the president led Tad outside.

Two orderlies from the morgue struggled on the steps with the thug's body. Carter stared at the sheet-covered form. He didn't even know the man's name. Juliet's bullet had hit him in the leg, but according to the coroner, it had managed to find an artery, and he'd bled to death in a matter of minutes.

Behind the morgue attendants, a pair of police officers herded out a manacled and morose Sean King. Carter's shot had disabled the man without killing him, so that only a few stitches to his arm had been required. The wound would have time to heal before he was hanged as a traitor and a spy.

Another set of footsteps sounded on the stairs. Carter turned. It was the doctor, looking tired as he rolled down his sleeves. It was not the face of a man bearing good news.

Artie looked up at Carter, clearly terrified. He managed to give the boy a wink and a smile. *Hope*. It was all they had, and Carter had no intention of letting go now.

Juliet's eyes were gritty. She was so tired. She would leave them closed awhile longer.

Someone was talking nearby. And somewhere else, further away, was singing. She frowned. Was it time for Emily's lesson? Surely it was too early in the morning. She risked a peek.

This wasn't her room. This wasn't even her house.

Miss Clara leaned over her. "Oh, my dear child. Praise God you're awake. We've been so worried."

"Where…?" Juliet's throat was so parched, the question came out as a croak.

Miss Clara handed her a glass of water. "You're in Mr. Pinkerton's lodgings. Do you remember what happened?"

With the hint, her memory flooded back, a kaleidoscope of impressions and feelings that stole her breath away. The glass seemed impossibly heavy, and Miss Clara took it from her and held it to her lips so she could sip it. "Artie?"

"He's fine. Wearing my patience thin because he's been in here trying to wake you up every five minutes since the doctor said you'd turned the corner."

Juliet let her head fall back against the pillow. She had never felt so weak or helpless. "Corner?"

"You developed an infection from the gunshot wound. It was touch and go there for a few days."

Juliet stared at Miss Clara. How long had she been asleep? Miss Clara didn't notice; she was busy straightening the coverlet as she chatted on. "The president came to see you. I have never seen a man so moved. He actually had tears in his eyes. I bet you could ask anything of him, and if it was in his power, he'd grant it."

"Carter?"

At that, Miss Clara glanced at her with a faint smirk. "Yes, your young man has been here almost constantly. He's been praying for you night and day. He wired Mr. Pinkerton and made arrangements for you to stay here so you wouldn't need to be moved, and he's brought groceries and taken care of everything so we didn't have to leave you."

"Is he here now?"

The door cracked open, and a small head peeked around it. Artie's eyes grew wide when he saw she was awake. "Juliet!" He bounded into the room. "Carter was right. You're going to be okay."

Miss Clara caught his shirt by the scruff of the neck before he could fling himself on Juliet. "Be careful."

More slowly, he approached the bed and then gingerly embraced her. "How do you feel?"

Juliet managed a smile. "Like I was trampled by horses."

Artie pulled back and gave her a saucy grin. "That's what nearly happened last time."

She laughed, then gasped in pain. Her body wasn't quite ready for that yet.

"I'll go tell Carter you're awake. He's going to be so happy."

She tried to stop Artie, but he raced from the room and clattered down the stairs before she could utter a word. There was only one thing Juliet wanted: a lifetime of happiness with Carter Forbes. But it was impossible. Not even a decree from President Lincoln could erase the differences between them.

A whoop sounded from below, followed by the thunder of heavier feet on the staircase. It sounded as if Carter was taking them two at a time.

He thrust open the door without knocking and stood framed in the doorway, a look of delight on his face. "It's true."

A bittersweet ache squeezed Juliet's heart at the sight of him. He was so handsome and so good. Far too good for the likes of her. She needed to let him go.

Miss Clara held a whispered consultation with him, then sat discreetly in the window seat.

Carter moved into the room carefully, as if stepping too hard might cause her to relapse. He sat in the chair beside the bed and gently took Juliet's hand in his.

"It's good to see you," she whispered.

"Seeing those lovely eyes of yours is an answer to prayer."

It was getting harder to breathe. How could she do this? How could she send away this amazing man, when all she wanted to do was profess her love for him? But if she really loved him, the answer was obvious. He was a Pinkerton. She was a fraud. Even though she knew he'd said those things to Sean only to throw him off the track, they were still true. There was no future for him with a woman like her.

His fingers moved to brush a strand of hair away from her face. "I've been think—"

"Carter, stop." Juliet could bear no more. "Please. I've been thinking, too. I'm going back on the road. Turns out I don't take well to staying in one place and being tied to a family." She cast an apologetic glance toward Miss Clara, willing her to understand.

His palm warm against her cheek, Carter looked into her eyes, his lips pressed together in a serious line. Then he broke into a smile. "There was a time when I would have believed you."

"You should believe me now."

"No. The only reason you became a medium was because you saw no other way to support your family. After all we've been through, I don't believe you can go back to that life. Is that true?"

Juliet nodded, amazed that he knew her so well.

"You have a good heart, Juliet. But that leaves you with no job and no way to support your family." He looked over his shoulder. "It's a dilemma, wouldn't you say, Miss Clara?"

"No doubt it is, Mr. Carter," she answered, without looking up from the book in her lap. "But the Lord always provides a way."

Carter chuckled. "Indeed He does. And that, Miss Button, is what I've come to tell you."

Juliet frowned in confusion. "What are you saying?"

"I'm saying the good Lord has provided a way. I've got a job offer that will enable you to keep your family together without returning to the stage."

Hope flickered in her chest, bright and hot. "A job? For me?"

He nodded. "Straight from Mr. Pinkerton. Considering your invaluable assistance in the Lincoln kidnapping case, it's his opinion that you'd make an excellent Pinkerton agent."

Surely she'd heard him wrong. She, Juliet Button, a Pinkerton agent? It was absurd. It was unthinkable. It was an answer to her heart's prayer.

Her lips parted. "But how—"

With the pad of his thumb, Carter stroked her bottom lip, silencing her for a moment. "I took the liberty of telling him you'd